HIGH PRAISE FOR CLAUDIA DAIN!

THE MARRIAGE BED

"For an unusual, sensual story set in a very believable medieval world, I strongly recommend The Marriage Bed."

THE HOLDING

"A marvelous and fascinating read . . . this book hits the home run."

—Mrs. Giggles from Everything Romantic

"*The Holding* is a romance that brings historical detail and passion together. The strong characters hold appeal as does the backdrop."

—*Romantic Times*

TELL ME LIES
RITA Award Finalist (Best First Novel)

"Ms. Dain has created memorable characters and a lusty tale. . . . This is an author with a bright touch and an erotic future."

—*Romantic Times*

"Claudia Dain has penned a sizzling tale that will warm your heart and sate your romantic soul."

—Connie Mason, bestselling author of
The Dragon Lord

"Claudia Dain heats things up from page one and keeps the reader at a slow burn throughout this appealing debut novel."

—Thea Devine, bestselling author

KINDLING THE PASSION

"Taste me again."

He bent to her mouth, holding her face between his hands so that she could not turn from him. She could not turn, but she did resist. Her lips were firm and tight against his mouth and her hands pried at his. It was a futile struggle. He would not release her; not tonight, not when he had already tasted the fire within her. He would ignite her again and this time, they would not stop. She was now his wife. And he had disarmed her.

Her kiss was cold, but he was still hot from their earlier fondling; mere coldness on her part would not stop him or even slow him. He burned for her. He would have her burn again for him.

Other *Leisure* books by Claudia Dain:

WISH LIST
THE MARRIAGE BED
THE HOLDING
TELL ME LIES

CLAUDIA DAIN

TO BURN

LEISURE BOOKS NEW YORK CITY

To Tom,
who rescued this manuscript from the ashes of the fire.
You are ever and always my hero.

A LEISURE BOOK®

April 2002

Published by

Dorchester Publishing Co., Inc.
276 Fifth Avenue
New York, NY 10001

ISBN 0-8439-4985-6

Visit us on the web at www.dorchesterpub.com.

"First of all, they killed and drove away the king's enemies; then later they turned on the king and the British, destroying through fire and the sword's edge."

—*The Anglo-Saxon Chronicles*

Prologue

Water, gray and wind-bruised.
Wood, rough and sweat-stained.
Sky of slate and torn cloud, lying heavily on the sea.
Savage people with a savage tongue
Speaking distantly of destruction and destiny
As the lash whistled.
Hands mauled and lifted
Unlocking chains that had for a year
Remained untouched.
Up and over.
The sky touched but briefly
What the sea now enveloped.
Enveloped and protected
Rushing northward in a buried stream
That revived and uplifted even as it concealed.
Pain, constant companion, dropped away

Claudia Dain

Subdued by the sea.
Lost in the depths.
Hopelessness followed eternal exhaustion
Sliding over slashed flesh
To feed the swimmers in the dark.
Of all
Only rage remained.
And grew.

Chapter One

Melania tried moving her right leg to ease the cramping and banged her knee against the rough wall of the clay vent instead. Reaching down to rub the throbbing joint, she managed to wedge her hand against her rib cage so that she could hardly breathe and then scraped off half the skin on the back of her hand as she wrenched it free. As tight as the hypocaust was, it in no way warmed her. Through the funneling of the hypocaust, she could hear the scrape of movement above her. And the crackle of fire. It would be wonderful to bake herself warm in front of a fire, her very own fire in her very own house, its light warming the room as much as its heat. It was very cold in the underground hypocaust and very dark.

Her father was dead. This she knew. She had

heard the full-throated cry, like wolves howling in animal unison; she knew it meant the Saxons had won. In the winning, they would have killed. It was their way.

Was it night? Probably. They had attacked at the cusp of daylight and darkness. It must be full dark now or perhaps even morning. She had no sense of the passage of time. She knew only that the raging heat of her fury had hardened to a cold knot of revenge fed by pride. They would not gain victory over her, and they would never defeat Rome. She was hidden according to her father's plan. Let them think they had won. She had eluded them and they didn't even know it. *Stupid barbari.* They would move on, attacking some other poor villa or town, as was their barbaric way, and she would emerge and build her life back to what it once was. They had most assuredly damaged the villa—they were just the sort of stupid oafs to do such a thing—but that meant only that she would have the freedom to rebuild in a more aggressive fashion. Let them come again. Just let them. She looked forward to it. But they had to leave first.

Cuthred threw another one of the library scrolls onto the fire. The satisfaction he received from the act was minimal, but all of the bigger items had already been hacked and burned.

"We are finished here. Let's move on," he said.

"You may be finished, but Wulfred is not," Cenred said lightly.

"This place is finished. There is nothing left to

take or destroy. I want more fun out of this isle
before we return home."

"Cuthred, you have absolutely no ability to entertain yourself. Must there always be a battle
found for you? Can you not find other ways to
amuse yourself?" Cenred laughed.

"No," Cuthred answered.

"He says no," Balduff said, "and yet I have tried
to get him to see the pleasure that a woman can
provide. Look at the process as a battle if you must;
she has defenses which must be overcome, terrain
which must be explored, secrets and hidden places
to be revealed. I tell you, a woman can entertain a
man for hours before she wears thin!"

"I like battle," Cuthred stated.

"Yes, you like battle, as do I," Balduff said, "but
women are more plentiful."

"There cannot *always* be a battle," Cenred said.

"There is no more battle here. Let's go to a place
that can provide one," Cuthred said.

"We will stay until Wulfred says we go," Cynric
said.

"Of course," said Cuthred, "but why does he
stay? The battle is won. The enemy dead."

"Because," said Cynric, "he does not believe that
all of the enemy *is* dead. Wulfred is more and more
certain that there is a woman hiding somewhere, a
woman of this house. A Roman woman. He will
not leave until he sees her cry for mercy."

"He will grant a Roman mercy?" said Cenred.

"I did not say he will grant it, just that he would
see her grovel."

"Placing my foot on a Roman neck would give me great satisfaction," Wulfred said, entering the library holding an ornate woman's comb in his right hand. In his left he held a pot of face powder. There was a woman. He had proof of her existence. All that was left was to find her. Never would he give even one Roman a chance to escape. It did not matter that she was a woman. All that mattered was that she was a Roman.

Ceolmund entered the library silently, dragging a slave, Greek by the look of him, by the back of the neck. Without a word he tossed the slave at Wulfred's feet.

"Name," Wulfred said in hesitant Latin.

The man, of average height among his own kind, stared up at the colossus before him. "Theras."

Wulfred nodded in affirmation. It was a Greek name.

"Duty."

Theras swallowed heavily and struggled to keep his breathing regular. Wulfred saw all this. He understood the man's fear—and his struggle to contain it.

"I was companion to the master of this place and also assisted him in—"

"Slow," Wulfred interrupted, his Latin stiff from disuse.

"Companion. Helper."

"Slave," Wulfred added.

Theras bowed his head and said in submission, "Slave."

"The Roman is dead," Wulfred said.

14

"Yes," Theras said, his expression unchanging. "The woman hides."

Theras remained silent, his face a mask of blank submission.

"Woman of Rome," Wulfred said. "Wife, daughter."

"There is no woman," Theras said calmly, his dark eyes as blank as a starless night.

But there was a woman. Wulfred knew it. He sensed her. She was close, close enough to cause the skin on the back of his neck to tingle, but where? The room was devoid of hiding places, sheathed in tile with simple wooden shelves for the remaining scrolls.

"Tell me," he commanded the Greek slave. "Tell me. You are mine."

The Greek lowered his eyes, waiting for the death blow. He lowered his eyes, yet his eyes were not still. Wulfred looked down. In the looking, he found his answer.

On the floor was a vent, a black hole surmounted by grillwork. A perfect hiding place for a Roman, slithering around in the dark of the dirt like a rat or a snake.

"Go," Wulfred commanded the Greek.

Alone, the Saxon warriors said nothing as they looked at the vent and understood. At a gesture from Wulfred, they filed out of the small room. Still silent, they circled the villa. It was Wulfred who found the furnace hugging the rear wall of the dwelling. It was Wulfred who smiled when he saw that the stone was cold and that the ashes had been swept clear. And it was Wulfred who gave the command.

"Light the fire."

Chapter Two

Attack, loot, and kill; that was their method. Never did they stay. Never. But this time they did. This time, because there was a Roman who had eluded them. She had hidden herself away, knowing that they would not linger after their victory. She had been so sure of what they would do.

But a Saxon would never do what was expected, not when a Roman had been counting on that expectation.

Wulfred did not bother to stay and watch the building up of the fire in the furnace, though most of his men and all of the slaves of the villa remained to watch in smothered horror. Oh, he could feel it; not from his own people, but from those who dwelled here. They had thought her protected. Wulfred smiled coldly, fondling his blade. There was no protection for Rome from Saxon fury, and there would be no protection for her from the fire. She would die in the blast of scorching heat or she would beg for release from her tomb and find death in the blade he carried. But she would die. She was Roman.

He would not have long to wait for her bleating wails. He would not have long to wait for total victory in this place that smelled of Rome.

Melania heard the crackle of fire before she felt the heat of it on the soles of her bare feet. She knew immediately what was happening. Somehow they had found her out. Somehow they thought to force her from her pinched cocoon. They had blocked her escape with the very fire that now warmed her, and so they must expect her to call for help, or release, or mercy. Melania smiled coldly in the growing heat.

As if she would ask mercy of a Saxon.

If she stayed, the heat of the fire would kill her eventually and the hypocaust vent where she had gone for reluctant safety would become her tomb. Melania sighed as deeply as the walls of the vent would allow.

There were worse tombs.

At least she would die untouched by their foul hands, and they would not have the satisfaction they so obviously wanted of finding her and killing her in some bloody Saxon way. So she would die.

She would die.

All that was left to her now was the means and

the method, and she far preferred to die inviolate than to have a Saxon lay his hands upon her, even if it was only to hold her throat ready for the knife.

Melania crept forward, digging her nails into the clay of the hypocaust, toward the library vent. Yes, she would die, but there was light coming from the vent, and for all her bravery, she did not want to die in the dark.

Wulfred paced in front of the vent, his impatience growing at a pace with the heat in the room.

"More wood! Now! Build it till it blasts her out of her hole!"

Cynric hurried out of the room to relay his message, just in case they hadn't heard him outside, which was unlikely. Wulfred had rarely been in such a rage. Leave it to a Roman to be so obstinate, so imbecilic, so perverse. Safety, cool safety, awaited her if she would just call out for help. The vent grille was set in tile and plaster; it would come free easily at a blow. He would have her out in moments, if she would just open her arrogant Roman mouth and scream in terror as any normal Roman would.

Gyrating her hips, she edged closer to the vent. It was cooler there and the light brighter. Mostly it was brighter. The heat came in dry, crackling waves that sucked the moisture from the air she was forced to breathe. It flowed over her in a caress that scorched and blistered. Her eyes were dry and it hurt to blink. Not much longer now. Not much longer before the burning air would char her lungs.

She would die soon—an honorable death, eluding an enemy's grasp. She would die untouched by Saxon hands. Her body would not be mutilated by a Saxon seax. Her eyes would never behold the filthy barbarian who had murdered her. She would be as inviolate as a murdered woman could be.

It was inevitable that she would die; each searing wave told her that, but she wanted her death to be as painless and private as possible, and dying here would accomplish that. But more than anything, she wanted to deny him the victory of her death. Here he would never know. Never be sure. Here she would win.

Wulfred could not remember having endured such heat; it coiled about him like a viper and tightened, squeezing out all memories of ever being cool. Snatching his cloak off his back, he flung it to the floor and stood, naked to the waist, watching the vent with glittering eyes.

How could she stand it? Was she dead already? Dead, without a whimper for release? Impossible.

Striding to the wall sconce, he ripped it from its base and carried it to the vent, wanting to see what his senses told him was there. Dropping to one knee, he thrust the flickering light down toward the floor. From the deeply shadowed darkness of the hypocaust, hate-filled eyes sliced into his with unblinking hostility.

No tears, no hysteria, no pleading. Impossible.

Perhaps the hidden one was not a woman. And certainly not a woman of a defeated race.

Wulfred scowled into those eyes even as he gestured for her to come out. Not even a blink in response to his encouraging beckoning.

The heat was so terrible that he was light-headed; how much longer could she survive? It was a small hole she had wedged herself into; perhaps she was trapped. Yes, trapped and unable to escape, for certainly a creature of Rome would run toward any escape. She could not move forward and would certainly have no desire to move backward toward the blasting heat. He would help her achieve her destiny and her most certain desire; he would help her find her escape. He grabbed the bars and pulled. The plaster crumbled easily and the opening was clear. No excuse now. She had to come forth. She would die by his hand and she would do so now.

Still, she remained embedded in the earth. Demented woman, could she not understand the escape he had given her? The Romans were a perverse people, but this went beyond the normal. Perhaps she was a true imbecile.

Wulfred reached into the small dark hole to pull her out, his patience burned up by the heat of the furnace blast, and was bitten on the hand for his pains. He grunted an oath. Definitely an imbecile. But imbecile or not, she would come out.

"Hand," he called in Latin as he held his hand out to her. Could she understand even such a simple word, such a simple concept?

"Ass," was the response. He knew the word and

understood the insult; even if he had not, he could have read the meaning in her eyes. Ass? She had called him an ass?

With a strangled and throaty roar, Wulfred attacked the floor, his seax a gleam of moving metal. He had waited. He had coaxed. He had been insulted. Now he would take her by force. Oh, he would not kill her where she lay, half-buried in the dirt. No, he wanted her at his feet and begging. She was brave when protected by the hypocaust; he would see a different side of her when she lay exposed and vulnerable at his feet. She would beg and cry and he would laugh, as they had laughed.

The floor was a mass of broken tile and powdery plaster. He pulled her free easily and dumped her on the rubble-strewn floor. No doubt now: she was very much a woman, though slight of build. Her hair was dark and long and straight, covered in dirt and a dead leaf or two. She was too small to have stoked such a fire of anger in him; the heat of his anger rivaled the overwhelming heat of the room. She did not beg or cringe at the sight of his battle seax or heave her shoulders in racking sobs. No, the little imbecile glared at him out of light-colored eyes with undiluted hate; not the look of a beaten foe, but more the look of a warrior plotting his next assault, even with the knife at his heart. He was looking at a woman who would have chosen to die by fire rather than call for mercy. But he did not admire her for it, of course not; here lay the woman who even now thwarted his dearest desire by not pleading for mercy. Even now, when he had her in his grasp, he had never been so angry. It pulsed through him like the heat waves that washed over him, consuming his reason, firing his passion to destroy and punish and defeat.

Chapter Three

"Why choose death?" he asked with Saxon bluntness and appalling lack of courtesy.

Melania was enjoying the coolness of the tile against her skin and the soft quality of the air in her throat. He had, in brutal barbari fashion, ruined her plans for a pristine death; for that alone she would have gladly killed him. That he would kill her before she could even try was a certainty. Besides, her head was swimming and she was having trouble getting enough air. In such a weakened state, she was not quite a match for him, stupid barbari though he was.

She was free of the scalding confines of the hypocaust, against her will; she might as well savor the relative comfort of her new position before he killed her. Her last moments were precious ones to her; did he have to ruin them with talk?

"I do not choose to die, you oaf; the attack on my home and the murder of myself was your idea, not mine. I only chose to die alone, and since you have taken even that from me, at least kill me without the noise of your appalling Latin beating against my head."

Wulfred stared in mild bemusement at the woman at his feet. The heat had obviously not robbed her of breath. For a beaten foe, and a mere woman at that, she was certainly combative. And talkative. Perhaps she truly was deranged; it would explain much and made more sense to him than attributing her with valor.

"I pulled you away death, away fire," he stated.

"A fire you started, monster. I am not an imbecile. Am I supposed to believe that you have no wish to harm me when it was you who destroyed my home?" Melania raised her head from the floor and glared up at the Saxon monster who dared to challenge her intelligence. "Should I take the hand of a murderer because it is held out to me?" Smiling spitefully and raising herself still further, Melania continued, "I would rather have faced my death without having to face a barbarian at the same time, and I would also have wished not to see my blood spill on your hands, for you, with your marginal intelligence, will think that you have won, but you have not! Better for the fire to have taken me than you, but it is still not your victory, for I will not die unavenged."

"You not die silently, either."

25

"No, I will not," she said, inching into a crouched position. "You think, in whatever haphazard fashion you may, that Rome and its citizens cannot stand against you, but I know that you shall never stand long against the power of Rome. However, after seeing what you, in your savage ignorance, have destroyed here today, I would willingly choose death. Kill me quickly, barbarian, for I cannot bear to live in a world in which you have won the day and ravaged my home."

He had understood only some of her diatribe, but it was enough. More than enough. She had dug deep into old and seeping wounds with her runaway tongue. Rome not beaten today? It was a lie. Rome died a little more each day from defeats such as this. She would prefer death to seeing him in command of her little Roman world? Looking at her crouched at his feet and ready to spring, he found he could believe it. She had inflamed him with every word, pressing to the limit his ill-used and much-hated Latin vocabulary trying to understand her. She was pushing him toward her own death with such proud and punishing words. Wulfred smiled grimly in sudden and perfect understanding. She had said it, stupidly revealing her motive: she wanted death because she could not bear to have her rotting Roman world shaken by uncivilized barbarian hands. If death was her preference, then death she would not have.

The girl would live.

"You have flushed her," Cenred said, entering the library. "She is a little thing."

Wulfred did not glance at him, but kept staring at the Roman on the floor. "Snakes are little."

Cenred laughed, studying the little Roman woman who had kept them all waiting. She was very small, even for a woman. And she was very dirty.

Melania, though she could understand but a few words of their garbled language, sensed that they were not behaving in the way of men about to kill. Should they not be more enraged, more bloodthirsty? But then, they were Saxon; they probably killed as easily and thoughtlessly as they wet the ground with their water. She studied them as they talked. All the world knew that the Saxon barbari were big, but she had discounted much of it as myth. She still wasn't ready to discard her notion that tales of their prowess were exaggerated, now she found it hard to dispute the truth of their monumental size. They were, without exception, at least three hands higher than any man she had ever seen. They were monstrous giants. A man had to be terribly awkward at such a size. Certainly she could see that they were well muscled, standing halfnaked as they were and wearing their uncultured garb of leather covering each leg. It was so . . . so . . . primitive. They were each light of hair and covered in it; hair hung down their backs and swirled across their chests. Repulsive. Surely such backward oafs would kill her without a thought, killing being their only skill. Still, studying the biggest one, the one who had dragged her from her pristine tomb, she could well believe that he would choose not to kill her out of sheer perversity. Every choice he made seemed to have her misery at its heart.

"Wife, sister, or daughter?" Cenred asked, astounded by her flagrant animosity and apparent lack of fear. "She seems too bold to be an unwed daughter or unclaimed sister."

"She is too bold for a wife," Wulfred said.

"A widow?"

"She has the bile, but not the age."

"There's not much left that a woman can be."

"She can be a slave," Wulfred said coldly.

Melania's eyes did not waver from the one who had grabbed her from the flames; she found him the easier to read of the two, and she did not like the way he was looking at her with his unnaturally blue eyes, eyes of such intense blue that they seemed to burn. Why was he waiting? He must have meant to kill her; every action proclaimed it. She would rather die now than later; waiting made the whole thing more difficult to bear. How like a barbarian to delay so stupidly. He was little more than an unthinking animal; and as an animal he would react.

With a quick lunge, she buried her teeth in the muscle just above his knee. The feel of his hairy leg in her mouth was disgusting, but the taste of his blood was very satisfying. He would kill her now, blind with pain and rage; she had only to hold on and wait.

His blood filling her mouth, Melania felt a rough tug on her hair. Yanking viciously, he attempted to pull her off. She held on, biting harder. She would release him when she was dead and not sooner. She knew he was in pain and the knowledge fed her; he could not last. He could not hold back the primitive emotions running through his blood; he would have no desire to. Her neck was about to break and he was ripping the hair out of her scalp, but he would give first. And he would give her what she wanted.

Eyes full of challenge glittered with unrepentant hatred into his, defying him, daring him.

Cenred clubbed her from behind and she slithered down Wulfred's streaming leg to huddle in an inert mass on the tile floor.

Wulfred watched her dispassionately.

"Snake."

Chapter Four

The Roman was still unconscious when Ceolmund again dragged Theras to the library. A shadowy flicker of his eyes when he saw the little snake was his only betrayal and would have been discreet enough to have escaped notice if Wulfred had not been watching him so closely. He would have answers from this Grecian slave and he would have them quickly. The Roman's ridiculous perversity had all but destroyed his pleasure in today's victory. He was in no temper for patience.

"Who is she?"

The slave's eyes lifted hopefully and then lowered to the floor. Yes, he knew now that she yet lived and had found gladness in the knowing; this slave was loyal to Rome and her bastard offspring, though Wulfred could find no reason for it.

To Burn

Wulfred swung his sword in a clean and easy arc. The wound he left behind on the slave's belly was as straight as a lance. The blood flowed freely, but would heal, if left undisturbed. It was the slave who would decide if it would be left undisturbed. Wulfred would have answers, and without delay.

"I will not ask twice," Wulfred said softly, without a trace of gentleness.

"Melania," Theras answered, his voice filled with self-disgust. "Daughter of this house."

"Her father?"

"In the courtyard."

That meant that he was dead. None lived who had fought against them in the courtyard.

"Bring him," Wulfred commanded, and his men obeyed, carrying the mutilated and stiffening body of the old man of Rome into the library and laying it next to the warm body of his daughter. Wulfred was not moved to pity at the sight of them together on the floor of their ruined house. None of Rome would ever arouse less than complete hatred in him.

"Go," Wulfred ordered Theras, and, with a quick look back to the masters he had served, the slave left.

Wulfred and his comrades stood in a loose circle surrounding the pair as they lay prostrate on the broken floor. None spoke. The old man's blood had congealed, his bowels and bladder emptied, his hands half curled into fists in his death throes; he had died fighting for his place in the world. It was

31

the best death a man could hope for. He deserved no pity.

Wulfred's gaze shifted to the woman. He noted again that she was very small. He squatted on his haunches to study this woman who had sent his pleasure racing away with her perversity. Her hair was black as night and straight as straw. Her skin was the color of ripe grain, and while it was without blemish, it also was without the becoming rosy blush of a Saxon woman. In profile, her nose was straight but long by Saxon standards, and her mouth small but full. She was as small and lithe of frame as a snake, and as venomous. He knew enough of the world to know that she was a beauty by Mediterranean standards, but he could see nothing save that she was Roman.

Rome: gobbling the world in its greed and arrogance. Rome: an empire of soldiers and tax collectors. Rome: gorging itself on the people who stood between it and its next conquest. Rome: the enslaver of all, bribing those it subjugated to lick the hand that had destroyed them.

Wulfred watched the pulse beat beneath the fine skin of her throat. She was so small, so defenseless; she would be so very easy to kill.

He placed his hand on her throat, pressing against her windpipe as he dispassionately watched for her response. In moments she began to struggle for breath, squirming against his weight, clawing at his hand, kicking against his hip for release. He watched her fight for her life with as little interest as one watched a bee tremble and die. He had found out what he wished to know. She cried for death with false zeal; instinct still prompted her to fight for her life. He released her. Casually he looked toward where her father lay, white and bloodless in the pale light of dawn; she followed his look. Eyes of lightest hazel filled with tears that did not spill. She looked him full in the face, and those tears that hung suspended in her eyes served to magnify her hatred and determination. She blinked and they were gone. Again she had managed to surprise him.

"As you have done to him, do to me, Saxon. I will not live in a world overrun by such animals as you."

Wulfred rose to his feet, towering above her. "You live or die, I choose."

"Then choose death, barbarian," she ordered.

"You could have died at my hand just now—you fought death."

Melania rose to her feet to stand before him. If she was going to have a debate with this monster, she'd do it face-to-face. Merciful God, his Latin was disastrous.

"I did not fight death! I fought you! Death I welcome and embrace as warmly as a mother—"

"Or a father?"

Melania quivered before him in a glittering fury, and with one breath she turned the tide of the conversation, becoming the aggressor.

"Come, Saxon, see if you can kill me. You have tried and failed"—she smiled—"twice? Three times? Perhaps now, if you try very hard, you will succeed at your task." Her hands on her hips, she said, "Or is it beyond you?"

He understood her to the core. She wanted death's release and sought to goad him into giving her that which she wanted most, yet when unconscious, she had fought wildly for life. Would she so willingly plunge into the darkness of death when a part of her fought for life? Which part of her would rule? Her inborn thirst for life or her rage for death?

With no warning, Wulfred swung his seax out toward her chest in an effortless yet deadly arc. If she stayed still, he would miss her by the width of a finger. But she could not know that. He waited for her to shriek and fall back from the sharpened blade. She did neither. The imbecilic woman leaned into the blow, her eyes glowing with scorn—and victory. Ceolmund pulled her back against him, away from harm.

The glow of victory in her eyes dimmed, but not the scorn.

"Since you are so hungry for death," Wulfred pronounced, his voice hoarse with frustrated desire, "you will starve for it. You will cry for release and you will find none."

"I will cry for nothing."

Wulfred smiled bitterly, remembering. "If you can say the same in a year, I might believe you. Today you have suffered nothing, endured nothing. Your words are only . . . words."

"And your threats are nothing. *You* are nothing. You who know nothing and build nothing and believe nothing. You think to torture me with life, but you will not. You are a stupid savage, a barbari, a pagan, and I will not tremble before such an oaf as you. You are an ass, and since you are determined not to kill me, then you have acquired a Roman citizen as your lifelong enemy, and only a fool makes an enemy of Rome. . . ."

"You are good only for talk."

"And you are good only for destruction and death, so do what you are best at, Saxon, or will you admit that you are afraid to kill a Roman woman?"

Wulfred pressed his great length against her, letting her feel his strength and his lack of fear. Fear Rome? For Rome there was only rage. Lifting her head with his hands, forcing her to face him, he spoke the truth of her position.

"I know what you try, Roman; I know what you feel. I will not kill you. That will not be your escape. Talk. You will not win. Your fate is to be under my command for as long as you live. It is your living misery which will feed me."

For just a moment he thought he saw her quiver, saw the shadow of fear cross her face, but then it was gone, subdued. For the moment.

"I do not believe in fate," she argued, wrenching free of his hands and his touch.

"So be it. But you can believe in what I tell you: you are mine to use. When death comes, it will be when I decide it, not you."

"I place my life in God's hands, not yours, pagan."

35

"And I have taken it out. Your life is mine and your death—"

"Only God has the power of life and death over me."

Wulfred smiled and said almost softly, "Then I am your god, Roman."

"No," Melania answered proudly, her calm restored, "you are my enemy."

Wulfred took her measure before saying with almost grim eagerness, "So be it."

Chapter Five

"She cannot go with us. Women do not go to battle," Cuthred said in his typical single-minded fashion.

"No," Balduff agreed, "but battles don't last all day, and women do have their uses in the off hours. If Wulfred wants her—"

"Wulfred has never wanted a woman before," Cynric said.

"Not wanted a woman?" Balduff laughed. "Of course he has."

"I did not say that he hadn't had a woman, oaf, but that he has never . . . well, he hasn't ever seemed to care for any particular woman," Cynric argued, uncomfortable with the topic.

"If this is the way he shows his caring, then—" Cenred began with a sarcastic smile.

"Shut up," Ceolmund said, cutting Cenred off. They all stared at him for a moment in surprised silence. Ceolmund rarely spoke, and only when he felt it was important. That he would speak now was peculiar, since they only discussed the Roman woman.

"She certainly is a virulent little thing," Balduff said after an awkward pause. "She's not what I expected of a Roman woman."

"Not what you expect of any woman," Cenred said.

"She fought well enough, considering the limitations of her arsenal," Cynric said.

"Teeth count," Cuthred pronounced in impartial martial judgment.

"Yes," Cenred said, "but who would have thought that she would react as she did? I was prepared to see her on her knees and crying for mercy, not snarling for a quick death as she sprang to the attack."

"It was also not what Wulfred expected, but he will have his satisfaction in his own way," Cynric said.

"He wants her with us?" Cuthred said almost piteously.

"I want her with us," Wulfred confirmed, stepping from the shadows of the courtyard to join the circle of his men. "We will stay. You are right, Cuthred. To bring a woman to battle is foolish. But now the battle is here, with this woman. I will have my way with her. I will get satisfaction from her, and then we will go."

They nodded in acceptance if not full understanding, but they were his comitatus and they would follow him in all things. Wulfred could not put into words the pleasure he would get in tormenting her and breaking her spirit. It was a perverse pleasure, but nonetheless real.

"Cynric," he directed, "since we stay, direct the slaves to clean the place. We will not live in this destruction."

"Yes, Wulfred," he responded.

"And Cynric," Wulfred said, and waited for Cynric to face him fully before he continued, "the Roman snake will work. She is no longer free, but slave."

Yes, it gave him a great deal of pleasure.

Except that she did not cooperate.

The fool woman went about the cleaning and organizing of her former household with vigor and resolve. Worse, the slaves all did her bidding, as if she were still mistress of this place. Worse still, when he stormed into the midst of them and declared that she was not to direct their activities, the work faltered without her. He wanted to let it be so, just to thwart her desire to rule and command, but he truly did not want to live in chaos for however long it took to break her, so he reluctantly and ungraciously ordered them to proceed as they would. The Roman once again directed the slaves, and the work progressed well under her command. But the worst of all was that none of it seemed to bother her. In fact, she hadn't seemed even to no-

Claudia Dain

tice his involvement. Being a slave didn't appear to
have affected her at all.

Impossible woman.

Wulfred left the villa, a series of rooms facing
inward on a walled courtyard, and wandered into
the surrounding fields to get some welcome distance from the Roman.

The day was well on, a hot summer day of white
haze and little wind. The villa was settled in a small
valley surrounded by gentle hills covered with both
field and forest. Rocky outcroppings pushed up
through the earth like abandoned monuments, dot-
ting the green landscape with splotches of gray. It
was a landscape not unlike his own land—except
that there were no Roman villas among the Saxons.
Wulfred scanned the area as he left the immediate
vicinity of the villa.

The east slope was trellised with grapevine supports, but few vines grew, and those that did were
thin and yellow of leaf. The barley fields to the
north were small, and he could see that there had
once been cultivation to the south, abandoned now.
Wulfred climbed to the top of the soft slope of the
north hill, above the barley fields, which was covered in honeysuckle blowing in the early summer
breeze. From here he could look down upon the
villa, nestled as it was against the slope of the west-
ern hill, snug in a protected little valley. Protected
from the blasts of weather, but not from man. It
was an indefensible spot, as he knew well. The very
positioning of the house demonstrated the arrogance of Rome. But there was an air of dilapidation

40

to the whole scene that he could take no credit for; no, that belonged to Rome completely. The arrogant Romans; how far they had fallen in this distant place.

A pair of larks erupted from the woods behind him and sprinted across the air, dipping low and then curving to rise up again. They were the only movement in the still summer sky shining above him, and he spared a moment to enjoy their flight. Birds were always free.

They swooped low, and his eyes followed them as they disappeared into the wood bordering the overgrown fields to the south. As he did so, the Roman, with her train of slaves behind her, paraded across a corner of the courtyard below. Watching her, Wulfred felt his stomach tighten and his brows close in a scowl. Yes, the Romans had fallen far in their place in the world, but one Roman still had far to fall.

"Finn," Melania directed, "you'll need to use a basket of fine weave to get the bigger pieces of debris out of the cistern, and I'll have Dorcas bring you a sheet of linen for the rest. Drag it across the top and work your way down. That should clean off the worst of it, but we'll still probably be drinking ash water for the better part of two months." Melania didn't stop talking as she moved briskly around the courtyard, ignoring the Saxon pigs who watched her every move with open dislike. "Do the best you can, Finn, though it will be a difficult task. I'm certain that only a Saxon would be so stupid as to foul

41

drinking water. Still, we must do our best to clean up after their oafish practices. Of course, it may be that they do not understand that sweet water is necessary for good health, since they consume salt water as a rule, I've heard. And when they can't get that, blood must do. I'm certain that depraved taste must explain their penchant for wanton killing; they but feed themselves. We, however, must have clean, clear water."

Finn had long since bent his head to his task, flustered and frightened by Melania's prickly speech. He did not know that the Saxons could not understand her barbs. Nonetheless, they had no trouble understanding her meaning. It was written in her every expression and mannerism.

Just as easily read was Cynric's fury. His anger fed Melania's spite enormously. The rage to die had dimmed with the day, but not the desire. She wanted it just to spite the monster. If she could goad the Saxon who watched her to kill her, she would have a double victory: the monster would lose her and he would not have had the pleasure of the dispatch. A small corner of her mind declared such logic irrational, but she was past caring. She hated the monster, the oaf, that much. She would do anything to thwart him. Anything.

As if drawn by her hatred, he appeared, striding across her courtyard as if he had built the place himself. *Arrogant oaf.* But the one who watched her was red with fury, and that pleased her hugely.

"I cannot understand a word of what she says, but I know she insults me with every breath! She

is beaten. She does the work of a slave. Can you
not kill her now so that we can be gone from here?"

Wulfred clasped Cynric on the arm in support.
He knew well what rage the Roman woman could
fire in a man; he battled it himself.

"She is a snake without teeth," he said calmly.

Cynric all but shuddered. "But venom enough."

"And no way of harming you with it," Wulfred
said. "Let her rant. It is all she has. She cannot
touch you. She cannot touch me, and I can understand her speech," he said, smiling.

"Do I insult you if I say I pity you, Wulfred?"
Cynric smiled in answer, calming himself at Wulfred's words.

"Never," Wulfred said, clapping him on the
back.

Now it was Melania who could not understand a
word of what was being said, but she was not a
dim-witted oaf who did not understand when she
was being belittled. The fury that had begun the
moment her father had shoved her into the hypocaust vent roared higher at this latest affront.

"Look at me, Saxon monster," she commanded,
her hands fisted until her knuckles turned white,
"and tell me that you do not find me a worthy adversary." By the telltale widening of his blue eyes
she knew she had judged correctly the direction of
his remarks. "Certainly I, a woman of Rome, am
more than a match for the cowards of your land
who call themselves warriors. Here, in the civilized
world, when a man makes a vow and willfully
breaks it, he is below contempt. And you, Saxon,

are a vow-breaker. You and your kind came to Britannia for pay, to protect us from the Picts, and have turned on those you swore to protect. What kind of man turns on his vow the way the wind turns in the leaves? You have no loyalty and no honor, Saxon pig, to break a vow freely made. You are a wolf who runs with the pack, an unreasoning animal who thinks only of his stomach and how to feed his appetite. Come, Saxon, tell me I am wrong. Prove to me that you and all your kind did not break your vow to protect the people of Britannia."

Her body, slight as it was, could hardly contain her fury, and her words about honor and cowardice were designed to drive a man to kill. She was a woman who demanded death as a child demanded a trinket. He saw all this clearly. He even understood that it was in the interest of her own honor that she sought to ignite him to bloodlust. Wulfred found it easy to turn aside from the knives in her words because he not only had understanding of her motives but truth on his side.

"You are wrong, Roman," he said calmly, even cheerfully, "and this is why. A vow given to an enemy is not considered binding by Saxon law. And Rome has ever been an enemy of mine."

For once Melania was dumbfounded. And speechless. Her silence didn't last long, however.

"The horrible thing, Saxon, is that I cannot find it in me to doubt the truth of what you say. Only a Saxon would construct the world so and call it legal. Tell me then, is your vow not to kill me also false, since I am your enemy?" Melania waited eagerly; she wanted so desperately to catch him in a lie.

Wulfred smiled complacently and said, "You are not so worthy a thing as an enemy, Roman snake. You are merely a slave."

This time he saw her coming; also he was beginning to understand her style. She sprang at him with fists and feet flying, pounding against him with all the fury of her defeat. He had taken worse bruising in his tumbles as a boy, and caught her against him in a bear hug, unhurt. Still she fought and twisted, and he tightened his grip and lifted her from the ground so that her feet dangled. He squeezed her until he could feel her ribs and the slowing pace of her breathing. He was pressing the life from her lungs and would continue to do so until she either stopped fighting him or fainted for lack of air; he did not care which.

She stopped fighting, but the eyes that stared unblinkingly into his were filled with frustrated hate. *Imbecile.* Did she not understand that he was fed by her hatred? When he met that stare and loosened his hold to allow her to draw breath, convinced that he had subdued her aggression, she spat in his face.

Wulfred immediately released his hold on her and she fell in a tumble at his feet in the dirt.

Looking down his tremendous length and wiping the spittle from his face, he said in a snarl, "Do not seek to provoke me."

Melania stood and faced him, her neck arched back so that she could meet him eye-to-eye, straightening her yellow stola as she did so. "Why should I not? Have you not given me your vow that I will live? Am I to assume that you will be troubled by a little spittle on your face when your body has gone unwashed for a decade? Are you admitting that I have hurt you?"

She was full of venom, this little Roman snake, and as dirty as one who lived its life with its belly on the ground. She ranted at him about a little dirt? She could not see her position, as he could. She was a slave, covered in dirt, disheveled and beaten.

"Slaves do not attack their masters," was all he said.

"That is obvious"—Melania smiled falsely—"but I am not your slave."

"You are."

"But I cannot be. Have we just not agreed that slaves do not attack their owners? And yet I have just attacked you. Without reprisal. Shouldn't you kill me, if I were your slave, for such an affront?"

"By killing you, I prove my mastery of you. Is that your logic?"

"Yes, Saxon dog, you have understood my reasoning very well. Perhaps there are other sophistications which you may be taught—given ample time and sufficient reward. I have been successful in training animals in the past—"

Wulfred would hear no more of her vicious tongue; with the flat of his hand he knocked her down into the dirt again. She sat looking up at him, quiet for the moment. But not afraid.

"I have determined," he began slowly, "not to kill

you until a time of my choosing. That is all. If you push me to anger, I will be angry." He bent from the waist and brought his face close to hers, so close that the breath of his next words moved her dark hair. "But I will not kill. There is much that can be done to you without the release of death, Roman snake."

Melania ignored his attempt at physical intimidation and rose as gracefully as she could from the dirt. She would face him as an equal, not as a subjugated slave, which she was not now nor ever would be.

"You can do no worse than what you have already done! You have destroyed life as I knew it and murdered my father by treachery! You have done your worst and have refused me the solace of death out of malicious spite!"

Wulfred's eyes flamed with blue fire as he spat out, "You expect benevolence from me, Roman?"

"Not benevolence, not even mercy; from you and your kind there is only destruction and ruin and despair."

Wulfred towered over her slight form, held so rigidly erect and so painfully proud. Her very posture was an affront to him. Grabbing her by the upper arm, he dragged her up against him and said hoarsely, "It is good you understand. For you and your kind there will be no mercy shown. I will drive you to despair and then destroy you. Your spirit will be ruined within you, and when death has become an empty dream, then it shall find you."

Melania endured his vow in stoic and superior

silence and then yanked her arm free of his grasp. She understood that this was a battle without quarter; none asked and none given. She also knew that he would not be leaving her home anytime soon; no, it would take a very long time to destroy her.

Chin up and gaze level, Melania answered him with all the superiority of Rome at her back. "So be it."

Chapter Six

"You know, Wulfred, if you want to squeeze the breath and fighting spirit out of a woman, there are more enjoyable ways to do it." Balduff laughed.

They were relaxing in the main room of the villa, the triclinium. Wulfred had no idea where the little Roman was, and he did not care at the moment. He needed time to get control of his anger, an anger that she had carefully stoked, and which was so hot that he had been within a hairbreadth of killing her. He would not kill her. Not yet. Not when she so adamantly wanted it.

"Leave it to you, Balduff." Cenred chuckled.

"What? Because I can see the pleasure in a woman?"

"We can all see the pleasure in a woman," Cynric said, "but not this woman."

"Why not this woman?" Balduff argued. "She is young enough, and shapely."

"She is dark and tiny. It would be like mating with a mole." Cynric shuddered.

"Especially since she always seems to end up in the dirt," Cenred said with a smile.

"So take her in the dirt, since she seems to prefer it," Balduff said casually. "She is a woman. Her breasts are intact and her limbs are soft. What else is there?"

"How can you tell she has breasts, covered as she is in that yellow sack?" Cenred asked.

"Because I have a knowing and experienced eye, boy; I can always find a woman's breasts. Even in the dirt."

"But they were small," Cynric said. "Everything about her is small, like a malnourished child."

"Her anger was not small," Cuthred said. "She has a warrior's spirit, I think."

"Ox dung," Cynric pronounced. "She has no valor. She is a child throwing a temper tantrum."

"How old do you think she is?" Cenred said.

"Old enough." Balduff grinned.

"Of course, you would think so, but her hips were hardly wider than a boy's." Cenred's brow furrowed in puzzlement. "Are you certain she's a woman, Wulfred?"

"You're pathetic, boy," Balduff roared. "Of course she's a woman!"

"Wulfred?"

Wulfred turned to his men. "She is a woman.

Even without hips and breasts, she has a woman's
spite."

"Are you saying that she has no breasts, Wulfred?" Cenred pressed, more to annoy Balduff than
anything.

"She has breasts: small, round, and firm, and the
swelling of hip needed for breeding. She is a
woman," Wulfred restated.

"A woman," Balduff repeated, "and shapely."

"Well, you did have your hands all over her,"
Cenred said lightly.

Yes, he had. Wulfred had not thought of the little
Roman in physical terms before this. She was
small, true, and young, but she had hips and breasts
and long, thick hair. Had he ever asked for more
in a woman? But she was a Roman, first and fore-
most; her being a woman was secondary. It was like
Balduff to suggest mating with her to subdue her,
but he could never do it. Not with her. It would be
like joining with a serpent.

"She is alone, overrun, her father dead," Ceolmund the Silent said. "I pity her."

Now, *that* caught him unready. Pity her? Who
pitied a hissing snake?

Theras and most of the people of the villa had re-
treated to the kitchen. It was familiar, warm, close,
and away from the Saxons. Melania was with them.
She did no work, as they did, but she was with
them. None faulted her, slave though now she was;
she hadn't been trained for kitchen labor. Those
skills would come, in time, if they had to. Like the

others, Theras was hoping that life might still go on as before—after the Saxons left. But would they leave? After Melania's last bout with the Saxon warlord, Theras was beginning to wonder. Couldn't she see that mollifying the giant's anger was the better way? Slaves, the defeated and powerless, did not fight back and expect their lot to get better. He looked over at her, sitting quietly, dry-eyed and remote in a corner of the golden-hued room on a small folding stool; perhaps she was thinking of a way to soothe the giant's animosity into a softer emotion, one that would serve her better. The Saxon was a striking man, big and fair-featured. Melania was shapely and a classic beauty. Surely she could win some favor from him with a smile and a soft reply. Defying him was a fool's route. She had no power as a slave, she had only her rage, and that would do nothing to placate Wulfred. Yes, Melania was an intelligent woman; she would see the error of her tactics. Perhaps. With his help. Theras crossed the room to stand beside her. Looking down on the top of her head as she sat upon the stool, he could see dust on her scalp. Never had he seen her so dirty, or so deeply in thought. If he could only nudge those thoughts toward pacification . . .

"If he won't kill me, I shall kill myself."

Theras sighed in momentary defeat. Melania was intelligent. She was also strong-willed and passionate.

"Kill yourself?" he repeated.

"Yes." She looked up at him, her eyes glittering

and hot. "Kill myself. That will show the beast that I will have my own way and he cannot stop me."

"You plan to defeat him by killing yourself?" Theras said slowly. "What victory is that?"

"I don't want to die, Theras; you know I don't. But I can't let him have this power over me. You know he plans to kill me anyway. That he hasn't done it already is only because he wants to make me suffer first and take all control away from me. Then when he kills me, in what awful manner I can't conceive, I will have lost both my life and my power of choice, and he will have won it all! Can't you see that?" Her tone was desperate, strident, and, worst of all, strong.

"Killing yourself is no answer," Theras argued. "He is angry; appease him. Perhaps eventually he will lose this desire to punish you, and then you will be both alive and free. Dead, you give him what he says he wants."

"He doesn't want me dead, Theras. He wants me alive until he decides to kill me. There is a difference."

"There is no difference once you are dead."

"The difference is that I can die happily the one way and in complete and miserable defeat the other. The only way to win is to take my own life."

Theras paused to consider his strategy. On the surface, there was logic to her argument. But there was more to life than what lay on the surface. Melania was set like a boulder in the earth; only something celestial could move her.

"Have you considered what the Lord of hosts has

to say about taking your own life? To be murdered as an innocent victim leaves you blameless. To commit suicide goes against God's law."

Melania slumped down on her stool. She had worked it out so perfectly, but she hadn't considered that. She was a Christian. She couldn't commit suicide. She was called to suffer whatever the world threw at her; unfortunately, she wasn't skilled at suffering.

"But in this situation—"

"Does not God know all situations in advance? Are you the lone exception because you have been made a slave by a people abhorrent to you?" Theras smiled gently. He had been bought to teach the children of this house and stayed on as companion when they had outgrown the need for a tutor. He had been given his freedom by Melania's father many years past, as had all who lived here. The Saxon had named him a slave and he had acknowledged the term, but it was the Saxon who had again made him one. Yesterday he had been free.

He understood the workings of Melania's mind, a mind never still, never at rest, though she was seventeen and should have settled down by now. Certainly he and her father had struggled through the years to teach her moderation and restraint, with limited success. Melania had not yet achieved the calm control that her father had so highly valued; she had been a volatile child and she had matured into a passionately tempestuous woman. Melanius had not despaired, however. She was a Roman child who had received a sound Roman education in a firmly Roman home. Melania would, given time and training, achieve the dignity of her race. Her father had determined that it would be so. But her father was dead and Melania was now a slave. Though her place in the world had changed, Melania more urgently than ever before needed the discipline and order of a civilized mind.

"You know that Jesus spoke specifically of a slave's obedience to his master, Melania. Are you exempt?"

"Oh, Theras," she whispered, her raised eyes dark and her lashes spiked with tears, "I want to be."

Theras smiled and said nothing, knowing he had made his point for the moment, praying that she would accept it.

Melania slumped upon her corner stool, her hands clasped around an upraised knee, her black hair a veil that swept forward to shield her from the others in the room. She sat alone in the noisy midst of them, a heaviness upon her that was not upon the rest of them because the blond giant had singled her out as a target for his roaring hatred. They had the comfort of hazy anonymity. Melania did not.

Small and dark, Flavius approached her furtively, his every movement portraying jumpy anxiety. Flavius, his great-grandfather armor-bearer to Melania's grandfather in the days of the legion, was a boy of eleven and newly orphaned by the Saxon horde. He crouched in front of Melania clearly expecting to be slaughtered at any moment—an idle fear, for the Saxons had killed no children nor any women; in fact, they had battled only those who raised arms against them in their attack. A small mercy, but a welcome one. Theras had heard of much worse happening at Saxon hands, and he suspected that Wulfred, for all his consuming hatred, was responsible for the mercy. Melania, he was certain, would not agree.

"Will you fight him, Melania?" Flavius asked, his voice high and thin.

Melania pulled herself out of her reverie and brushed her hand against Flavius's dark hair, her smile gentle. "Am I not Roman, little one?"

Flavius rested his head upon her knees and wrapped his arms around her legs; he looked as if he were clinging to her for his very life. "Yes, but he is big."

"Rome is bigger," she said without hesitation.

Flavius chewed his lip and brushed his dirty face against the wool of her stola before mumbling, "He is nearer."

Melania sighed and ran her fingers through his hair as she leaned against the wall of the kitchen. They were a pair, these two, both dark of hair and slender of form, though Flavius was but a gangling boy who had not yet begun to reach adult size. Melania was full-grown and fully formed, slight as she was. They looked like what they were: children of Rome.

"Only for now," she said. "He will not stay. They never stay."

"Never?" His eyes looked into hers, his hungry fear consuming him.

"Never." She smiled down at him. "That is why I must hurry and fight him, before he runs away. I won't have much time to teach him what a fierce enemy he has made here, will I?"

Flavius lifted his head and said solemnly, "Do you need my help, Melania? Should we fight him together? I could help you. . . ."

Melania brushed her fingers against his cheek and said with matching solemnity, "You are valiant to offer, Flavius, but I must fight him alone, his fury against mine. If we fight him together, he will be too easily outmatched. A small victory for us and not a worthy one for Romans. You stay well away from him and his kind, Flavius, do you understand? Stay away from the Saxon wolves."

"I will, if you say, but . . . are you not afraid? He is so big and so fierce."

Melania's eyes burned bright, and she looked out over the top of the boy's head, her fingers stroking his hair softly. "I am not afraid."

"But—"

"Have you not noticed how fierce I am? Should he not be afraid of me? I think he should, but do not warn him of my ruthlessness. My battle plan is to catch him unawares—not a difficult task, since he is a Saxon."

Flavius looked up at Melania with all the love of a motherless child in a hostile world. "You are very brave, Melania."

"As are you, Flavius," she returned seriously.

Everyone froze as Cuthred stomped into the stone-paved room.

"Wulfred. Work. You," he said in simple and harsh Latin, pointing at Melania.

Pushing Flavius behind her, Melania glanced scornfully at Cuthred over her shoulder and opened her mouth to lash him like a wild horse; then she abruptly stopped herself and began to smile—a beautiful smile, certainly, but one that made Theras twitch in alarm and even caused Cuthred to scowl in suspicion. Grinning like a child, she jumped up from her stool and walked briskly out of the kitchen, waving Cuthred out of her way as she went.

Theras, watching her in surprise, was not at ease.

The moon drifted lazily through a cloudless night, a night as serene and untroubled as all summer nights should be. The air was still and soft, a fitting embrace for that luminous moon. All nature was somnolent and quiet, save for Melania, who was still hard at work. Working, though the sun had set long ago. Working, though others were asleep. Working, though none watched her at her labors, except the moon. And Wulfred.

She swung her hatchet with greater ease now than she had when she had first begun; she'd had hours of practice. Quartering logs was not a task he would have set her to, not thinking she had the strength for it, but she had attacked it with a will and of her own accord. Her blade was as dull as a post by now, but still she did not relent. The rest of the house slept while the little Roman toiled on. She could hardly lift the tool anymore, and her feet shuffled in the dirt, raising dust.

Wulfred was flatly perplexed.

Cuthred told him that the woman had gone directly to work upon command and had not stopped since. He knew that because the Roman was never unobserved. He didn't trust her not to attack one of them. He didn't trust her not to try to escape. He didn't trust her not to burn the place to the ground in feminine fury. He didn't trust her. So first Cuthred and then Cynric and now he watched her at her labors. And labor she did. What she had tackled was no light kitchen detail. No, hewing logs into quarters was man's work. Yet she had cut quite a tidy pile of lumber. But why did she not stop? Cynric had tried to get her to stop and she had almost bitten him for his kindness, hardly stopping long enough in her work to do so. Why?

As he watched her from his position on the slope, she suddenly dropped to her knees and then forward onto her face. He waited for her to move. She did not. Cautiously Wulfred eased down the hill, wary of a trap.

The moon was a white light in the sky; he could see her clearly. Just as she could see him if he was not careful. He had reached level ground and was just a hammer toss from her when a wolf howled from deep within the wood that surrounded the villa's lands. The girl jerked and rose to her feet clumsily, shaking her head and grinning like an imbecile. Before the sound of the wolf had floated away into the night, she was back at her task, swinging the blade with renewed vigor.

She was a far cry from the Roman lady of leisure she had been yesterday, before they had come to split open her pampered world like the rotten fruit it was. Her gown was split and covered in sweat and dirt, as was she. But why such zeal over a pile of wood? Did she think to fan his pity and obtain a release from her slave state?

"It is useless to hide, Saxon," she said between swings. "I can smell you."

She did not speak like one seeking pity.

"You could as well smell yourself," he answered, coming into the little light cast by her lamp.

"My sweat is of honest labor," she huffed, raising the blade for another swing. "Yours stinks of deceit and treachery."

"Sweat is sweat, Roman. There is no meaning in it."

She smiled at that and continued her downward swing. "You are an ignorant oaf, Saxon. Dull as the wood I chop."

"Not so dull as your hatchet," he answered. "If you would work, use tools that will help and not hinder you." Without waiting for her response, he stepped behind her and took the ax from her hand. At once he began to sharpen it.

"I am not surprised that you know well how to sharpen an ax to an edge. Your own ax must often grow dull from hacking at bone and tissue," she said in a hiss. She was uncomfortable at his interference and her voice revealed it.

Wulfred smiled. "The flesh does not bother my weapon. It is the bone that dulls my blade."

He watched her pull herself erect and grab for the ax. Had she almost been asleep?

"Go to the hole you sleep in, monster. Leave me," she commanded in ringing tones. "I have much to do."

"Here is my hole," he answered, gesturing toward the villa with a grim smile. "There is much to recommend it. I took it from one not strong enough to keep me from it."

She ignored him. Or pretended to. Up came the blade in the moonlight and down again toward earth to mark its passage with a solid *thunk*. Again. And again.

Wulfred moved off into the shadows near the villa, but he continued to watch her. She did not work for show; she labored intensely, pushing her slight body to the limit and beyond. Why? Why work so hard for an enemy? The muscles in her biceps bunched and twisted, as did the muscles across the tops of her shoulders; he could see no more in the garb she wore. Her hair was a loose and tangled braid down her back, and that braid flicked outward and back with each stroke, the ends brushing against her bottom, visibly round and full despite the loose gown that draped her. The rhythm of her movements unveiled a grace that he had not noted before. She moved fluidly, quickly, like a small and energetic stream rushing away to the sea. Lithe, she was, and sinuous. Sinuous . . . like a snake.

Wulfred shook himself like a dog coming out of water, disgusted. Turning away from the snake at her slave labor, Wulfred strode into the villa, through the courtyard, and into the triclinium. Cenred was sleeping closest to the door. It was Cenred who was kicked into wakefulness.

"Watch her."

No need to ask who. There was only one "her."

"Watch her do what?" he asked, rubbing his hand through his hair and stifling a yawn.

"She seeks to leave not a tree standing," Wulfred said in a growl. "She may kill every tree. She may not harm herself."

"When she tires?" Cenred was afraid he already knew the answer.

Wulfred smiled. "Then you may rest."

Chapter Seven

"It's been four days and I've slept no more than a handful of moments," Cenred complained to Wulfred. "What is wrong with her that she does not tire? I am tired and I but sit and watch!"

Wulfred had also been watching her, as he watched her now. "She tires," he answered. "It is only that she does not rest."

Cenred had been set to the task of watching, but Wulfred had not been able to ignore the Roman. Surreptitiously he had watched her. She had given up chopping wood and proceeded to wash linen, then dig a latrine, then patch a hole in the wall and one in the roof. The results of her various labors were not worthy of praise, but she attacked each task furiously. And she never stopped. She never slept, or at least, no one could catch her at it. No

Claudia Dain

one drove her to such extremes; she drove herself, hardly taking time to eat. Now, hard at work on her latest effort, hoeing the fields clear of weeds, he watched her. Her movements were slow and clumsy, the lithe grace of earlier days gone. Her back was bowed with effort and exhaustion and her eyes were dull. Her tirades had stilled long ago. She didn't seem to have the energy for anger.

Wulfred frowned as he ambled toward her, the sun warm on his skin and the dirt soft under his feet. What drove her so? She was on the verge of collapse, that much was obvious, yet she resisted, working herself into a stupor. He understood what she was enduring, the effort demanded of her small frame, and wondered at it, but he felt no glimmer of pity. Four days was nothing. Yet she was a woman, young and very slight. . . .

And determined to get him to kill her. Yet she had not provoked him since she began her labors, having no time for him or anyone else. No time even for sleep . . .

Wulfred lifted his head as suddenly as a dog lifted its nose to the scent. He knew, in that instant, what his little Roman was about.

He strode across the furrows to her, his anger a living thing, as hot and pulsing as flame.

"Get out of my field, barbari; have you no concept of the order of my rows? Of course not, you are a stupid pagan and know only disorder and disharmony and disloyalty and . . ."

Wulfred did not interrupt her so much as allow the wind in her sails to die out listlessly. She did not even have the strength to fight him with one of her endless tirades. Oh, yes, he knew what she was about.

"Cease your work," he commanded. "Even a slave must sleep if she is to live." Grabbing her by the chin to turn her face up to his, he added one further command: "And you will live, Roman." Her eyes flamed gold in the strong summer sunlight. Her anger flared against his spark.

It was true; she was almost too exhausted to speak. She was not too exhausted to attack. As she swung her hoe up for a blow to his big, ugly, yellow head, the monster knocked it easily from her hands.

"You would have done better with the ax," he jeered.

"Your weapon? Never."

"Your pride is easily stirred." Wulfred smiled coldly.

"That is because it never sleeps," she countered.

"But you shall."

"You cannot force me to sleep," she said, stiffening her sore spine.

"Slave," he said under his breath, closing the scant distance between them, "I can force you to do anything."

So saying, he grabbed her in a rough grip by the upper arm and pulled her from her work, dragging her down the incline to the villa below. Literally dragging her, for Melania dug in her heels and fought him every step. Fought him unsuccessfully, though this latest confrontation fired her blood and fed her sluggish brain as nothing had in days. No longer was she tired. She was embattled and she was alert and she would not sleep. He was making it all the easier for her to refuse to do so. Fighting him was the best and most enjoyable work she had had in days.

The Saxons and the Britons who composed the population of the villa watched Wulfred drag Melania toward them with delight. Cenred was grinning from ear to ear, and Ceolmund was nodding approvingly. The Britons were less obvious in their pleasure, but Theras looked plainly relieved. All this Wulfred saw in a quick glance as he pulled the twisting and clawing Roman behind him. She hadn't been this energetic for two days. Fighting him pleased her as no other activity had yet, and he understood well that she was using this fight as a way of keeping herself awake. But she would not succeed. He had determined that she would sleep. She *would* sleep.

When they reached the level ground of the villa, Melania's fight against the monster's hand that held her doubled in intensity, and she punched the oaf's shoulder with all the strength of her anger. Her fist landed with a solid *thunk*, but the pagan fool did not stop and so she hit him again. And again. Most satisfying, even if it didn't seem to do any good. And then the barbarian grabbed both of her hands in one of his and continued his march into the villa courtyard.

"Let me go, you stupid barbari! You cannot make me sleep if I do not choose to do so, and you will soon find that I will not be forced to do anything not of my own will. Son of a monstrous toad! Blind and leprous ass! I will not go! *I will not!*"

Wulfred had known she would resort to curses and proclamations; it was her nature. But she was tossing out her words at such a furious rate that he could make out only a word here and there. However, even that paltry sum was enough for him to understand her meaning. And her anger.

It was then that she bit him.

He was not surprised.

Giving her a hard yank, Wulfred dragged her through the courtyard, to the pleasure and entertainment of his comitatus, and tossed her into a small chamber that was not too badly destroyed. She landed on the only furniture in the room, a couch.

"Sleep," Wulfred commanded in ringing tones, clearly not expecting to be disobeyed.

"I do not choose to," Melania answered in just as regal a tone as he had used, springing up from the couch and its softness.

He took a step farther into the plastered room, his very size intimidating. "Slaves do not choose. Slaves obey."

"You are so right." She smiled thinly in response. "Slaves obey, and if you command me, I will not obey. I am no slave."

"Your logic is faulty, Roman. I have the might to make you what I will. Your denial means nothing when I have the strength to prove you wrong."

She stood proudly before him, defying him with every gesture and every word. Four days of no sleep had not softened her spirit or her resolve in her pointless fight against him. Her plan was to push herself physically until she sickened and died of exhaustion. He had seen too many men die in just the same way not to recognize the signs now. She was living on will alone, her body ravaged by unending labor. He had not thought her capable of it, not a pampered Roman. And not a woman. She was not what he had expected when he had thought to smoke her out of her hiding place. But he was coming to know her, and to know what to expect of her. This challenge she had created by refusing to sleep was like meat and drink to her; it fed her diminished energy and allowed her to ignore her exhaustion. This fight must stop.

"Why are you so afraid to sleep?" he asked, changing tactics.

"I am not afraid!" she said, bristling.

"Nothing will harm you," he promised, backing away from her to ease her tension. "The couch is soft and the chamber quiet." He said it so quietly, his voice hushed in the still air. "No one will disturb your rest."

"I do not want to rest," she responded wildly. "I do not . . . unless it is the rest of the dead."

"That rest you will not find!" he shouted, past his brief attempt at patience. She was impossible, completely unreasonable.

"Then I'll have none at all!" she yelled, the cords in her throat standing out in sharp relief against the thin column of her neck.

"You'll have what I choose for you to have," he

said, and advanced on her as he said it. She'd lie upon that couch if he had to hold her there, and that was what he fully intended to do.

She fought him, of course, but she was no match for his strength. In a matter of moments he had her pinned on her back, one long leg thrown over both of hers and his arms pinning hers to her sides. She hissed her fury and threw her weight against him, cracking her head against his chin in the process. That slowed her enough so that she reverted to her favorite weapon, her adder tongue.

"You stink, barbari pig, and your hairy body irritates me at every point." He could feel her breath on the hair of his chest, an odd and not unpleasant sensation. "I could not have planned a better torture for you than to force you to touch your enemy for as long as I choose because . . . I will not be still . . . and you will . . . have to . . . stay. . . ."

And she slept. Exhausted and spent, relaxed to her very bones, nestled in his arms. She was as petite and light as goose down, and as soft. She was very small in her sleep, without the fire of her spirit burning bright and hot. She jerked suddenly, her muscles in sudden spasm, and he stroked her arms to quiet her. She sighed lightly and mumbled something before turning in to him. Her feet, small and dirty, she buried under his calves. His hand slipped easily into the gentle indentation of her waist as her hands, cupped together, pressed into the hairy hollow of his underarm. She burrowed in her sleep.

Wulfred looked down at her as she nestled against him. His thoughts were a jumble and a mys-

tery to him. One thought, so familiar, rose up from
the tumult. One thought: how very simple to kill
her now. Wulfred's left hand moved over her torso,
the flat stomach, the flattened breasts, the slender
line of throat and clear angle of jaw. If he killed her
now, he and his men could meet Hensa, the Saxon
commander, on his march south. There would be
more battles and more victories before leaving this
isle at the end of summer. Wulfred brushed his
thumb against the thick fringe of black lash that
shielded her eyes. He had not known lashes could
be so black, from root to tip, sooty black. She
twitched her head at his strange caress and murmured softly as she buried her black head along his
ribs.

He did not want to kill her now.

He could have left her. He had achieved his purpose and thwarted hers. But he stayed. He stayed
until the sun slanted in long yellow bolts across the
mosaic floor. He stayed, holding her, until the rosy
sky of a summer sunset washed the room. In the
end, he decided that she had been right: she could
not have devised a better torture.

She awoke in the late afternoon and for a moment
wondered if she had fallen asleep for mere instants.
Her happy delusion could not last, for two reasons:
one was standing in the doorway, watching her,
and the other was that she felt too rested. And defeated. She did not feel any closer to death. She felt
muscle-sore and wooly headed.

"How long?" she asked, her voice gravelly with thirst.

He didn't hesitate, knowing exactly what she meant. "A night and a day."

A night and a day. It was a serious setback, and she could almost have wept at the thought of having to start all over again. But she did not weep; her resolve to outwit the hairy oaf was greater than her frustration at losing so much time and effort in her plan to work herself to death.

Sitting up and swinging her legs over the side of the couch, she became entangled in a light cover. Someone had covered her in her sleep. The monster had probably tried to smother her. But watching him standing in the doorway, his revoltingly big arms crossed over his hideous chest, she decided that to kill her in her sleep would not satisfy him. He would want her awake and, preferably, screaming for mercy. One thing was certain; as stupid as he was, he had understood her motive in working so hard and would not now simply watch and wonder when she set about her tasks. In fact, knowing how perverse and obstinate he was, he might make it very difficult for her to outwit him in that way again.

What to do? If she could not die by exhaustion, what way was left her?

"Get up, slave, and cease lingering on your couch," he rumbled, not moving from his place in the doorway. "It is time for you to eat."

Melania smiled slowly at his words and then dipped her head to allow the tangle of her hair to

hide her satisfaction. She should have known the
barbarian half-wit in front of her would provide her
with the perfect solution. She would die and it
would be in her own way. It wouldn't actually be
suicide. Suicide was jumping off a cliff or falling
on a sword. This new way was perfect.

"Then stop blocking the door, you monstrous
oaf, unless you've hidden the food under the
couch? I can't smell anything, but then the stink of
you would foul any aroma of food. Step aside, pagan pig, unless you wish to serve me on my couch?
It is the Roman way. . . . Try not to trip over yourself in obeying my wishes, Saxon; merely step away
from the portal so that we may both have the pleasure of being out of each other's sight."

Oh, yes, she was rested and back to her full
strength. Wulfred watched her stride across the
courtyard to the kitchen like a soldier on parade.
But why had she obeyed his instructions so readily?
And what was she so happy about?

He rethought their most recent conversation. It
had been short. He had told her how long she had
slept; that had dismayed her. He had seen the
thoughts and plans flying through her mind like
larks sweeping the sky, searching for a new method
of having her way and thwarting his. She was so
easy to read, like a child hiding a sweet behind her
back. Hiding a sweet . . . She had brightened when
he had mentioned food. Of course, she was hungry.
She had done much labor on little food and no
sleep. Hunger must be riding her hard. She could
ill afford to lose the weight. But why such glee? He

did not trust her happy, though he hardly trusted her snarling. He did not trust her at all, but there was something in her suddenly bowed head that screamed deception. But what?

She was better watched, that much was certain, and Wulfred followed the path she had taken across the walled courtyard to the kitchen hugging the wall. It was a low-ceilinged building, built of timbers, clay, and plaster washed white. He stooped to enter through the timber-framed doorway. The room was small in comparison with the other rooms of the villa—certainly the triclinium was four times its size—but it was a spacious room by Saxon standards. The ceiling was of timber, planed and beveled, and the walls painted a warm white that glowed golden in the reflected light of the massive hearth. Long tables of polished oak paraded down the center of the room and were covered with bowls, platters, and the disarray of food being prepared. The room had four windows, each a perfect square. With all he could say against the Romans, Wulfred forced himself to admit that they excelled as builders.

His eyes scanned the room from his position in the doorway; she was nowhere within. The former slaves of Rome stopped their labors and stared at him in silent fear; he did not want their fear, only their obedience. And their cooperation. A bowl clattered to the floor and broke into three pieces; a smallish boy stood above the mess in stricken silence, his eyes wide and still. Wulfred ignored him.

The boy was not Melania, and it was Melania he wanted.

"Where is she?"

There could be no doubt in anyone's mind whom he meant, yet they remained silent.

"I sent her to the kitchen. She is not here. Where is she?" he repeated, his voice a throbbing drum in the small space.

"Do not hurt her!"

Wulfred turned to the sound and again saw the boy. He held the shard of pottery in his hand like a weapon, and on his face he wore a look of terrified resolve. Wulfred's mouth twitched in reluctant humor; little Roman warrior, hiding in a kitchen with a dish for a weapon.

"You would fight for her? Against me?" he asked solemnly, seeming to consider his young opponent.

The boy swallowed and clenched his shard, his knuckles white. "Am I not Roman?" he asked, mimicking the snake.

Wulfred stroked his belly, considering. "I don't know. Are you?"

The boy seemed to wither. "Can't you see that I am? Can't you tell?"

"What I see is a young warrior who lacks a proper weapon. Do you also lack a proper name?"

"Flavius is my name."

"Ah, a Roman name."

"Of course," the boy huffed, his grip on the shattered pottery loosening. "Just like Melania."

"Not like Melania," Wulfred said. "You are soon to be a man, a warrior. She is a woman."

"She is Roman, like me. And she is something of a warrior," Flavius argued.

"No," Wulfred said, crossing his arms and leaning against the doorway. "She is a fighter. There is a difference."

"Oh."

Wulfred watched the boy in his defeat, the fight in his eyes replaced by confusion. A small boy, too small to be a true Roman, but not too small to begin learning.

"Would you be a warrior or a fighter, Flavius? I give you the choice, since you are so near to being a man."

Flavius chewed his lip in concentration and rubbed his thumb along the rough edge of the dish. He looked Wulfred over carefully before answering.

"Are all Saxons warriors?"

"Not all, but most. It is the way of pride for us."

"And all Romans?"

"More in the past than now," Wulfred answered truthfully, admiring the boy for his logic. "Rome is well known throughout the world for her warriors."

"I would be a warrior," Flavius said firmly.

"A wise choice." Wulfred smiled, uncrossing his arms.

"When?" he asked, striving to keep his voice level and mature.

"You begin now. Go find Ceolmund and tell him of your desire." When Flavius moved abreast of Wulfred, Wulfred stopped him with a broad hand on his narrow chest. "It will be difficult."

"Of course." Flavius shrugged and moved past him and out into the light. Wulfred watched him go with a smile. The broken shard fell from the boy's hand without a thought as he went to begin his Saxon training.

Turning again to face the room, Wulfred repeated, "Where is she?" His smile had departed with the boy.

Theras stepped forward to face their new master. "She has been here. She was given a dish of food. She has gone to a quiet place to eat."

He spoke clearly and plainly. Wulfred appreciated the effort, but the Roman's long-winded tirades made it unnecessary. His Latin was once again close to effortless. Another reason to want to see her dead.

So she had obeyed him. Strangely the knowledge brought no comfort. Why would she obey so readily and so completely? The only answer was that it had also served her own purpose, and her purpose was ever at odds with his. He would watch her and be sure of her obedience to his will.

"Where?" he asked the Greek.

The man hesitated before answering, yet what choice did he have? He was a slave. He had no choices.

"There is a flat rock on the hill to the east, overlooking the vineyards. She is there."

Wulfred had been there. He knew the spot.

He turned from the kitchen, feeling the relief of the Roman hybrids he left behind as palpably as a touch. Cynric saw him and made to follow; Wulfred waved him off. He needed no assistance in handling the Roman. Cynric's brows met over his nose in an irritated scowl, but he slowed his pace, staying within the courtyard as Wulfred passed through the open gate. When he was beyond the vineyards, he could see her, a white blur in the fading light. He knew she had been able to see him from the moment he had crossed the courtyard into the kitchen. From her vantage point, the villa and all its environs were visible. He approached her laterally and from behind. The sunset was splayed out like a banner, leaving her in black silhouette. An empty dish was on the rock next to her.

"You follow me like a dog, barbari. I choose to be alone. I have no doubt that you can find your way back to my villa," she said with calm disdain. "Unfortunately."

He was more comfortable now, his guard relaxed. She was behaving normally, in her spiteful, vicious Roman way. This way was better than quick obedience; this way he understood.

"You have nothing, Roman slave, except a sharp tongue," he answered, standing on the rock next to her, staring at the rapidly sinking sun.

"And a will, Saxon, a strong will that you will find impossible to break," she said in a snarl, standing to be eye-to-eye with him, or as much as she was able given her stunted size. The woman came hardly to his chest.

Wulfred smiled, relaxing. "I do not want to break your will, Roman. I want to break you—a thing not so difficult to do."

He said it easily, confidently, and it shook her courage. He could see it. He could feel it. She was not the same woman she had been; his coming, his defeat of her and her kind, had changed everything. This he knew and this she was coming to know. It was sweet knowledge and he gloated in it.

She reacted to this knowledge in predictable fashion; she threw the empty dish at him.

He caught it with one hand and threw it at her feet, where it shattered into shards and powder on the massive rock.

"You are a clumsy slave," he said when the sound of the breaking had echoed away into the night.

"It was my dish to break if I chose," she responded with heat.

Wulfred stepped closer to her and clasped her chin between his fingers. He looked deeply into glittering eyes, the last rays of the sun turning the hazel into earthy gold. He could feel her breathing quicken and feel her stiffen under his hand. He hoped it was in fear.

"But I did the choosing," he reminded her softly. "So it will always be."

She stared up into his eyes for a moment or two longer before breaking away from his touch and hurrying down the hill, escaping the truth of his words. Escaping him. Wulfred smiled easily and followed her down, content.

When the scent of their passing had cooled, a young wolf skittered out of the shadow of the wood, making a quick and direct path to a spray of honeysuckle not far from the rock. The contents of Melania's dish were consumed in no time.

Chapter Eight

Remembering how she had labored through the nights, Wulfred did not wait until the morning to gather all the inhabitants of the villa in the courtyard: Saxon, Roman, Briton, and Greek. Two torches lit the space with a hazy glow as sparks flew upward to mingle with twisting smoke before being lost in the pitch of night. He stood with his back to one torch. All could see him clearly, even those on the fringes who were indistinct shadows to him. He could be seen—seen and heard. Heard and obeyed.

"The Roman," he began, pointing directly at her as she stood against the kitchen wall, ignoring him, "will do no labor. If she is caught raising a sweat, all will suffer for it." When they said nothing, when not a Briton raised a brow and not a Saxon murmured an oath, he repeated, "She will not work. If she works, you will not eat."

He watched her as he spoke. She was standing alone, apart from them all, leaning her shoulder back against the wall in negligent ease and unconcern. Torchlight left her face in shadow, but outlined the curve of breast and hip in sharp relief. It was a trick of the light; he knew she was not so shapely beneath her Roman sack. He could not see her eyes, but he could read her mockery of him in her insolent posture. Her very lack of concern set a fire to his suspicions, and when she remained coolly unconcerned and looked down to brush a careless hand over her skirt, he knew without doubt that she had devised some new plan to rob him of his goal. A plan at which she would fail, but which would cause him no end of annoyance.

"Are you saying that it is your wish that Melania do nothing?" Theras had the temerity to ask.

Wulfred thought that over for a moment; he did not want her living the life of a pampered woman of Rome, even though that was exactly what she was. There had to be some work that would keep her idle hands busy that would also not threaten to kill her.

"Does she know *how* to do anything?" he finally asked. He had the satisfaction of seeing her jolt upright at that insult.

After a somewhat uncomfortable pause, clearly wishing that Melania would speak for herself, Theras said, "She can weave and dye and fashion jewelry."

To Burn

None of that sounded too strenuous. "Acceptable." Wulfred nodded and then commanded, "Go."
He looked at Melania as he said it. Melania looked
back at him and, when she stood alone facing him,
when he understood that she left of her own inclination, she sauntered off.

The group drifted back into the shadows of the
night until the two torches lit only the dust of the
courtyard ground. Wulfred and his men went into
the triclinium to begin the light evening meal that
ended their day.

"Well, that will hardly kill her"—Cenred
laughed—"unless she manages to throw herself
into the path of the shuttle in her weaving."

"No, she will live long enough to give Wulfred
his revenge, now that he understands her deviousness," Cynric said.

"What weapon does a woman have beyond her
deviousness?" Cuthred said tersely.

"A woman has an arsenal of weapons"—Balduff
chuckled—"but this one is too stupid to use them."

"Stupid?" Ceolmund asked. "Or proud?"

"What pride is there in trying to work yourself
to death doing menial labor?" Cynric said.

"What pride in meekly waiting for the ax to
drop?" Ceolmund countered.

"Come," Cenred said, "what pride in dyeing
linen? This talk of pride in a woman is foolish."

"She could well be proud of her hair," Balduff
murmured into his cup.

"Her hair?" Cynric said. "That snarled and dusty

81

mess? It is as appealing as a swarm of flies over meat."

"Just because you do not like black hair . . ." Balduff huffed.

"If pride is a word you will not ascribe to her, then what of valor?" Ceolmund persisted. He had not spoken so much at one time in ten years.

"What valor in chopping wood?" Cenred smiled.

"No," Cuthred said slowly, "there is valor in her fight against us. All that she has, and it is not much, she throws against us. She has courage." It was his highest praise.

"It is true," Cenred admitted, "that I did not expect such a fight from a Roman woman. There is more to her than first appears." Stroking his chin, he smiled ruefully. "She is a determined adversary."

"No."

Wulfred had been listening to their talk, surprised by most of it, content to let the conversation drift until it died naturally. But he would not allow them to talk themselves into attributing valor to the little Roman.

"It is not valor that drives her," he said into the sudden silence. "It is desperation. As her desperation grows, so will her frenzy." Looking at each man lingeringly, he said, "She must be watched carefully."

"She is being watched, Wulfred," Cynric said.

"Yes, she is being watched," Wulfred repeated, "but she must be made to suffer that which she fears most: a world ruled by Saxons."

Wulfred's eyes blazed vivid blue from the yellow

tangle of his hair. In his eyes they saw what drove him to vengeance and they did not question it. They understood his motivation and supported it, to a man.

Yet . . .

"It is unfortunate that we did not stop in another valley."

Balduff looked askance at Ceolmund, considering his comrade's whispered words.

"Does your heart grow soft for her, this small Roman slave?"

Ceolmund shook his shaggy head, the ends of his dark blond hair brushing against the crease of his elbow, and said softly, "I am concerned for Wulfred. This vengeance against a girl barely into womanhood will not sit well with him in years to come."

Balduff lifted his cup for a long swallow before answering. "I admit to not being overly fond of it now. It is no secret that I like women and, no matter what is argued, she is more valorous than most."

"She is determined," Ceolmund said.

"She is desperate, according to Wulfred," Balduff responded. "Time will prove what she is."

They sat in silence, the two of them, ignoring the ribald conversation of their brothers in arms as they drank cup after cup of good Roman wine. In time, Wulfred rose from the floor and left them, his step steady. He had consumed but one cup, as was his practice. Balduff watched him go and, without turning to Ceolmund, who sat quietly at his side, murmured, "Whatever she is, she is set against Wulfred." Sighing deeply, he added, "It is a hopeless defiance; she has no chance of besting him."

Ceolmund could not disagree.

"I shall outsmart him," Melania said almost lethargically three days later. "I wish I could take more pride in it, but it is too easily done."

"In what way will you outsmart him, Melania?" Theras asked over the productive din of meal preparation. The Saxons ate lightly after dark, a point on which to be grateful. Still, the warmly lit kitchen hummed with purposeful activity and Theras closed the distance to Melania so as to hear her better. Though he dared not expect that he would be cheered by her words; she had that stubborn gleam again. Even Finn, not known for his intelligence, had learned that when Melania carried herself just so and when her smile was as cold as three-day ash, it boded ill. Theras wondered if Wulfred understood as much about her yet.

"He is such an oaf," she went on, "a league behind me in tactics and incapable of reason. He shall be so easy to best; when I lie dead he will but begin to understand how I have outmaneuvered him." Sighing and brushing her loose hair back behind her ears, she finished, "Stupid barbari."

"What do you plan, Melania?" Theras asked again, suspicious at her refusal to answer directly.

"Plan?" she answered with innocence. "Why, certainly not to work until I drop. Does he not have me set at the very tasks I have always done and always loved? And in my own home?" Shaking her head, she said with a little smile, "Ridiculous and pathetic barbari."

"You must not take your own life, Melania," Theras urged.

"Suicide?" Her eyes glittered as she thought of swords and cliffs. "Never. But he will not win in this game of wills against me. I will best him. And he will know it."

"There are other ways to win," Theras said slowly, eyeing her carefully as he continued, "less aggressive ways." When she did not flare in fury, he continued. "He is a powerful man . . ."

"Yes, I am sure his life of killing has led him to believe that."

". . . and not unattractive . . ."

"He is as attractive as a boar in the mud, except the boar has finer teeth."

". . . and he does not seem . . . that is, I think he could be attracted to you . . ."

"Attracted to me!" She sprang to her feet, knocking the stool over. "I would that you had continued in comparing him to a muddy boar and the wandering murderer that you know he is. Attracted to me!" she spat out, her hair flying like a black war banner behind her as she paced in front of him. "He is attracted only to the idea of making me suffer, and I would sooner die than give him the pleasure, so speak to me no more of his being attracted to me. My stomach is heaving at the thought. If I so much as believed what you . . . Why, I would carve his eyes out of his head and feed them to the ravens, and then I would cut off his hands and stick them

on the wall in eternal farewell to his hellish comrades, and then I would—"

"Melania!" Theras interrupted her tirade, which was growing hotter with every breath she took. "Your course is most unwise. You are a slave now. You cannot fight him and you cannot win, not this way."

At that, she stopped both her wild pacing and her diatribe against the Saxon. Facing Theras, Melania said with icy control, "I am not a slave. I will never see myself as a slave. And I will fight. And win."

Theras watched her leave the kitchen and walk away across the courtyard. "But Wulfred sees you as a slave," he said softly. "His slave."

She heard him, but it didn't matter. She was no one's slave.

Stalking away from Theras's unpleasant speculations had felt wonderful, but she suddenly realized that she did not have a destination. For the first time in days she had nothing to do. Melania slowed her pace and considered her options. The triclinium was occupied by the oaf and his band of bloodthirsty arsonists, and she had spent too much time already in the little room where she had slept away her head start at beating the Saxon. The kitchen, where she had found herself more and more since the coming of the salivating horde, was not a wise choice, given her recent decision and the steps she'd taken to implement it. She had not been to the baths and the exercise room that comprised one arm of the villa since the Saxons' arrival. It was a likely destination since *they* would certainly have no inclination to visit the baths.

The caldarium was at the rear of the wing, closest to the furnace. Next to it was the tepidarium and then the frigidarium, each open to the other by a narrow doorway, and at the farthest end was the exercise room. It was a fairly elaborate affair for a country villa, but her family had always prided itself on staying fit. Of course, it did not have the shine and finish it had once had. None of the villa or the surrounding grounds did. Once this had been a country home, used when life in nearby Duroli-pons had become hectic and noisy; her family had come here for solitude, and from the villa had come much of the food and wine that had fed her ancestors when they dwelled in the town. But that had been many years ago. Her father had been a boy when they had left the town for good, coming to live at the villa. No one had planned for it to be a permanent move. No one had planned on the Saxons and their never-ending raids. No one had thought that the legions would leave. Nothing was as it should have been. Still, she thought, shaking off her gloom, the legions would be back and she would still be in possession of the villa. Her home.

The shade of the portico was welcome after the heat of the courtyard. It was a hot summer, hot and dry. Unnaturally hot. The notion bordered on pagan superstition, but she was almost certain that it would rain if only the Saxons would leave. Everything would be right again, safe, if only he would leave.

Starting at the back, in the caldarium, Melania cataloged the destruction; the decay she was already familiar with. Missing benches, broken tile, dirt: all new since the Saxons' arrival. New, but not unexpected. Moving through the connecting rooms, making her way carefully over the broken tiles, Melania finally arrived in the exercise room. It was not unoccupied.

In the dim light she could just make out Dorcas and one of the filthy Saxons copulating on the floor.

It took her a full three breaths, shaky and deep, to find the words, but find them she did.

"Dorcas," she said clearly and almost calmly. "Get up. Dress yourself. And take your dirty hands off her legs, Saxon pig! Get up, Dorcas; push his hands away if he will not do the decent thing. The decent thing, what am I saying? There is not a Saxon alive who knows what is decent, so certainly none have the ability to actually do it, unless the only decent thing they do is die, and I would have them do it decently by the thousands! Get off her, you imbecile!"

"You have intruded upon our privacy," Cenred said with a placating smile. A smile? He could smile? As if their fornication were no concern of hers, except that she had intruded upon it? Breathing became more difficult; she couldn't seem to get enough air. There were red spots shifting in front of her eyes.

"Shut up, monster! Just . . . shut up and go away! Privacy . . . did you say privacy? You expect privacy in the exercise room? In my home?"

"Is that what this room is for?" Cenred said easily, with Dorcas lying tense and frigid beneath him. "Well, I am getting—"

"*Don't* say it!" Melania threatened. "Revolting! Disgusting! That's what you are, what you all are. Get out before I lose the contents of my stomach . . . and I don't require privacy to do it!"

It was when she began to gag that Cenred took her seriously and, quickly adjusting his scanty clothing, left the room, leaving Dorcas to Melania.

Melania scrutinized Dorcas carefully as she adjusted her clothing. Dark of hair and eye, Dorcas had been born within the villa walls. Melania had known her since birth, but had she really known her at all?

"Have you always behaved like a whore?"

Dorcas finished pulling her tunic down to cover herself and kept her dark head bowed. Still, Melania could see her jerk at the question.

"I had little choice in this," she answered with quiet dignity, raising her brown eyes to face Melania. "I have chosen to make the best of the situation. Cenred is kind . . . and . . . It could have been worse," she finished with a catch in her voice.

"It could have been worse? You spread yourself for a Saxon, practically in public, and it could have been worse? What of your commitment to God? What of the fact that they came here to murder and steal and burn? Perhaps it could have been worse for you," Melania said with stiff dignity, "but it could hardly have been worse for me."

"Oh, yes, it could be worse for you," Dorcas answered, her own ire rising. "You are a slave now, as much as you deny that truth. Why do you think that you have been spared? Do you not know that they take their pleasure where they find it, even to the burning of this place? Didn't you wonder that they didn't touch you?"

"Touch me?" Melania asked in numbing horror. It had never occurred to her. Those . . . animals, touching her? She could as easily imagine Optio, her father's mount, suddenly reciting Greek poetry.

"Yes. It is because of him, of Wulfred. He is in charge of his men and he is in charge of you. They will not touch you because of him. They dare not."

"He is *not* in charge of me!"

Dorcas responded with a cynical raising of her brows and said nothing. There was no need, Melania realized. He controlled her home, her servants, her labor. Her life. But it was only for a season of her life—a season as unnatural and miserable as this hot, dry summer. Like all seasons, it would pass. It had to pass. There could not be year upon year of this domination, this contest of minds and wills that fired them both; this could not continue past the summer season. She did not think she could endure more than a season of him in her life. He hounded her through the day, and she was certain that he watched her at night while she slept. He had taken her home and made it into his camp. He had taken every familiar and cherished thing in her life and put his Saxon mark upon it; she wondered sometimes if he had not somehow put his mark upon her.

"I . . . did not understand," Melania said, her thoughts whirling. "I didn't know." Looking into the dark eyes of Dorcas, Melania came as close as she could to an apology. Melania was not accustomed to being in the wrong; she had little skill in the art of apology and even less desire to learn. "Do what you must, Dorcas, to survive. I will find no fault in it. And I will pray that God will also find you guiltless. It is the Saxons who are guilty."

Before Dorcas could voice a reply, Melania was gone, hunting for the Saxon the way fire hunts for air. She did not care to listen to her tumbled thoughts; she preferred to act. Fortunately he was so very easy to find; the smell alone would have led her. He was where she had known he would be, lounging with his gang of murderers in *her* triclinium, that seducer of the powerless with him. *Oaf.* He would answer to this charge of debauchery and licentiousness; he would have a chance to defend himself. She would be civilized.

"I have just been informed that your men have been taking . . . liberties with the women of my home, women to whom I have a responsibility. It has also been pointed out to me that I have been spared these atrocities because of you and the control you have foolishly convinced yourself you have over my life." Her anger growing with every breath she took, like a living flame that was fed by the charged air between them, Melania said, "Is it true, if you can find it in your deceitful Saxon heart to acknowledge truth, that it is because of you and your interference that I alone have remained unmolested?" Her charge was clearly stated. He was being given the chance to defend himself publicly. She astounded herself with her superior sense of justice, but it should not be surprising: she was Roman.

Wulfred had not moved during her fiery speech, but remained kneeling at the table, negligently sipping his beer. He had not looked at her, firing her anger at his insolence even higher, and when he finally spoke, it was to his men. But he said it in Latin.

"She sounds insulted."

Her anger stuck in her throat and she choked on it, speechless.

"You have managed it," praised Cynric, watching her struggle for words.

"I had almost given up," said Cenred.

"You monster!" she screamed, her hands arching into talons.

Balduff smiled and toasted her, saying, "Never underestimate a woman."

"For a moment," Cuthred said conversationally to the table at large, "I thought—"

"Shut your foul, Saxon mouths!" she commanded them.

To their own surprise, they fell silent. The Roman looked closer to killing than they had yet seen her.

Of them all, only Wulfred was unmoved, his blue eyes lazily on her face, his hands relaxed on his bulging thighs. Didn't the oaf have the sophistication to know that meals were taken in a reclining position? Didn't he even have the grace to look embarrassed? Blue eyes raked her body insolently and she stiffened as if he had touched her. As if he would dare.

"Is it true?" she asked, breathing hard through her mouth, her eyes bright and hot in the whiteness of her face. "Have I alone been left untouched by you barbari?"

The monster had the gall to grin. He ran his hands down the length of his thighs and then slowly back up to his hips. His hands were long-fingered and covered with a sprinkling of blond hairs that gleamed gold in the firelight. Why was she staring at his hands?

"Only you can confirm the truth of that, if you can find it in your deceitful Roman heart. . . ."

"No one has touched me!" she shouted in ringing proclamation, forcing herself to look away from his hands which were now resting on his narrow hips. "Is it because of you?"

"Perhaps it is because of you," he answered simply and irritatingly.

Because of her? Because she was clearly superior to them and they knew it? Because she had them cowed, in awe of her? It was not impossible; in fact, it was more than likely—

The disgusting oaf interrupted her speculations.

"There is little about you to commend you, Roman. You stink."

It was easy to subdue the prick to her pride when he was smiling up at her so spitefully. Never would

93

she allow him to win in a contest of insults, not when he gave her so many weapons.

"No more than you, Saxon," she said, smiling coldly back. "My smell is of good, honest work while you smell of deceit. I prefer my own smell."

"In that it seems you are alone."

His eyes, so blue, so intense, stared into hers, and within the very heart of his eyes she saw that he was laughing at her. Laughing at her when he had ruined her world with his filth and left her alone to clean it up. She turned to leave, ignoring his men, who were laughing at her expense. Oh, he was having a fine time.

"Alone is my preference," she said over her shoulder.

"It is my preference which should occupy you," he called to her retreating back. Retreating . . . she would not retreat. And she would not be mocked by such as he.

"Which it does not," she said, turning to face him across the triclinium's width. "Will you kill me, you who claim mastery over me? Shall it be death by knife or club or ax? Or will it not be death at all because you fear the retribution of Roman justice? Roman justice, the truest this world can give, protecting the weak against the monstrous and keeping the murderer from the innocent."

"Keeping me from you?" he interrupted with a scowl. "I will not speak with you of Roman justice," he said in a snarl, the smile completely wiped from his face. She couldn't have been happier.

"I can understand why, barbarian, when you—"

"No," he interrupted harshly. "You cannot. Leave, Roman; obey your stated will if none other will serve. Leave. Now."

She backed up a few steps at the intensity in his voice and the look in his bright blue eyes and then forced herself to walk away from him casually, as if it had been her decision to leave the triclinium. He had actually looked angry. In all she had done, in all the words they had thrown like daggers at each other, in all the moments when she had physically attacked him, he had never looked angry. But he was angry now. And the worst of it was that his anger didn't give her one moment of pleasure.

Chapter Nine

"He is fascinated by you," Dorcas said to Melania as she paced in the courtyard.

"Who?"

"Wulfred." At Melania's blank look, Dorcas added in superfluous explanation, "The great Saxon oaf."

"Is that his name?" she casually asked. She knew his name, and it was more than she wanted to know. It was more important that he know her name, which she was sure he did, even though he had never called her by it. *Roman* was what he called her, as if it were an insult. *Stupid oaf.* But he must know her name so that when she bested him he would have her name to howl to the sky in defeat until the day he gave the civilized world a gift by dying. A day that could not come soon enough to suit her—as long as she died first.

"Did you hear . . . ?" Dorcas finally asked.

"Yes, he is fascinated by me, as well a worm should be in awe of a hawk. It does not surprise me. It does repulse me."

She had not seen him for five days, and it had been eight since she had begun her latest campaign to thwart him in his determination to keep her alive. Five days . . . the villa was not large enough for that to have happened naturally. No, she had worked at it, avoiding him like the disease he was, bothered by the anger she had sparked in him. Angry that she was bothered by anything he did. And worse, disgusted that she found herself wanting to get a glimpse of him. She had not seen him for five days. This odd wanting could be explained away as morbid curiosity to see the effect she was having on his composure; surely he must be curious as to what she was doing, maybe even worried that she was getting the better of him in some way. Of course, she was. If only he would seek her out. If only he would demand her presence so that she could refuse him; there would be great satisfaction in that. Had he forgotten her in the past five days? Had he forgotten that she was his enemy and needed watching? Had he forgotten the anger that she had unknowingly sparked in their last exchange? Had he forgotten their hatred of each other? She hadn't, not in five days. She couldn't in five years. But where was he?

Melania paced restlessly, like an animal tethered.

Claudia Dain

She had a pounding headache behind her eyes. She'd had it for days.

"You could use it," Dorcas said, relentless in her efforts at conversation.

"Use what?" Melania asked, reluctantly being drawn away from her angry preoccupation.

"His fascination."

"What are you trying to say?" Melania stopped her pacing.

"Do you know nothing of men, of him?" Dorcas asked, her tone almost exasperated.

"I know he is a monstrous oaf, hardly a man at all, but more a beast or a pestilence. A deadly pestilence that destroys all before and behind it. Yes," she continued, warming to her topic, "he is like a worm, feeding on death. Why?" she asked, letting her pain feed her anger.

Dorcas did not answer. Wulfred, the worm, was standing in the gateway to the courtyard.

Of course, he'd heard every word. When had she ever hidden her thoughts? Or her venom.

She'd been hiding from him. It had been five days since she had stood before him spouting words on Roman justice—words she hardly knew the meaning of. It had taken him the better part of two days to be certain that the anger she had sparked in him was within his control.

Five days. She looked smaller than he remembered her, if that was possible, little more than tendon and bone. And so agitated, as if she would fly out of her skin if she could. But what did she do

98

with herself? He knew that she did no hard labor—
she was too carefully watched for that—but what
of the light tasks that were more comfortable for
her? How did she spend her time?

He had watched her intermittently, though he
had men enough to do the duty if he had demanded
it. He had not. She was his enemy and he would
see to her. He had watched her. She charged the
air around her with her energy as she moved from
one room to the next, directing, leading, comforting. He had watched her with Flavius, the boy, and
seen a gentleness that seemed odd for her. At least
in his experience of her it was odd. One thing was
constant: she never acted the part of a slave. No
matter the task, no matter the hour, no matter the
place, she was in command of both herself and all
within her sphere. It served to make her seem all
the more Roman to him, though he would not have
thought that possible. He looked at her now, her
black hair braided into a thick mat down her back
that touched the roundness of her bottom with a
playfulness that he found irritating. Distracting.
Disturbing.

She looked exhausted, her skin as thin as air and
her eyes dark bruises against her face. Yet she was
not still, but pacing, pacing in front of the kitchen
doorway. What was she about? Nothing good, certainly.

When Dorcas said nothing to her question, Melania turned quickly to face the other woman.
Turned quickly and swayed on her feet, her balance
almost lost. Her equilibrium lost over such a simple

act? This from the woman who had swung an ax with agility and grace? Wulfred scowled, studying her, rubbing his knuckles over his belly in abstract concentration. There was something about her behavior that tugged at a dark memory, something from that black time he had hoped revenge would wash away from him. Wulfred's hand scraped along the hairy ridges of his abdomen in a rhythmic caress, reminding him. The hand stopped and dropped to his side. He had seen such weakness before, even felt it himself. It was then that he knew exactly what she had been about for the past five days. She had been starving herself.

"Has she eaten?" he called to Dorcas, striding toward them.

"It is not yet time for the meal," the girl answered easily, confusion in her voice. She did not know.

"Get her some food. Now."

"I am not a child to be spoken over!" Melania declared. "Speak to me, oaf, if you have something of import to say, though that is hardly possible, is it?"

Wulfred's turquoise blue eyes pierced hers in smoldering anger as he waited for Dorcas to return. In moments she appeared with a plate of bread and fruit. Wulfred took the plate from Dorcas and held it out to Melania in challenge.

"Eat."

Turning up her arrogant Roman nose, she said with a sniff, "I am not hungry."

"I have not asked you anything. I have told you—eat."

"What a lovely world it would be if each of us had his way in all things. Never to have our desires thwarted, never to want something we could not have." Her eyes glittered like a writhing serpent's. "Don't parents in your pagan country teach their children that you can't always get what you ask for? But then, you were probably cast out to fend for yourself at a toddling age, like an animal. And just look at what became of you."

Wulfred held his ground, continuing to hold the platter under her arrogant nose. "You are ignorant of many things, but know this: you will eat this plate of food or I will hold you down and force it down your Roman throat. Just like a stubborn child."

"I am no child," she said, pointing her nose into the air.

"Prove it," he said in a growl.

She hesitated before taking the plate from his outstretched hand, and he could read her desire to throw it back at him. She resisted the desire. He was almost sorry. She looked at the food. He watched her swallow down her saliva. Finally, looking him in the eyes, she reached for a slab of bread and, breaking off a bite-sized piece, put it delicately and very deliberately into her mouth. She chewed the crust of bread into pulp before swallowing it down. Slowly, deliberately, methodically she ate the bread and the sliced apples and the ripe olives. He watched her every swallow.

"From now on you will eat every meal with me,

where I can watch you. This is not a request," he added.

The fire of direct confrontation flared behind her hazel eyes and then was tamped out and covered by a screen of deviousness. She would obey, but she also had a hope of thwarting him. Again. Wulfred allowed her to walk away from him, flinging her braid over her shoulder with enough force to cut him had he been a step closer. He had the victory in this latest battle and they both knew it. He also knew that she had not exhausted her arsenal, limited as it was. But she could not starve herself, not with him monitoring her every morsel. Still, she had the look of a warrior rearming. He knew her well enough to be suspicious. And wary.

Chapter Ten

He watched her like a wolf watching a newborn lamb, watched her eat as little as she could get away with without inciting a direct confrontation between them. She had learned enough to know that she had little hope of winning against him in a direct assault; he was too huge, too powerful. And still she grew thinner. Melania wanted to crow her delight over the success of her latest strategy, but she didn't. She didn't want him to become even more suspicious than he already was, and he would know something was amiss if she let the light of victory shine forth from her eyes. Oh, yes, she felt a thrill of victory every time she outwitted him, though he had made it more difficult with each passing day.

He had begun by forcing her to eat in the triclinium with the rest of the Saxons, directing the positioning of her plate himself and watching her as she ate. Of course, she had positioned herself as far away from him as was physically possible, though the room was hardly large enough to permit her to eat without seeing him and his horde of murderers. Their table manners weren't as bad as they could have been; they certainly did not wash sufficiently between courses and definitely did not appreciate the delicacy and intricacy of the dishes served, not when they wolfed them down as they did. Still, it could have been worse.

After a few days passed and she still continued to lose weight, Wulfred insisted she sit next to him during meals. Melania smiled slightly to herself. He still did not understand her method, and she was winning before his very eyes. *Pitiful pagan fool.* After giving him her most superior look, one she had certainly perfected by now, she deigned to accede to his wishes. The head of the table was her accustomed place, after all, and this was her home, her table, and her food. Of course she would sit next to him in the place of honor. It took him out of her direct line of vision anyway, a definite blessing, though now they shared a platter and sometimes their hands brushed, making her stomach tighten uncomfortably. Hardly surprising, since he was such an animal, but she should have hardened herself to his presence by now; these disconcerting tremors should have abated in intensity. Instead they had increased. His blondness no longer aroused her attention. His bulging physique hardly caused her to turn her head. His growled commands incited only a shrug. She had not quite developed an acceptable response to his flame-blue eyes, but she would. She had no doubt as to that. She was a Roman and he a mere Saxon.

Now he was even more demanding about the amount of food she consumed. She had her winning method, but still, it was better if she did not eat too much. And much, much better if he did not watch her too closely, or sit too close, or rub his hip against hers as had happened once or twice, causing that odd sensation in her belly. Really, he was too big to sit in such civilized surroundings. It was obvious, at least to her, that he should root around in the dirt with the rest of the pigs instead of squeezing in next to her.

These mealtimes were most trying.

Taking a small mouthful of wine to cleanse her mouth, Melania began to rise to her feet. Another meal blessedly over. It was her usual practice to exit as quickly as possible after the meal, a practice that suited her winning method to perfection. Today Wulfred broke his own practice of silence during the meal.

"Stay," he commanded, his voice a deep rumble in his hairy chest.

No need to ask to whom he spoke. Only she was the recipient of such terse commands. To everyone else, both Saxon and Briton, he was almost jovial. She paused, standing facing his back, wondering what he would say next. Such a wide and well-muscled back. Melania shook off the rolling in her

Claudia Dain

belly and redirected her thoughts. Such a lovely, exposed target.

Turning to look up at her, his vivid blue eyes piercing in their intensity, he pointed back down to the cushion, indicating that she sit.

She crossed her arms in clear defiance and waited, standing, expelling a large sigh in the doing.

"You seem to do nothing," he said, toying with a crust of bread, looking at it and not at her. "I will have no idle slaves."

"I am not a—"

"Show me your handiwork," he interrupted her familiar tirade. "Or was the Greek lying when he said you had some skills?"

"Only you lie, Saxon, as do all your kind, so it is understandable that you think all other races are as you." She paused and dropped her eyes for a moment before adding grudgingly, "But Theras did not lie."

"Do you lie, Roman?"

She raised her eyes to turn back at that, instantly furious.

"I have certainly never lied in telling you of my hatred of you and your pack, Saxon, though I have never told the whole truth of my rage because I cannot find the words to express the loathing I feel and the vengeance that will be mine."

"*You* cannot find the words? That surely is a lie," he taunted, rolling the crust into a ball between his fingers. "And what vengeance can a slave wreak? And that slave a shriveling, shrinking female."

Melania smiled in silent superiority and unspoken victory; what a dolt he was. "To be small is the Roman fashion."

"And to be lazy?" he asked, picking up a small bit of cheese to toy with.

"I am not the one who wishes to linger at the table, Saxon; it is you who plays with your food." When he said nothing, merely staring at her with those too-sharp eyes of summer blue, she understood that he had also been toying with her. She was most definitely not a woman to be toyed with. Melania turned on her heel and announced, "I'm leaving."

"And I'm going with you," he said, rising quickly to his feet. How could such a monstrous oaf move so fast? "To see you at your labors, light as they are," he added.

Not at all what she wanted. Naturally. It had already been too long since her eating, and now he dogged her like an unwelcome cur. If she didn't already know how stupid he was, she would suspect that he knew . . . or almost knew. But he could not know how she was defeating him with every day that passed, even every meal that they shared in such loathsome proximity. She had to endure his company at meals; she saw no reason to endure it now. Her temper fired, fed also by the explosive headache that had been as much a companion to her as the giant Saxon oaf now tripping along behind her like a monstrous bear.

"I do not need you, dog, to shepherd me to my tasks. I do them, as you surely know since you have me watched nearly constantly by that pack of fools you call friends. Now leave me, Saxon. What I do will not hold your interest."

"You seem very sure," he said mildly.

"I am always sure of what I think and, therefore, what I say. It is the mark of the intelligent."

"It is the mark of the arrogant," he contradicted.

"You would think so, Saxon, you who say whatever you will, no matter what you are really thinking or planning, but I say what I know, and I *know* that you are bothering me and I *know* that I want you gone. I want to be alone and I don't want you tagging along behind me like a burr on the tail."

"And you get everything you want?" he said in a quiet snarl, rubbing his hands along his thighs in irritation. "I can well believe that in the past you had but to whisper and your will was accomplished, but that is in the past, Roman, and today you must do as I want."

"So you say, again and again," she spat out, twisting her hair between her fingers, hating the sight of him, hating the feel of the food sitting so solidly in her stomach. "I am not an imbecile! I understand what you want of me. Exactly what you want of me!"

He wanted her death. It was what he had planned for her from the start of this strange summer, and there was no surprise in it. But now he was not some nameless Saxon barbarian slicing down at a Roman landowner with his seax; he was Wulfred and he wanted Melania dead at his feet. The image appalled her suddenly. Turning, she ran out of the courtyard and up toward the vineyards, running away from him. Running away from the anger and impotent rage that choked her whenever she had to face what he had done to her life and how he was trying to manage her death.

The hill seemed steeper than before and left her gasping before she had gone far, but that was good. It meant she was weakening, sickening. Winning. She stopped at a rocky outcrop, her breath coming in gulps, and hung her head, holding back the length of her hair with a hand. With very little effort, she vomited up the contents of her stomach. It was not so difficult as it had been. In fact, it was almost effortless after so many times. But it was still a miserable exercise. It was why she ate as little as she could; it suited her better to keep such a disagreeable practice to a minimum. It would not be an easy victory, but she would attain it.

Wiping her mouth with the hem of her skirt, Melania straightened and pushed a few strands of hair away from her face. Revolting business, but such was the price of victory over the Saxon. And it was a victory. She felt so weak, so empty, so light in the head. How much longer before she simply dried up and blew away? Let him catch her then; let him try to catch the dried leaf she was becoming. In spite of the headache, she felt almost euphoric.

Until she turned around.

The Saxon was watching her.

He stood with bulging arms crossed over his naked chest, one foot resting on a small rock, his eyes full of contempt. Surprise rolled through her. She had not anticipated his contempt.

"You are as devious as a child," he stated.

"No," she argued, wiping her mouth again. "I am as determined as a Roman."

"Determined to starve yourself."

How horribly he said it; how awful it sounded when he said it.

"Determined to escape you," she answered.

"That you will not do," he said, uncrossing his arms and walking toward her, his step long in spite of the uneven ground.

"You cannot force me to live when I have chosen to die. You cannot force me to eat. You cannot stop me from rejecting my food!"

Standing over her, crowding her, pressing against her, he gripped her by the arms. It hurt. And as often as he seemed to touch her, each touch carried a spark that burned—a quick burning that sparked something within her that she couldn't tolerate, wouldn't investigate. It was because he was so vile, so barbaric; it was the only possibility. He said two words, two words that chilled the fire he had started in her.

"Watch me."

"To do that you would have to be with me constantly," she argued. He was such an imbecile. Did he not know that she would defeat him?

He only smiled and slowly released his painful grip on her arms.

"So be it."

It was worse than the vomiting. A chain around her throat would have been kinder. It was torture and nothing less.

He was with her every moment of her waking. They ate together. He followed her when she relieved herself and told her that he was listening carefully to be certain that she was not also relieving herself of her food. *Animal.* He watched her clean her teeth. He watched her talk to Theras. He watched her instruct Dorcas. He watched her preparing her dyes. He watched her forming delicate balls of gold for a brooch. He watched her and watched her and watched her.

She was gaining weight steadily, and she knew she was the source of his increased good humor.

She was miserable.

Of course, he not only accompanied her on all her tasks, but forced her to accompany him. *Odious oaf.* They stood now in the courtyard watching his men practice with their clanging weapons. He did not touch her; he did not have to physically force her to stand by his side; they had passed through that phase of their warfare. At first she had fought him, fought his constant proximity, but he was bigger and stronger and more primitive. He had held her to him, along the hard and unyielding length of him, held her until she was painfully aware of every bump and bulge, held her until she thought she'd vomit from the heavings in her belly. His touch had been worse than anything, and so she had relented. To keep him from touching her. To keep him away from her.

Balduff, his perpetual grin firmly in place, faced Wulfred in the courtyard they had claimed as their place for mock battles. Their sword tips touched briefly in metallic salute before the battle dance began. These Saxons were so battle-hungry that they fought each other when no other foe was at hand. She had seen such play many times now. She had watched Wulfred countless times raise his sword above his head and charge down upon his opponent. She had noted the play of muscle beneath his golden skin. She had seen his biceps bunch at the contact of steel to steel and traced with her eyes the sweat that ran in a languorous trickle down his breastbone to soak the waist of his leather leggings. Melania ran a hand across the sweaty line of her collarbone, suddenly very hot in the treeless courtyard. She had seen him perform in the sun of the courtyard day upon day but only because he had forced her to attend him. Only that. She would not be here now if not for his bullying, as he well knew. It was not for love of looking that she waited now, not when the sun beat down and her knees felt weak with the heat.

He was an oaf of a man to keep her waiting for him while he played away the day.

Balduff blocked Wulfred's blow and swung in, throwing an elbow to connect with Wulfred's belly as he spun out of sword reach. It was a devious and dishonorable move: a Saxon move. Wulfred absorbed the blow without even a catch in his wind and stuck his foot between Balduff's feet, tripping him neatly. Melania smiled in spite of all her best intentions and watched as Balduff rolled to his feet, covered in dust and still grinning like a fool, sword in hand. Wulfred also grinned as they continued their sparring.

It was beyond tolerable for him to have such a knee-buckling grin and to throw it so casually at Balduff.

The circle of spectators around the courtyard was growing, as it always did when the Saxons played their barbaric games. Melania had abandoned all ideas of trying to stop them.

Balduff was backing away from Wulfred, his brow sweaty and his cheeks red. Wulfred, the oaf, looked much as he had when they began. He clearly had the endurance of an ox. Melania could hardly let herself be impressed by that; he was an animal. All Saxons were animals.

Wulfred charged boldly, his sword gleaming white-hot in the sunlight of the summer day. Balduff blocked, metal rang, Wulfred twisted, and Balduff's sword whizzed through the still air.

Flavius watched, mouth agape, as the sword flew at him like a hurled missile.

Before Melania could run more than a handful of steps toward Flavius, Wulfred threw himself into a roll that raised a cloud of dust, lifted his sword, and blocked the flying blade. Metal clanged and echoed as Balduff's sword dropped to the dirt near Flavius's bare feet.

Flavius looked down at Wulfred, crouched at his feet. He began to shake, the tears rising to fill his dark eyes. Before they could fall, indeed, before any of them could think what to say or do, Wulfred pulled the boy down into his lap.

"I've got you," the Saxon said gruffly, his hands rubbing the boy's slender back. "I've got you now."

Flavius snaked thin arms around Wulfred's neck and clung, his sobs smothered against Wulfred's chest, his legs curled upon Wulfred's lap.

None spoke. Balduff walked softly near and rubbed a hand across the boy's head before retrieving his sword and edging his way into the circle of people in the courtyard, disappearing, as had his smile.

When Flavius had settled somewhat and his legs had uncurled, he wiped frantic hands across his reddened eyes. Wulfred continued to rub his back, his movements measured and supremely unhurried. His expression showed no embarrassment at Flavius's emotional display.

Melania frowned in confusion. Such had not been the way with her Roman father. Such a display of fear would have elicited brusque rebuke or poorly masked distaste. But for Flavius there was tender compassion and a warm embrace. From a Saxon.

"Swords are fearful things when they come at you," Wulfred said easily. "It is why a warrior trains, to learn to defeat his fear of them in mastery."

"I . . . I was not afraid," Flavius whispered, his voice full of unshed tears.

"I was afraid," Wulfred admitted with a small smile.

"You were?" Flavius said with another swipe

across his eyes before looking up at the man who held him.

"Yes. Weren't you?"

"Well," Flavius said, holding his shoulders stiff as he took a shaky breath, "I am Roman."

Wulfred smiled. "I think even Romans are allowed to be afraid . . . sometimes."

"You do? But . . . but Melania is not afraid. Melania is never afraid."

Wulfred turned to look at her, and she hoped her frown was still firmly in place; she knew her confusion was. Wulfred bent to whisper something to the boy held within the curl of his arms. Melania watched Flavius shake his head as Wulfred shrugged and nodded, his smile a gentle gift to the child.

"Then you will continue your training," Wulfred said firmly, raising the boy to his feet with one hand, the private moment and their whispered words over. "It is a good lesson for a warrior: beware the sword not in your own hand; it seeks your life."

"I think I knew that before," Flavius mumbled to the dirt at his feet.

"But now, I think, you will never forget it." Wulfred chuckled, raising the boy's chin with his hand and looking into his eyes. "And stand farther off when you watch us train. I will let you know when you may enter into the circle for your own game. For now, use the stick and the club given you, strengthen your arm, train your eye, and tame your fear. These are the lessons for now."

"Yes, Wulfred," Flavius said, walking off. He was without shame and it showed in his walk. Wulfred had given him that.

It was not what her father would have done. It was nothing like what her father would have done. But Melanius, her father, had been a wonderful man, an honorable man, a Roman. That was the important thing, the only thing. The only thing worth remembering. The only thing worth knowing.

But she would love to know what it was that Wulfred had whispered to Flavius.

The courtyard, once a place of refinement and peace, was now a place for arms practice. It was a sight that physically pained her. Her father had so loved this place, this home of theirs. He had cherished it as a bright jewel of Rome in a land that was coming to forget its heritage. Rome had flourished in Britannia for hundreds of years; Britannia was of Rome, yet some now, in these uncertain times, had lost the use of Latin. Unthinkable, yet true. But it would never be so with her. She was Roman. She would remain Roman. As her father had remained Roman.

Her father . . . it was better he was dead than to have lived to see this occupation of their home. He had died fighting while she had lived on, well fed and well rested, thanks to the Saxon. It felt almost a sacrilege to have survived. She hadn't thought much about her father since . . . since the moment she had seen his bloodless face and mutilated body. And seen the Saxon's face just behind it, greedy to feed off of her grief and despair and defeat. She had pushed her sorrow for her father to the depths of her being, focusing instead on outwitting the Saxon murderer and stealing his ultimate victory, but now . . . now she had time.

She had believed in the beginning that her own death was hovering over her like an angel, ready to pluck her from this horror and carry her to God's arms; but she had already lived longer than she had planned and might live longer still. It seemed the barbarian wasn't quite as stupid as she had hoped. Suddenly she wanted to say her farewells to her father, even if only in her heart.

The Saxon was absorbed in watching his men play with their stupid weapons, smiling his approval, grunting in that pagan language of his.

"Where is my father?" she demanded.

Wulfred turned to look at her over his impossibly large shoulder, his eyes very blue against the pale gold of his skin. He was shirtless—again and always.

"Where do your beliefs tell you he is?" he asked mildly.

"I know where he is, imbecile. He is in heaven with the saints of God and where, I am thankful, no barbarian will ever touch him, but where are his remains?" She asked it fearfully and hated knowing that Wulfred could detect the emotion in her voice, but she was so afraid that her father had been burned or dumped in a heap of slaughtered bodies. Christian she was, but she had a Roman's sense of burial.

117

Claudia Dain

His eyes clouded with something she would have named sympathy in another man, and he turned away from his sport, taking her arm to lead her away. Melania pulled her arm away from him, never wanting his touch and certainly not now when she felt so painfully exposed. He let his own hand drop and said softly, "I will show you."

She followed him, positioning herself just slightly behind his left shoulder; it was a position that kept him in view and yet made it unlikely that he would touch her. They left the walled courtyard by the side gate and walked slowly over the parched grass. It rustled beneath their feet, heralding their arrival to the birds and the wind. After only a few paces, she knew where he was leading her; all of her people had been buried here. This was Theras's doing, and she thanked him in her heart for his thoughtfulness. Her mother was here, as was her mother's sister and a brother of her own who had died in infancy. And now her father. The stone was new and the lettering crude; still, it was a respectable monument to the man.

> Here in
> the tomb lies
> Melanius.
> In peace.

In peace. Yes, now he was in peace, and she was left behind to battle their common enemy. She who had no peace and would find none until she joined her family in heaven, where Jesus the Christ had

118

promised his followers that he had a place prepared
for them. At least she had a place somewhere; the
villa seemed less hers and more pagan every day.

She turned away from her melancholy thoughts,
refusing to be crushed by the knowledge of her father's peace and her lack of it. Her time would
come. Either way it would come. If she won against
the Saxon, she would die. If the Saxon defeated her,
she would die. Oh, yes, she would be with her father soon. It couldn't be too soon. Melania sighed
and glanced at the golden animal who stood silently
beside her, blue eyes scanning the treetops. Was he
giving her privacy in his barbarian fashion? It was
possible—he had the ability to surprise her—but
she found it inconceivable to believe that he would
do anything that touched upon kindness. He was
Saxon, an animal.

"Is he really there?" she asked suddenly.

"Yes," he answered simply, looking down at her.

"Why?" She did not know what had happened
to the others, but she had seen no other stones.
They had not received this treatment.

"He fought well," he said.

A Saxon answer. Oddly she found she could understand it.

"He was not so very old," she said softly, touching the rough stone with her fingertips.

"No," he agreed with an answering softness, staring down at her.

Lifting her eyes to the sky, she marked the flight
of a pair of larks skimming the treetops. Birdsong

119

caressed the air and the wind played in the trees. It was almost music.

"He loved this place, his home."

"He fought well," he repeated, his highest praise.

"Yes," she agreed, knowing it must have been true. She looked at the trees as they were moved by the wind's invisible breath, ignoring the building tears behind her eyes.

They stood a pace apart and said nothing for a while, watching the changing pattern of the clouds as they rushed across the sky. Was heaven as beautiful as this place she had known all of her life? Could it be?

"He fought for you as well," he offered after a time.

Melania smiled and ran her hands over the inscripted letters. "Yes."

"He loved you," he said with the barest hesitation. How had he ever learned the Latin word for love?

The tears rising, she choked out, "Yes."

It was true: he had valued her, taught her, disciplined her. Fathered her.

"Was it you . . . did you . . . did he . . . ?" She could hardly ask, hardly get the words out, but she suddenly had to know. Was her father's death on this man's hands, this man who stood in solemn silence with her at her father's monument?

"It was not I, Melania," he said without hesitation. He had understood her fear and her question without her having to belabor it. He understood so much about her—perhaps too much. And he had said her name. It was the first time. It sounded strange on his tongue, rougher and wilder, not the cultured name it was. She was suddenly glad that he was not the one who had taken her father's life.

"Not you?"

"No," he said solidly.

Strangely, she believed him. For all of his barbarity, he had never lied to her. He would never see the need, but also she did not think it in him to lie. There was no lie in the blue eyes that blazed into hers now; there was sincerity, earnestness, even compassion. But there could not be compassion. He was too cold, too merciless, for compassion. The image of Flavius sobbing against his chest came instantly to mind, and she pushed it down; just because he could be kind to a child did not unmake him from the monster she knew him to be. A single act would not erase a lifetime of experience. She was no fool, and no Saxon was merciful.

"Then who?" She turned to face him, her eyes clear now and as sharp as ever. Her tears were gone as quickly as they had come.

He took a step nearer and said firmly, "It was not I."

He would not tell her. He did not want her to try to take vengeance against one of his men. In the end, did it matter? Her father was dead. Wulfred had not killed him.

"Did . . . he die well?"

"He died fighting," he began. It did not mean to her what it did to him. "He died well."

"He never gave up, did he? He fought until . . ."

She stared up into his eyes of blue, searching for . . . something. Understanding? But that was the same as compassion, and she had already decided that he could not give it. He was Saxon. He stood before her, blocking the sky and the swaying trees with the warm gold of his body, and his eyes burned to give her . . . what? Comfort? Could she wrap her arms around his neck and would he hold her to his chest while she cried out her loss and her isolation in a world without parents? Would he hold her and whisper to her until the pain went away? Could he, who had thrown the sword into her world, make everything right again? Everyone was gone; the legions, the wool merchant, the tile setter . . . her father. Even Marcus was gone. She was so very alone. The tears rushed back.

Who would whisper against her hair, "I've got you now"?

"He died well, Melania," he said softly, his hand almost touching hers.

He did not touch her; she was thankful for that. If he touched her the tears would overwhelm her.

"That was like him." It was all she could think to say. He had died well, as she had not.

Chapter Eleven

As she had not. As she was not. Starving herself to a skeleton out of spite was not dying well. Sticking a dirty finger down a parched throat was not dying well. In the thoughts she'd had of her father, thoughts born at his monument the day before, the last weeks shone with a disturbing clarity; what she was doing was not well done. There was no victory in this.

It was especially demeaning that even the Saxon had seen her efforts as childish rather than noble. Viewed through his eyes, she wondered if she looked more pathetic than anything else. She would die honorably, not pathetically. She would not have him think poorly of Rome because of muddled reasoning on her part. Better to die as her father had. Strong. Fighting. Clean.

She rubbed her grimy hands against the filth of her stola. Dirt had been one thing when she had been near her own death; what had dirt mattered then? But she was well rested and well fed and was no nearer her goal of outwitting the Saxon than she had been when he had first arrived in her valley. All those comments he had made concerning her appearance and her desirability, or lack of it—she supposed there could have been more truth and less insult in them than she had thought at the time. Certainly it was no fitting way for a Roman to go into battle against the barbari. She was a disgrace. She was a far, far cry from her father and his valiant and noble effort, but it was not beyond her; she could honor him still. She was weak now and exhausted. It would take some time to build her strength. It would take strength to fight the oaf on the new terms she was just now formulating. Her path had been self-destructive—perhaps Theras had been right in that—but she would hack out a new path for herself. A path of destruction for the Saxon. A path of righteous vengeance for herself. It would take time, time to plan and grow strong. It would take no time at all to become clean.

Not one to ponder a new resolution, Melania left her small room, the room that had been hers since the Saxon had first carried her there to sleep, and made her way across the courtyard to the three-room system of baths. She was ashamed to admit it, but she had avoided the baths since finding Dorcas and that grinning imbecile of a pagan stripped and tumbling together like a pair of animals on the floor. It was her house, but there were some things she preferred not to see. She didn't know if they'd ever been back, certainly she'd never been back, but, stiffening her spine against whatever awaited her, she was going back now. It was the first step on her new path and she strode firmly. She would own and command every inch of her home, and no copulating Saxon would get in her way.

The sun was high and bright, the shadow cast by the portico deep and dark. She did not hesitate as she penetrated the darkness. She marched right in, holding her breath unconsciously. Thanking God, she hissed out her air; it was empty. The frigidarium was littered with broken shards of pottery, a few burned scrolls from the library, and a small pile of tattered leaves, but the small pool was intact and holding water. Dirty, leaf-strewn water. Still, it was not beyond repair. Moving through the doorway to the tepidarium, she saw at a glance that this room was now being used as a place to sleep. Cloaks, an odd pair of shoes, and a wide-toothed comb lay in comfortable disarray. The caldarium, just beyond the tepidarium, was in much the same condition, thought it also boasted a mat of pale yellow straw laid over a thick pile of pine boughs. They had turned her baths into a dormitory. Melania sniffed in disgust and folded her arms over her chest. The flea-infested Saxon hawks would not nest here, not in her baths, not when she was suddenly so eager for a bath and a fresh change of clothes. The Saxons would have to vacate the trio of rooms in order for her to indulge in her bath; she would, of course, be bathing daily. Melania smiled slowly. Why, she was still in the same garment she had worn when she last ate with her father. That would change. When she disrobed, it would be burned, in memory of him.

Yes, the rooms must be cleaned and returned to their original purpose before she could be clean herself, and the Saxon mob would clean what they had soiled. Unfortunately, the barbari would do nothing on her word alone; eating with them every day had taught her how slavishly they followed their leader. Melania swallowed hard. Wulfred. She supposed she must somehow become accustomed to using his name, graceless as it was. Wulfred. It sounded like a bark, which was hardly inappropriate, now that she thought about it. Wulfred. She needed his help. She would be courteous. She would be pleasant. She would be agreeable.

He would not be difficult to find; he never was. He was so huge that he was impossible to miss. This was perhaps the only time when that fact did not irritate her. She was going to be pleasant because she was, very simply, going to get her way. But a quick circuit of the rooms of the villa, the expanse of courtyard, the grassy area just beyond the gate, brought her no sight of him. *The oaf.* Could he not once do what was convenient and expedient for her? Ridiculous question, since she was dealing with a Saxon. She found him in the stable, where she had never before seen him, running his hands over her father's horse. Her father's most beloved horse.

"That is my father's mount, oaf. Take your manure-encrusted hands off her before you ruin her coat with your mauling."

Wulfred, the oaf, did not even look at her. He continued calmly brushing the dust from Optio's ruddy coat, brushing dust all over himself in the process, not that he seemed to care.

"Your father is dead," he said on a downstroke.

He was stripped to the waist, as always. Did these pagans have no decent clothes? His leg coverings were of braided leather and looked most uncomfortably tight to her. She had no idea how he managed to sit. Was cloth beyond their Saxon skill? Animals all, they lived in the skins of dead animals. Except that he did have a cloak; she had seen him once in a cloak. Where had he hidden it? Must he always be so revoltingly disrobed? It was so completely barbaric and so uncomfortably distracting.

"Then she is mine by Roman law," she barked out, stepping closer to him to claim her right, angry as much with his nudity as with his flagrant touching of her horse. "She is not yours to touch, Saxon. Can't you see how agitated she is becoming at your nearness?"

Optio had begun stomping and shifting the moment she had come upon them and grew more disturbed with every word Melania spoke. Still, the Saxon did not look at her. No, she was not worthy of eye contact. His attention was all for Optio, whom he now soothed by stroking her muzzle with a wide hand.

"There is no Roman law here, little snake, only

127

my law, and this horse was calm until you crept in."

She had never been good with Optio; that much was true. But she had now talked herself into a corner and could not think of a way out. Would the Saxon never leave and go plunder another Roman's house? Would he stay and torment her until her hair turned white? Would he never fully dress?

"Will you take her when you leave?" she asked in a snarl. It was all she could think to say. How long would he stay? She had pondered it long and often.

Wulfred gave Optio a long and lingering rub before straightening to gaze at the ceiling of the small room. *Oaf.* He would make her wait for his answer. When what little patience she had was disappearing in a vortex of flame, he finally looked her straight in the eye.

"Probably."

Ha. So he was leaving. *Good.* She'd begun to wonder if he hadn't put down roots like an obnoxious weed.

"And when are you leaving?" *Now. Today. Please, God.*

Now he did not hesitate. He looked straight into her eyes and said with sober deliberation and ominous intent, "When I am finished here."

She knew what that meant. He would not leave until he had broken her spirit and then killed her. He had never made any secret of his goals, but then neither had she. She had fought him from the beginning, without relenting, and so she would continue, emulating her father. And like her father, she would not fight for her own death; why should she when his death would be so much sweeter? He would not leave until he had finished with her; so he thought, but he would not leave until she had finished with him. He would be here a long time, because she had decided to fight, now that her own death seemed beyond her reach. He had assured his own death by withholding hers. She would die as had her father, and nothing less. *Stupid barbarian.* Let him keep protecting her from hard labor, seeing that she ate well, keeping her ever at his side or within call. He was making it very easy for her to kill him.

"Is that why you came?" he asked.

"What?" She started. It was as if he had read her mind. But that was impossible. He was a dirty pagan: stupid, uneducated, ignorant, dull. He could not know her thinking or read her heart. "No . . ." she managed, and then regained her composure. "I want to take a bath, and the murderers at your command have almost ruined the rooms. Tell them to clear out or I will."

That was as nicely as she could put it, more nicely than he deserved, to her way of thinking.

But not to his.

Wulfred, his hands resting firmly on the back of the horse, found himself marveling at her arrogance. Her home lost to her, her people dead by his word, her very freedom a memory, and she still held herself with head unbowed, spitting orders like a little Roman general. From what source sprang her unswayed confidence in her own inbred superiority? Even for a Roman she was excessively proud.

"Tell me of your father," he said, stroking Optio again, his movements measured and swift. It was hardly a question.

"What has my father to do with the baths and their deplorable condition, except to say that he was scrupulously clean in his habits?"

"Your father was Roman?"

"Of course he was Roman, you oaf; what else could he have been?"

"Born in Rome? Educated in Rome?"

She bristled like a cat poked with a sharp stick. Wulfred felt the beginnings of a smile move the corners of his mouth. He lowered his head to his task to keep her from seeing it. He hardly wanted her to imagine that she brought him pleasure.

"No," she said in a snarl, her eyes hot and glittering, "he was born here, in Britannia. Educated here, in the Roman way."

"It was your mother, then, who was Roman born and inspired in you a love of Rome?" He smiled with empty charm, knowing the answer before she spoke.

"She was of Britannia also, from Durovigutum, just west of here. A fine Roman town."

"A fine British town with a Roman name," he countered with a sharp smile.

"Britannia is of Rome, imbecile, as you know well," she said.

"You are too young to have journeyed to drink

from the Tiber," he said calmly, enjoying himself enormously, "so it must have been your grandparents who taught you so well to revere and mimic the Roman way, the land of their birth. What brought them to this isle? Conquest?"

He had struck close enough to the truth to hurt and just enough off the truth to bite. He could read the pain in her eyes and it fed him. This was even more fun than watching her eat.

"My father's mother was a Briton," she said. "My father's father was a legionary."

"Out of Rome?"

She hesitated before answering, anger flaring in her eyes like a live spark. His smile struggled for life.

"Out of Syria."

"So it is from the east that you come by your black hair, and not from good Roman stock. And from a warrior as well."

"Does that surprise you?" she said sharply.

He looked her over appraisingly, marking her rigid frame braced for attack and her hot, aggressive eyes.

"No." He smiled, finally giving in to the urge. "But for one who screams her Roman-ness with every breath, you seem to be more of Britain than of Rome."

"You are a fool if you believe that only the city of Rome births Romans," she said with heat, "and that only touching the dirt of the seven hills confers citizenship. I am as Roman as the emperor. My feet are even now on Roman soil, the air I breathe is Roman air, the—"

"Soldiers protecting you Roman legionaries?" he interrupted.

"They'll be back," she said with authority.

"Not while you live," he said with just as much confidence. "The Roman world is shrinking, Melania, breeding fewer Romans every day. Do not link yourself to a dying race."

"I do not link myself. I *am* Roman," she stated flatly.

They stared in silence at each other, measuring the evidence of their race in each other's faces. He stood tall, blond, and muscular, a Saxon to the very bone. She faced him in the dusty stable room, small and proud and black of hair, the pride of Rome stamped upon her features. She was a slender torch, a brand, filled with the fire of pride, the fire of battle. Perhaps the fire of passion? He shocked himself with the thought. And then smiled. Melania was passionate about everything, in both her hates and her loves. He had never known a woman like her; he didn't think one had been created. She was passion and intellect embattled, blind rage and cool plotting, towering pride and fragile femininity. And she was Roman, always Roman. He knew that all born within the Roman sphere and with Roman citizenship were Roman, but she was also Briton, even if she would not claim it. He could see it if she could not. There was more to her than Rome could give.

"And as a Roman," she said, breaking the cord

of fragile understanding that was being forged between them, "I have a need to bathe. Tell your maggots to vacate the rooms. I will see to their repair."

She said it almost magnanimously, though her eyes would not meet his. He could not hold back the smile that curled his lips.

"If you wish to bathe, there is the river."

Her head jerked up and her strangely colored eyes blazed her anger even before she spoke.

"Do not tell me what is on my own property! I am fully aware of the river, having heard its voice since my birth, but I do not bathe in the river, as does a horse. I bathe in my baths! Of course, you, in your pagan stupidity, would know nothing of proper bathing. Or do you bathe at all? I have seen no evidence of it since you have overrun my home and my land. Certainly the baths have not been used . . . in their proper way."

He watched her gaze shift and slide to the ground as she twisted the ragged end of her dress. And he knew why. Cenred was hardly discreet. When her next sentence veered off the topic of her bathing rooms, he was not surprised. He was pleased. Her clear discomfort brought him heady pleasure.

"Why, the Roman bath is the envy of the world, not only for its structural beauty but for its elegance of function. To bathe in a river has not been done in centuries . . . in either your culture or mine, though for entirely different reasons," she finished bitingly.

Wulfred had listened to her diatribe in pleasant silence, arms crossed and leaning against the stable wall. She was so full of hiss and rattle, this little Roman snake, and so empty of teeth. Why had it taken him so long to find the joy in baiting her? She was so wonderfully predictable in her responses.

"Well, then," he began, pushing himself away from the wall, crowding her, "you have convinced me. I'll see that the rooms are immediately cleared. I can't wait to experience a Roman bath." He smiled as he brushed past her and left the room.

Melania stood in stunned silence, a look of horror growing in her eyes. He wasn't gone long, and then was back again, grabbing her by the hand and pulling her along behind him. Pulling her toward the house. And the baths.

"You are going to use *my* baths?" she asked in a hiss.

"Certainly." He grinned. "I can hardly wait after your description of them. You *were* trying to convince me of the superiority of the Roman bath, weren't you?"

"Well . . ." she huffed.

"Well?" he echoed, slowing down so that he could look back at her face, a face suffused with fiery, outraged red. She seemed to be having trouble keeping up.

"My purpose was to prepare a place for my own bath," she said.

"You'll get your bath," he responded lightly. "And so will I."

To his back, Melania muttered softly in resignation, "It's not as if we'll be sharing the water."

Wulfred only smiled in predatory anticipation and kept walking, her small hand a tight fist in his.

Chapter Twelve

It had taken more time than she would have liked
for the rooms to be cleaned to her satisfaction. Five
workers had scrubbed and rinsed, herself included,
before she was content. Now, near dusk, she began
her final survey of the quartet of rooms that comprised the baths. The tepidarium, where the bathing began, was no longer a disgrace. The floor was
clean, the broken tile swept away, and the cobwebs
cleaned from the corners. There were many missing
tiles, but nothing to be done about them. None here
had the skill for setting tile, and her father had been
a young man when the craftsman who had known
the technique for creating the brightly colored tiles
had moved out of the area. The villa did not look
its best, but she couldn't blame the Saxons for
everything. To be honest, the tepidarium looked as

135

good now as it had before they had descended.

Melania stripped off her dirty yellow stola and laid it next to the fresh stola of soft amber and the palla of brilliant saffron that Dorcas had laid out for her. Her clothing would travel with her from room to room during her bath, and she would bathe unattended because she had Dorcas engaged in a more important duty: guarding the entrance to the room. She would not be intruded upon by any of the yellow-haired vermin without ample notification; it was even to be hoped that Dorcas could scare a stray Saxon off if one happened near. Dorcas had spent some time with them, because of her Saxon bedfellow, and they now regarded her with something of fellowship and goodwill. Not so Melania. Not that she cared. It was enough that she had to tolerate Wulfred. More Saxons she did not care to know, however distantly.

She stood nude for a moment, listening for unwelcome footsteps on the courtyard side of the door. It would be just like that big oaf to come charging in, hoping to catch an eyeful of her in such naked vulnerability. These Saxons had the morals of pigs and the manners to match. She knew what he would want—to shame her with her own nudity—but he would fail. She'd been seen nude by half her household in the course of her life. Of course, no man had ever seen her body, but the Saxon could hardly embarrass her, since he was hardly a man. Hearing nothing, she smiled in relaxed anticipation and walked to the bath, eager for the feel of the warm water against her skin, so very eager to be clean again, so eager for the pure indulgence of something so completely Roman. As she stood staring into the water, her foot poised, she realized that she had not *really* looked at the water before. She had looked at the tile and the absence of rubble and the clean walls, but she had not really looked at the water.

It was dirty.

Human hair, yellow and long, floated in swirled patterns on the top of the water. There was a dark scum line on the polished rock walls of the pool, and there was a trail of water leading to the doorway of the frigidarium. There was only one man with the perversity to bathe in water prepared for her: the great Saxon oaf who had taunted her about the superiority of the Roman bath.

She'd been gracious in allowing him to take advantage of her baths; he was certainly in need of a bath, though mere water could hardly wash away his barbarism.

Furious, she hurriedly wrapped the palla around her torso, flinging the long end over her shoulder; she wouldn't take time to do more, not when that oaf had dirtied her water. If he weren't such an imbecile, she'd suspect him of doing it on purpose and out of spite, but she couldn't credit him with having the wits to know that he had ruined her bath.

Following the trail of water, she marched to the doorway of the frigidarium, the linen of her cloak slapping against her calves and the long end trailing in the water at her feet. It was empty. Where . . . ?

A low, rippling laugh from the exercise room caused her to jerk her head in that direction. So he hid from her there, but that laugh . . . it was a woman's.

A vision of Dorcas and that leering madman of hers rushed upon her. They had used the exercise room, too. . . . A rush of pure, hot fury rose up from her belly and lodged itself in her throat, choking her. She could see his mouth on a slender, female throat, his strong hands on a firm bosom, his golden body lowering a woman's fragile form to the ground . . . where he would hold her to him, covering her and sheltering her even as he pierced . . . large hands entangled in dark spilled hair as his mouth moved to devour a hard-tipped breast . . . his golden hair falling across her torso as his hands moved down . . . as his mouth . . . and his eyes. His eyes would burn blue as he thrust into her. . . .

Melania hurtled through that doorway like a launched spear and would have struck him with the same slicing force if she hadn't been so stunned by what she saw. She locked her knees to keep them from buckling. Oh, it was Wulfred, as she had known it would be, and with a female of her household, Ness, but what they were doing . . . It was a complete and disgusting flaunting of Roman tradition.

Ness was giving the oaf a massage!

Melania ignored the wash of relief that tumbled through her and focused instead on this latest affront to Roman ways.

"You are an ignorant fool, Saxon, to let her attend you. Only males serve males in the bath. Ness, you should have told him what error he was in when he forced you to this duty; never think that I will hold this against you. I know you have been taught better. Now go back to the kitchen, where you are more needed, while I speak to the Saxon."

Ness did not move. Worse, she looked very happy to rub her hands over the back of the Saxon, who had only a linen sheet draped negligently over his buttocks, and that slipping with each pass of her hands. In fact, the Saxon looked rather content himself. And they both all but ignored her.

Melania smiled coldly at Ness. "Do you have trouble understanding me, Ness? Is my Latin suddenly difficult for you to decipher because you have grown used to the Saxon tongue?" When Ness only smiled in feminine superiority and trailed her hands down the oaf's back to linger on his buttocks in a touch that was blatantly a caress, Melania walked to the table, ignoring the near-naked Saxon. "Very well," she said, then I will use a language that you will have no trouble understanding.

"Go, Ness," Melania commanded in Saxon, her color high. "Go the kitchen. Stay there." Melania grabbed Ness by the arm and propelled her toward the door, her feet barely touching the tile floor.

Ness ran out of the baths, Wulfred apparently forgotten. If Ness had thought Melania powerless because the Saxons had come, she had just been shown how wrong she was.

Wulfred had said nothing during the exchange. Alone with Melania, he continued to say nothing.

Turning on his side and supporting his head with a hand, he watched Melania expectantly, an odd smile on his face. The sheet was held in place by miracle alone. Melania moved briskly away from the table where he lay in insolent arrogance.

"You dirtied my water," Melania began, tightening the sheet that sheathed her, wishing he would do the same to his own slack sheet. "If I didn't know you for a fool and a pig, I would think you did it intentionally."

Wulfred eased himself onto his back, the sheet slipping down past his hip joint, and crossed his arms under his head. The size of his muscles could only be described as repulsive; there could be no grace in such monumental bulk and bulging lack of smooth symmetry; her father had looked nothing like this man with his mass and his definition. Romans did not look like this. Civilized men did not look like this. Only barbarians had such height, such breadth, such formidable dimensions, such blatant and unrefined . . . strength. Even his belly was ridged with muscle; his digestion must be crippled by such rigid bands.

"We have argued before about what you *know*," he said easily. "I am too relaxed to argue with you now. You were right about one thing: this is far better than the river. I wonder why you have waited so long for a bath of your own."

"I had other things on my mind," she said, twisting the sheet tighter around her, in direct defiance of his casual disregard for his own covering.

"And now?" He slid his glance sideways, amused

as he watched her battle with her sheet.

"And now the water is foul," she barked.

She would have struck him—certainly the urge was upon her—but he was so . . . so . . . unclothed. She kept her distance.

"I am but one man."

"But so very foul," she answered. "The cleaning of the rooms will have to begin again, and from the ground up. Tell me, exactly which rooms have you used? No, never mind. The smell will guide me."

He smiled, the cords in his throat moving in silent laughter. His hair was lighter, brighter, washed of its film of dirt and oil. Even the hair on his chest was golden, and the soft hair of his underarm was the color of clear amber. He was golden and yellow all over, mountains and valleys of muscle that shone with massage oil, long lashes of umber shielding such intensely blue eyes. Eyes that were the solid blue of lapis, but so very much lighter and hotter and brighter. Saxon eyes. Uncultured. Unkempt. Uncivilized. And laughing at her.

"I amuse you?" she said coldly.

"In your Roman way, you do," he answered, rolling again onto his side. The sheet fell with silent grace to the floor, revealing layers of muscle, a long frame, golden hair: stark male nudity.

Her eyes covered the length of him, refusing the urgent commands of her thoughts. She had never seen such a body. She had never imagined that a male body could grow to such dimensions or that muscle could bulge so high that it made its own shadow. And she had certainly never seen a man's most private parts before. Even at that point he looked muscular, growing and hardening even as she watched. Melania dragged her eyes away from the stunning metamorphosis and looked at his face. He was smiling in male delight.

Understanding flared like a sudden fire.

He was baiting her, knowing how the sight of him repulsed her, unnerved her, distracted her. Knowing that this was but a new battle, she summoned the resolve to fight him as she had always fought him and as she would always fight him. He was Saxon; he would not defeat her.

"How very intelligent of you." At his questioning look, she added, "I wouldn't have thought that your kind could be amused by anything less than a murder or a rape or a fire. That you could find it in your limited range of thought and purpose to be amused by a conversation with your intellectual superior is a sign in your favor. Perhaps you have learned something in the time you have spent among Romans here."

"I have learned much in the past from Roman hands," he answered, his smile vanishing. She did not look at his body, so hypnotically large in its formation. She kept her eyes on his face; she had learned to tolerate his face.

"Bravo," she cheered falsely. "You do credit to your race. Someday you may be taken as an exhibit to Rome, to show the scholars that some Saxons are able to learn. You may change the history of your kind."

"It is the history of Rome that I will change," he said with suppressed rage.

"And so you begin in Rome's backwater; oh, yes, I know that Britannia is not the hub of Roman thought. Why attack the heart when you can slice a finger? Yes"—she smiled, arranging her sheet to fall about her like a royal robe—"you do show some signs of intellectual promise."

Melania left him there, naked and enraged, defeated in his purpose. Once she had arranged for clean water for her bath, it would be a perfect day.

In clean water, Melania enjoyed her bath. This time Dorcas attended her. Theras watched the entrance to keep all at bay while she was within. She knew Wulfred would not intrude; he had left the baths shortly after she had, in an obvious rage, and gone for a walk in the hills, the somber Cynric his only companion. Sighing and sinking lower into the water, Melania smiled in contentment. It had turned into a wonderful day.

She leaned forward against the coping of the pool so that Dorcas could scrub her back. She had already been to the tepidarium for a warm soak, followed by the caldarium to build up a healthy sweat and cleanse the pores, then back to the tepidarium for a rubbing with soap, which Dorcas was doing now. Glorious. Even remembering the hairy oaf in his nakedness could not destroy her victorious mood.

"You have lost much weight, Melania," Dorcas

noted. "Your breasts have lost some of their full-ness."

Melania shrugged. "The men of Rome favor small-breasted women."

"There are no Roman men near. Do you think Saxon men share the same preference?"

Melania glanced over her shoulder.

"Why should I care what Saxon men favor? A wolf would be their preferred mate, I should think. Or a sow."

"They do prefer women," Dorcas said gently in reproof.

"Excuse my callousness, Dorcas," Melania said softly, and turned to face her. "I had forgotten that you couple with them."

"I do not couple with *them*. Just one: Cenred," Dorcas said, blushing and dropping her head.

"If you are not displeased, then I will not make trouble over it, but have a care, Dorcas. The Saxons are little better than animals. I would not have you mauled."

Dorcas seemed on the verge of saying more, but Melania rose from the water and waited for the cloth to be draped around her. They walked care-fully on the stone-and-tile floor to the frigidarium. Melania dropped the cloth and stepped into the cold-water pool, washing the last remnants of soap from her body. The icy water made her catch her breath. It was no pleasure to linger in this pool. Rising again, she stepped out and walked quickly to the exercise room for her massage. Dorcas rubbed her briskly with a woolen cloth and then laid it aside, ready to begin kneading Melania's muscles. Melania groaned in contentment as Dorcas's fingers pressed against the tight muscles of her shoulders. Why had she waited so long for this?

"They are not such animals," Dorcas said with some hesitation; servants did not begin conversations, but things at the villa had changed since the coming of the Saxons. Thinking of Cenred and his perpetual grin, she blushed. "Their ways are different, but they can be kind, even thoughtful. . . ."

Melania sighed in weary concern. "He is using you, Dorcas, and you are allowing it to make your way easier," Melania said bluntly. She did not want Dorcas hurt when this dream she had constructed shattered. "If you make more of it in your mind, you will only add to the hurt he has brought you."

Dorcas manipulated the disks of Melania's spine gently for some time before she said, "I will not dispute what you say, but have you considered that you could use the same method to protect yourself?" When Melania wrenched her head around to glare at Dorcas, the girl rushed to explain. "It is just that Wulfred shows signs of being attracted to you. . . ."

"Yes, he is very attracted to the idea of killing me."

"He spends so much time with you, he truly seems intrigued by you, and his looks are often so heated, even intense."

"Murderous," Melania said, flopping down on her stomach again and pillowing her head on her arms.

"Why not use his attraction to encourage him into treating you more kindly? I worry for you, Melania. He is a man who has much anger in him and it all seems to be directed at you," she finished awkwardly.

Melania rolled over so that Dorcas could massage the large muscles of her thighs. She tried to answer patiently; truly, they no longer seemed so much servant and mistress as sisters from a civilized world trying to survive in a barbarian wilderness.

"Dorcas, I am already as pampered as a cat. He prohibits hard labor, watches what I eat, and feeds me only the best of the table; only his constant company clouds my days. I certainly do not want to encourage him to get any closer to me than he already is. What would I gain from feeding this attraction for me that you tell me he already has? And let me hasten to say that I do not see it at all. He can hardly stand the sight of me, and I return the feeling."

"You have been very sheltered here," Dorcas said. "I think you do not understand what you are seeing in him."

"I know bloodlust when I see it. He wants me dead, after he has seen me grovel, of course."

"What he feels for you is strong, that is true, but it was a Roman whom he sought to kill. You have become more to him than that. You are a person now, one he knows . . ."

"With that feeble mind?"

". . . and one whom he has come to respect."

"As well he should."

"He has seen that you are more than just a Roman. Can't you see that he is more than just a Saxon?" Dorcas said, urgent in her appeal.

"I can see that he is a Saxon pig." Melania snorted. When Dorcas looked at her with pitiful appeal, Melania reasoned, "And again I say, to what purpose? Could my life here be any easier? Why should I dupe the fool into believing that I return whatever attraction you say he feels for me?"

Dorcas said nothing. She kept her dark head lowered and vigorously rubbed the muscles of Melania's right calf. Melania propped herself up on her elbows and asked again, "Well?"

"I had thought that you might feel some softer emotion toward him, in time. He is not such a—"

"Ha!" Melania interrupted with a burst of victorious laughter. "Give up your schemes, Dorcas. I will not soften toward the Saxon oaf. If your Saxon brings you some comfort in this disaster, take your comfort with no censure from me. But do not expect the same of me. The Saxon is my enemy. I have not forgotten it. Neither has he."

Dorcas said nothing further on the subject, for which Melania was grateful. Cuddle up to the Saxon oaf? Where was such insanity born? No matter that Dorcas thought her an innocent in such things; she knew enough to know that all such a plan would get her was a large and hairy body pressing her down on her cot and crushing the wind out of her. What victory there? Oh, he would have fun enough; it would be an added victory for him, but what gain for her? No, it was beyond foolish. It was ridiculous. Not to mention repugnant. Just remembering the planes, ridges, and shadows of his body caused her stomach to fly up into the cage of her ribs. If he ever touched her in an embrace tinged with anything other than pure hatred, she would probably throw up.

"She doesn't throw up her food anymore."

Wulfred grunted in affirmation and kept climbing. Cynric kept pace with him, holding his sword casually, ready. He would always be ready to fight for Wulfred, especially against the little Roman in the villa below them.

"She eats when you tell her to."

Wulfred didn't respond by so much as the shrugging of a shoulder. He kept climbing the small hills that surrounded the valley of the villa; it was not difficult climbing, but they attacked the hills with a will. Wulfred had much to occupy his thoughts. The little Roman always occupied his thoughts lately.

For Cynric, it had become a very disappointing summer.

"How will this kill her?"

Wulfred stopped at the question. They were at the top of a small rise, the wind moving softly over the waving grass, pushing well-formed clouds across the sky like boats coming in on the tide.

"Do you think that I won't?"

"I think that I do not understand this way of

fighting. I do not understand a battle where food is a weapon and a good night's sleep is a blow. I do not understand—"

"You have said it," Wulfred interrupted softly and with buried force. "You do not understand. She is Roman; this will not be a battle as you understand it. There will be little of logic in it," he said.

"We have been here half the summer."

"She is devious, resourceful."

"She is a woman, easily killed."

"She is a Roman woman; killing her would be her victory, not mine."

Cynric sucked in his breath and clasped Wulfred's arm in exhortation. "She is Roman, Wulfred, and you have sworn—"

"I have sworn to make her suffer. She is."

"She doesn't seem to be suffering," he mumbled. Anyone that arrogant, well fed, and pampered was not suffering.

"Her foot is in the trap, comrade; I only tighten the noose and watch her silently gnaw herself to death."

"Nothing that one does is in silence."

"True." Wulfred smiled, looking away across the hills that stretched out before them. "But she gives me pleasure in her misery. It is a pleasure I would not hasten from."

"The summer is half-gone. Hensa will wonder—"

"We are here to fight and take. I have a fight that I would not turn from. I have all the treasure I need in this place. We will stay. And she will live, unharmed, until I say otherwise."

"When?" Cynric asked, ignoring the implied threat in that statement.

"I do not know. She is determined, stronger than I thought at first, and with a passion that I did not expect of a Roman."

"She is a woman. They are emotional."

Wulfred laughed and stroked his seax. "It is more than emotion. There is a fire in her that I find I can understand, even respect, though she is Roman." When Cynric only grumbled, Wulfred added, "Tell me of another woman you have known who is like her."

Cynric was silent, uncomfortable with the thread of admiration he could hear in Wulfred's voice.

"We stay until the end of the summer at the latest. I will take my pleasure from her. I will face Hensa when the time comes. You need only follow me, as you have sworn."

Cynric straightened from under his load of concern. "I do not need to be reminded to whom I have sworn myself, Wulfred. I am your man. Do not doubt."

"I do not doubt you. Now do not doubt me. I know what I am about in this place. Everything I wanted to find in attacking Britannia, I have found here."

Cyrnic listened and tried to understand as he walked alone back down to the villa, but he could make no sense of Wulfred's words.

* * *

Having no duties other than the ones normally performed by the woman of the house, Melania had the leisure to have her hair coiffed in an elegant, multibraided, upswept style. Dorcas was very good with hair. Feeling more feminine than she had in weeks, Melania decided to apply a modest amount of makeup as well. Antimony she brushed lightly over her lids, darkening them and accentuating her oddly colored eyes. What could you call a color that was not brown, not green, and not exactly hazel? Her father had told her that her eyes were a turmoil of green and amber brown and bright gold. Not an unpleasant mixture, he had assured her, but also not quite standard. But her black hair was her glory and she knew it. It might be very well for the women of Rome to wear wigs of blond and red, but in Britannia lighter hair was more often seen, and so her black hair stood out. She loved it. It was true black, she could see that for herself, with not a trace of brown or red or even blue to alter the hue. Admiring herself in a small mirror of beaten silver, she decided to apply a touch of red to her lips and cheeks. She was wan after her various efforts to defeat the Saxon; the added color was almost necessary to mimic more vibrant health. Not that she was ill; it was just that she had felt more vigorous in her life. Curse the Saxon for that.

With Dorcas nodding her approval, and the woman's unspoken hope for peace shining from her dark eyes, Melania arranged the folds of her palla and left the exercise room. Dorcas followed at a discreet distance. It might be fun to see how the Saxon responded to her now; she looked nothing like the bedraggled and dirty girl he had pulled from the hypocaust. Perhaps he would even be intimidated by the overt stamp of Rome in her demeanor and bearing, though she did not put much hope in that. The man had proven to her repeatedly that he was too dull to know when he should be impressed.

Not so his men.

She walked across the courtyard, where they were engaged in their usual mock battles, and first one, then another, then all stopped to stare at her. Dirty and sweaty and pagan they were, but they stopped to stare—no, to gawk—at her.

It was quite enjoyable.

"Who is it?" asked Cuthred.

"It's Melania, you dolt," Cenred said. "Who else could it be?"

"I thought it was your woman, Dorcas."

"Dorcas stands behind her, Cuthred, which you could see if you saw anything but the gleam of your seax."

"I see her," he said gruffly. It was clearly a new experience for him.

"Melania," Balduff said under his breath, dropping his seax and his shield so that they hung limply from his two hands. "She's a beauty, as I knew she was. And you said she was a mole, Cynric."

"She doesn't look as small and dirty now," Cynric said slowly, still staring and not able to stop himself.

"And she certainly doesn't look like a boy," Cenred said.

"*I* never said she looked like a boy," Balduff huffed. "I have always seen her worth, her femininity, her shapeliness."

"What compliment is that?" Cenred argued. "You see the worth of every tadpole of a girl."

"She is no tadpole," Cynric said.

"Bravo, Cynric, she has escaped being a mole and now a tadpole by your wise judgment. It would be best if you left the discussion of women to your superiors. You seem to lack the ability," Balduff said, pushing Cynric to the rear of the group they had formed to marvel at the glorious transformation of Melania.

"She looks very Roman, doesn't she?" Cuthred said, gripping his seax, his knuckles white.

"And you find that a curse?" Cenred said. "She *is* a Roman, fool, but I can find no fault with it, not as she looks. Do you think all Roman women look like her?"

"No," Ceolmund the Silent pronounced. "She is unique."

"I agree," said Balduff. "Never have I seen . . . Almost I would not have thought . . ."

"Ho, so you admit to being stunned by her beauty," Cynric said, pouncing. "You, who claim to know all there is to know about women."

"I never said she reminded me of a mole, Cynric. You alone have that distinction. . . ."

Melania listened avidly as she slowly glided across the courtyard to the doorway of her room.

This was wonderful fun. Why, oh, why, had she waited so long to bathe? It was just then that Wulfred stormed through the gate and into the courtyard. What would his reaction to her transformation be? She only hoped it would be as soul-satisfying as that of his men.

"Is this how you serve me? In childish bickering? I could hear you halfway up the hill," he snapped, not looking in Melania's direction. Very deliberately, she thought.

"Wulfred," Cynric said, almost blushing, "the woman, the Roman, she . . . we . . . well, *look* at her!"

Wulfred glanced at her over his naked shoulder and said gruffly, "Have you never seen a clean woman before?"

"No," Cynric tried. "I mean, yes, but Wulfred, she . . ."

"She's beautiful," Balduff said, his voice soft and emphatic.

"She's Roman," Wulfred spat out.

"Fine," said Cenred. "She's a beautiful Roman."

"A beautiful Roman woman," Cuthred summarized for them all.

"And?" Wulfred demanded. "This is something you have not known before now?"

"Well, she was very dirty," Cenred said haltingly.

"And now she is clean. Does that mean that she will rob you of your purpose simply by bathing her filthy body and replacing her encrusted rags with proper clothing? Is that the extent of your commitment?"

"No, Wulfred," they said, almost in unison, shamed.

Melania watched and heard all from the shadow of her doorway, learning, observing, planning. What a fool she had been. What a self-destructive fool. If a simple stroll across the courtyard had caused such bickering and splintering, what would a more concerted effort yield? Wulfred would be harried in trying to control them, the dogs who claimed him as master. He would be exhausted within the week, and how could he retaliate against her? She had done nothing, except to bathe.

Oh, and Wulfred would not escape unscathed. No, him she would taunt and beguile until he was a besotted fool. If Dorcas was right—and she now prayed to God she was—then Wulfred felt a flicker of attraction for her, though he had hardly glanced at her and was acting in his normal obtuse way. He hadn't taken one step toward becoming besotted that she could see; but he would. With some effort on her part, a look, a smile, and that blessed proximity he insisted upon, she would have him howling in frustration as easily as she would have his men at each other's throats. And when the game had paled for her, when she was sick of watching the Saxons fall over themselves for her, she would kill him. Thanks to his own proclamation, she would be close enough to accomplish it. God willing, she would have him enamored enough to have weakened his guard.

Melania smiled suddenly and smoothed the folds of her palla. This was going to be a lot more fun than starving.

Chapter Thirteen

She took a piece of bread soaked in oil and spices and held it out to Balduff, her head lowered and her smile beckoning. Balduff, his smile radiating all the way to his eyes, leaned forward to take the offering with his fingers. She pulled back, laughing, coaxing, until he finally opened his mouth in submission and took the food from her hand—all the while wearing that besotted smile.

She leaned toward Cenred, leaned so far that the neck of her stola gaped and he surely had a view of her breasts, and made a motion of brushing dirt off his shoulder. With her other hand she tickled him, and Cenred jerked and laughed at her touch, his light brown eyes shining.

She winked at Cuthred. Cuthred, who smiled

only when he was killing, grinned and turned away, pleasantly embarrassed.

Ceolmund, still silent, could hardly bear to look away from her.

Wulfred watched and wondered.

Melania had changed more than her clothes. She had been the personification of spitting and hissing fury; she was now smooth and silky temptation. She had insulted his men at every turn; she now charmed them with seductive smiles of promise. Promises she did not keep. Promises he would not allow her to keep even had she dared. No one would touch Melania. She was his alone.

He knew she would not dare. This display of hers was a ploy, a new method to thwart him; he understood her well enough to know that. Unlike other women he had known, Melania was consistent in both her emotions and her goals. He knew that she was still determined to defeat him and, at the very least, rob him of his joy in defeating her. So this new familiarity, this exuberant flirtation, was only a new means to the same goal.

But how did she rob him with this display? Did she think that watching her breast brush against Balduff's arm would bother him? Balduff, his eyes glowing with suppressed desire, instantly grew hard enough to be seen from across the room, but he did not touch her. Wulfred tightened his jaw until his teeth ached, but he kept watching her, his face a careful blank.

When she leaned close to whisper into Cenred's

Claudia Dain

ear, brushing a finger down his arm to the back of his hand, did she cast half a glance at him to see if he watched? Wulfred crossed his arms over his chest as he leaned against the plaster wall; he knew she did. Therefore he would not allow her antics to make his guts twist upon themselves in angry turmoil, though they did each time she touched a man and smiled her sudden smile. He would not give her his anger or his interest. He would give her nothing on which to sharpen her viperous teeth.

Not everyone had his control.

Cynric lurched to his feet and strode away from the table, his eyes an angry blaze of lust and fury; Cynric was finding it difficult to reconcile his distrust of the Roman with his desire for the woman. Cynric found his temper pushed to the edge by the little Roman snake.

"You can see the trouble she is causing," Cynric fumed, "and the pleasure she gets from it." Balduff and Cenred were debating, loudly, the quality of the wine from Melania's vineyard. They competed to see whose praise would soar the highest.

Wulfred, studying Melania's pleased expression with studied stoicism, said only, "She thinks she is causing more trouble than she is."

"She is a viper, slithering among us. A fire, burning each of us."

"I am not burned," Wulfred said easily. "And I am not afraid of snakes."

"Perhaps not you . . ."

"The solution is simple, Cynric," he said, facing

158

his friend. "Walk away. If the fire is too hot, turn your back on it and walk away."

Cynric grimaced his anguish at the idea of retreat, before he did just that, but not before turning for one more glance at Melania.

Melania, always reworking her battle plan. She had the appearance now of one content, at peace with her situation and with her life, but he did not believe the pose. She was not happy. The hatred and violence of weeks did not turn easily to acquiescence; none knew that better than he. Melania was consistent, true to her stated goals, passionate in her vow of hatred. No, this was a new tactic, a new strategy to best him.

She was a resourceful adversary; he'd give her that.

She'd maneuvered him into prohibiting her from hard labor, into eating each meal at a place of prominence at his side, into daily baths; it had not been her initial intent to win these luxuries from him, but the result was the same. And now she teased his men into fits of desire and jealousy and he spent more and more of his days controlling them, redirecting their passions, because he would kill the man who touched her. His men did not act on her blatant invitation and they never would; he had declared her his alone, which all within the confines of the villa knew very well. Now she turned his protection of her to prick him. Oh, yes, she was very resourceful, very devious.

How to turn the trap she had set back on her again? What would eat at her? What would cause her to crash against the restrictions of her life until she drowned in endless despair? That was all he wanted for her, this Roman, to be crushed by his hand, as he had once almost been crushed. To taste the despair he had once known until she choked and vomited on it.

He watched her. It seemed he always watched her. Her hair was up, crafted into swirling, minute braids, the black gleaming in the torchlight, inky, shining, smooth, a perfect foil for her glittering eyes. The black makeup she wore accentuated the large almond shape of her expressive eyes—eyes in which he could read the shadows of spiteful pleasure. She was an exotic beauty like nothing his men had ever seen or ever known, even beyond his own experience of women, but she was Roman. He understood Romans.

She leaned back on her elbows and Balduff fed her. It was very seductive and she knew it well. She had filled out since her attempts at starvation had failed, but she was still petite, hardly more than a handful, hardly as high as his chest. A Roman to the bone, she was; they were not a large race, but they were proud and domineering. She was dominating them now, subjugating his men with desire. She, being Roman, would not be content until she ruled them all. An arrogant race. A seductive race.

Though he had never found anything about Rome to be seductive before knowing her.

She knew what she was doing. Every smile and tilt of her head was by design. She was clever. She was determined. And she had proven herself to be ruthlessly devious.

Spitting her fury at him, she had defied him. Demanding rights that were no longer hers, she had tried to bully him. Even when she was afraid, anger came spitting out of her. Anger, so often rolling out from her to slap against her foes, was her defense.

Wulfred smiled, knowing he had unearthed a weakness in his adversary, and then he laughed lightly; he could only appreciate her unflinching bravado. She did not give up, this one, and perhaps he might have admired her for it. Perhaps he would have felt desire for her himself, for her hair was as thick and dark as the night and her eyes as bright as the sun and her shape and form as delicate and feminine as the lark, and her spirit . . . her spirit was a blazing fire that would not be doused. Perhaps he would have felt these things, thought these things, if she had not been Roman.

Wulfred pushed away from the wall and dropped his arms, forcing himself to look away from her. She was like a fire in the night; if one looked too long, it became impossible to see anything but the fire.

How to stop her? How to turn this latest strategy against her? How to end the friction among his men? How to destroy her slowly, so that he could lengthen his own pleasure in this revenge? That was all he wanted, no matter her beauty and her fire; her defeat was what fed him, as planning his defeat fed her. She had not changed. She would never change.

161

He looked back at her over his shoulder. How long had he looked away? A moment or two? Had it even been that long? It had felt longer.

Wulfred, watching her sip her wine and wink at Cuthred across the rim, smiled as the perfect revenge burst upon his mind with the shining force of the rising sun. His smile was so full and so unexpected that Melania choked on her drink, eyeing him with instant suspicion. It was well she was suspicious, for he knew exactly how to stop all the trouble she was stirring up. This little Roman snake would cause no more trouble. He laughed out loud as he left the triclinium.

He could not see her, but he could feel her eyes on his back. And he could almost hear her rattle her alarm.

They stood in the dark of the wood, the scattered yellow lights of the villa twinkling warmly in the narrow valley below. Clouds of ice blue skidded across the night sky in tattered, tortured strips, running away to the east. A wolf cried sharply in the night, a broken cry of hunger. The leaves of last autumn twirled and hissed in a sudden strong gust of night wind, stirring the moist decay at their feet for a moment before dying off. It was just such a night as this that he had taken her world for his own, taken it and destroyed it. It was fitting that this night should be so much like the first time he had seen her villa, so helpless and indefensible against the dark, for now he would destroy again, though in different fashion.

Why could his comitatus not see it as he saw it?

"I honor you always, Wulfred, but think again on this plan. This is no way to defeat her!" Cynric said, his voice quavering with tension.

"Better to kill her, be done with it, and move on," Cuthred said flatly, fingering his blade with a reluctance odd for him.

"Without my pleasure from her?" Wulfred smiled, with no thought at all of killing her.

"There is pleasure in killing," Cuthred argued.

"But there is more pleasure in torment, especially of a Roman," Wulfred said. "Especially of this Roman."

"If it is because she has . . . well, if it is because she is beautiful . . ." Cenred stammered guiltily.

"And?" Wulfred prompted, squatting on his haunches and turning his shadowed face to the quiet villa below.

"If we have driven you to this by our attention to her . . ." Cenred continued, his guilt almost choking him.

"No one drives me to anything, Cenred," Wulfred said slowly, pulling his knife free and resting its tip on the ground at his feet. "You are not the cause of this. She is. As to her beauty, I have seen it always."

"Have you?" Cenred said, amazed.

"Certainly. Do you throw your seax away because it is covered in blood and mud? Do you not see its shape and form? Is it without virtue because it wants cleaning?"

"She has no virtue," Cynric mumbled.

"She has one virtue that I prize above all," Wulfred said, standing, holding his knife easily, aggressively. "She is Roman, and only a Roman can give me my revenge. For this I value her."

The group of warriors were silent at that. The night wind died to nothing. The leaves dropped from the branches and hung lifelessly in the dark. A large insect, black and armored, scuttled through the leaves; Wulfred flicked his knife and the insect was impaled, his armor a useless thing against a Saxon weapon.

"She is courageous and she is hostile, hating Saxons as you hate Romans," Ceolmund said softly, looking away from the quivering knife in the ground and down into the villa courtyard.

"Hating us?" Balduff asked, his light blue eyes round in disbelief. "She has been delightful, at least to me." He eyed Cynric judiciously.

"Hating us," Ceolmund repeated.

"You were not fooled?" Wulfred asked, looking at his companion with quiet respect.

"No," Ceolmund stated seriously. "I think that her hate is as strong as yours, Wulfred."

"Perhaps, but *she* is not as strong as I. She cannot win."

"No, she cannot win, but why do this to yourself? This method wounds you as it enhances her," Cynric said, his voice hot in the still night.

"Wounded?" Wulfred asked, flexing his right arm. "I shall not be wounded because I marry her."

The words settled into the darkness like a stone, sending back ripples that struck against their very bones. Only Wulfred was oblivious to their bruising. Only Ceolmund suspected why.

"No, but you will be tied to a Roman for the rest of your life. What vengeance is that?" Cenred argued.

"And she will be bound to a Saxon throughout her life, a very miserable life. There is my vengeance."

"You honor her with your commitment," Cynric said in a snarl, angry because the contrary woman *would* see it as a punishment. "She will be brought into your house. What greater honor for her?"

"She will not see it as an honor. For her it will be torture, and that is all that is important," Wulfred stated, closing the subject, he thought.

"Slavery can end at your will, but the marriage bond is binding. You will have her in your life for the rest of *her* life," Balduff said with a shudder that had little to do with Melania.

"Which is all the more reason for her to hate it and all the better for my purposes. There will be no release for her, and she will know it."

"She sees no release for herself as a slave," Cuthred said, "and yet she does not behave as a slave."

"As my wife, she will be tied to me with the tightest bonds possible, bonds nearly impossible to break. It will be my greatest joy to watch her spend her lifetime thrashing against these bonds of marriage."

"Wulfred," Cynric asked, taking him by the arm in gentle admonishment, "are you certain? Will she

Claudia Dain

feel the bonds of marriage when she did not feel the bonds of slavery?"

The villa lay in peaceful repose, the lights winking out in the heavy darkness below. All were abed, or soon to be. Unsuspecting. She was so very unsuspecting of what he planned for her.

Wulfred smiled and his teeth gleamed white in the moonlight. "She will."

Chapter Fourteen

It wasn't turning out at all as she had planned. Oh, it was going well enough with Wulfred's men, or it had been going well until just recently. Recently, in just the past few days, they had all but run from her whenever she approached. Cynric had looked close to throwing stones at her to drive her off. Inexplicable behavior, even for Saxons. Still, it was mostly Wulfred's response, or lack of one, that puzzled her.

He didn't act anything like a jealous suitor, or even an interested suitor. He didn't act like a suitor at all. *Stupid, perverse, pagan barbarian.* Why, when all his men had fallen over themselves at a crook of her finger, did he remain so aloof? He did not treat her any differently than he ever had, the oaf. She was oiled and perfumed and coiffed and draped in beautifully worked wool, and he was just as surly and distant and dull as he had always been. *Imbecile.* Could he not see that she was more beautiful than any woman he had yet encountered in his miserable life? Could he not understand that she was higher in intellect and breeding and culture than any woman he could have possibly met roving through the woods, as was his natural routine? Could he not see her worth, her beauty, her desirability?

Not that it bothered her in any personal way that he was so obtuse. No, it was only that it would have been so delightful to watch him tear himself up with desire and jealousy. It would have been a wonderful game, one that she would have enjoyed completely until the time had come for her to kill him.

Melania licked her lips; they were trembling.

She *would* kill him. She was strong and rested and more determined to defeat him than ever. If he were intelligent, he would run from her villa, for she was set on destroying him. And she would succeed. He would never anticipate violence against him, not from her, not now. None of them would; she had donned the role of beguiler too completely for any of them to see the role of executioner she had planned for herself. It would not be murder, not when it was retribution for what he had done to her. She had not forgotten her father, though the soil of his grave had settled during the summer and grass had seeded itself over the bare earth, gentling the raw reminder of his recent death. She had not forgotten, would not allow herself to forget, and

Wulfred would pay the price for that murder, for murder it had truly been.

He would murder again if she did not stop his plans for her. His attitude toward her had not changed, despite her primping and smiling. What was the matter with him? It could not be that her lures were invisible to the Saxon eye.

No, Balduff alone with his silvery hair, ice blue eyes, and wide smile would have convinced her otherwise. He was, or had been, delightfully submissive, eloquently ardent, and blatantly obvious. Cenred, too, she had charmed, though he had been more reserved out of regard for Dorcas. To be honest, she could well understand what Dorcas saw in him; he was beyond good-looking, with light brown eyes and wavy golden hair. His build was slim-hipped and muscular and his smile constant. His two front teeth were slightly overlapped and the effect was charming, even for a Saxon.

Cuthred, light blond with soft blue eyes and a broken nose to match a chipped front tooth, had surprised her with his docile adoration. He was built like a bull and had the same aggressiveness; so she had hardly thought he would turn his thoughts from battle long enough even to notice a woman. He had most certainly noticed her; in fact, his tongue-tied longing was almost endearing.

But it was Cynric who had been her greatest victory to date. Cynric, who had scowled at her from beneath dark brows from the moment he first had laid eyes upon her. Cynric, who would have chosen to spit on her before having to speak to her. Cynric, with his thick red-blond hair and deep blue eyes, had outrageous freckles across his nose and on the backs of his large hands. Cynric, hating every moment of it, desired her. Or had. What had happened?

Ceolmund had not changed, but he had never been a violent enemy. He was a strange Saxon: quiet to the point of silence, gentle as much as it was possible for a warrior to be gentle, and almost kind. Very odd behavior in a Saxon. He was handsome, too, though they were hardly an ill-favored race. Ceolmund's golden hair was quite dark and hung in waves to his elbows. His brows were heavy and sweeping over eyes of cool grayish blue. He was the tallest, excepting Wulfred, with wide shoulders and narrow hips, and his long nose was blunted at the tip. A most impressive man, for a Saxon, and second in size and strength and appearance to only one: Wulfred.

Wulfred, the only one among them to have remained her constant foe and completely blind to her transformation. If she had needed proof that he was an imbecile, she had it in this blindness. If only she could be as blind to his appearance. He was taller than any of them, his shoulders, arms, and back enormous with well-defined muscle; she couldn't help noticing his form, she rationalized, since he was never decently covered. His hair, golden blond and falling to the middle of his back, didn't cover him. Those skins he wore on his legs didn't cover him. A linen sheet certainly didn't cover him. She'd never forget the grin of arrogant and shameless satisfaction that he had worn when the sheet had crumpled to the floor. Or the gleam in his large eyes of intense blue.

She'd had ample time to study him during the last weeks, even though he'd kept his distance, emotionally. Physically he was as close as ever. Why, of them all, did he seem so unmoved by her transformation? He still called her a Roman snake on occasion, and she had hardly hissed her temper in weeks—an incredible feat of forbearance. He hadn't changed at all, and that meant one thing: he would kill her eventually. If she did not kill him first. It was that simple. It was a battle of wills between them that would end only when one of them lay dead. She didn't want to die. She didn't want him to win. But how to kill him?

A knife through the heart would do, but it had occurred to her that he was so muscle-bound, the knife might not make much headway. Her strike must be swift, and she did not have much weight to put behind the blow, so the chest had seemed to her more and more unlikely. A long, deep slice across the throat would work and leave lots of his Saxon blood pooling on the ground besides, a definite plus, but he was very tall. She could never do it when he was standing, not being able to comfortably reach his throat, and he did not sit very often. It was a puzzle. If only he had fallen at her feet, as she had planned.

Melania left off her pacing in her little room. There were no answers there; the answers were out with Wulfred and the rest of them. Perhaps Cenred would give something away; he was fairly easy to read.

Leaving her privacy behind, something she had a little more of these days because of their foolish trust in her, she walked under the welcome shade of the portico, ambling toward the triclinium and keeping her eyes on the courtyard. Cenred was there, with Dorcas. He liked Dorcas well enough; that was obvious from the shine in his light brown eyes and the grin on his face. Dorcas returned his smiling regard, despite the fact that he was a murdering, hairy Saxon. Still, Melania had to admit, Cenred was charming. She'd spent enough time with him by now to know that, but how could Dorcas forget even for a moment that he was a Saxon? She had never been able to. And certainly the oaf had never done a thing to encourage her to forget it.

But Cenred was different with Dorcas. He was smiling fully at Dorcas and, though she kept her dark eyes lowered, she was smiling back. They looked pleasant enough together, though not what she would call easy in each other's company. Melania leaned against a pillar of the portico and studied the lovers, really studied them, for the first time.

Cenred and Dorcas swirled around each other, drawing apart and swinging close in turn, never allowing the distance to grow too great. It was like a strange dance. He walked toward her and she backed up, smiling. He stopped. She stopped. He spoke and she drew a step nearer. He took a step toward her; she stopped and gave him her profile.

He stepped forward again and again until he was close enough to reach out and brush a finger down the length of her arm. Dorcas whirled away, smiling, and then stopped but three paces off, facing him. Cenred said something in a low tone, almost a whisper, that caused Dorcas to laugh and run toward him, her face alight with happiness. Melania had never seen such a look on anyone's face as she saw now on Dorcas's. Never had Dorcas looked so beautiful. When she was a step away from Cenred, when Melania fully expected her to stop, Dorcas flew into Cenred's arms, arms that enfolded her with ease. Laughing, he let her go, sliding her down his body until she struck him playfully on the shoulder; he let her drop and she shrieked in exaggerated alarm.

But beyond all this play, this play that Melania knew led to the couch and originated on the couch and mimicked the antics of the couch, beyond all this, Melania saw something in Cenred's eyes, and in the eyes of Dorcas as well. But it was Cenred she studied. Cenred, who was of the tribe of Wulfred. There was a hunger in those eyes of warmest brown, and a claiming when he looked at Dorcas.

She had seen something of the same look in Wulfred's eyes just this morning. She had been on her knees in the antechamber to the library, a room that for two generations had served as an altar. The Chi-Rho of Christus had been painstakingly pieced into the tile floor, the work clumsier than the original tilework, but beautiful because of its meaning. She prayed there daily, and he had always left her to it,

173

Claudia Dain

but today . . . today he had not left her alone.

He had said nothing. He had demanded nothing of her. Still, it had angered her that he had intruded upon her privacy when she wished to converse with the Christ. He had stood in the center of the library, the room an unsalvageable wreck since his arrival and of no use since he had burned all the manuscripts in his pagan violence, stood on the very spot where he had first seen her those long weeks ago. He had watched her, his arms folded across his bare chest, his eyes brilliant blue and blazing with a look she had never seen. A look she could not name. A look that was a shadow of the look that Cenred used when he looked at Dorcas. It was a claiming.

When he called her slave, he had not had that look. This was something different altogether, and knowing what it was that Cenred and Dorcas did together sent a chill racing along her skin.

Was it so? In all her efforts to tempt him, had she succeeded and not known it? Did he desire her after all? Had she not understood him at all? But what use was it when he did not fall all over himself in clumsy and ridiculous admiration of her? What victory was there in this cold appraisal?

Still, she had tempted him, if she could trust the look she had read in him. He wanted her. Wulfred, the Saxon, wanted her.

Melania turned away from the couple in the courtyard and grinned. She had him. She had him exactly where she had planned for him to be, caught in a net of desire for her. It was a little disappointing that he did not act in any way the be-sotted fool, cross-eyed with lovesickness and loping after her like a dog seeking a treat. Still, it was al-most perfectly plain that he wanted her.

She turned back to the courtyard and walked the perimeter, deep in thought, her hands playing with the folds of her palla. He had watched her through her prayers while she had rigidly ignored him, aware of his every breath and determined that he not know it. He had not moved. Neither had she. The larks outside in the summer air had warbled in happy chorus until a raven had disrupted them with its hoarse croak and sent them flying off into the trees. This she did not see, but heard, the mental picture very clear though her eyes were closed in prayer.

Had she seen a glimmer of desire in those cold eyes of his? It had not seemed so, but if a thread of claiming, of possession, was in him, would there not also be desire? It seemed so to her. How could there be one without the other? Melania smiled somewhat smugly and wrapped her arms around herself. He desired her. She wanted to laugh with the joy of it, but that would be an undignified dis-play of emotion, and so she contented herself with grinning. Wulfred had fallen prey to her. Wulfred wanted to possess her. Melania grinned so fully that her cheeks ached with gleeful satisfaction. Of course, it was only the joy of winning, nothing else.

Melania turned out of the courtyard, suddenly stifled by the sun and the wall and the air and the tightening sense of enclosure. She walked briskly with a light, tripping step to the river. It was low now—the rains had been few this summer—and the river was sluggish. Still, it was running and it soothed her. Nothing else moved on this still, summer day. The sun was hot and dry; no wind stirred the treetops. Even the birds were still. It was too hot to fly, too hot to sing, too hot to sweep the sky for food. Melania turned her eyes back to the water; she watched the ripples of gray and silver as the water sped by, reflecting the golden sun in fragmented snatches. The water looked almost like molten metal as it flowed past her spot on the low bank of grass; almost, except that she could feel the cool air rising from the surface of the stream. She lifted the stray hairs off her neck with a casual sweep of her right hand, keeping her eyes on the water. It was a pleasure to watch moving water on such a hot day. It had been hot all summer, and so dry. Would this freakish and unnatural summer never end?

Of course it would end. Autumn was no more than a month distant and the weather would cool. With the chill, the Saxon horde would retreat. Finally he would leave. She would have her home again. He would take his men and his weapons and his arrogant orders and he would sail away. He wouldn't come back; he probably wouldn't be able to find his way if he wanted to. He wouldn't want to; what Saxon returned to a place plundered of all worth? No, when he was gone, he would be gone forever, and she thanked God for it.

She couldn't wait for him to leave, taking his

hopeless desire for her with him. He would leave. She would never see him again. She would forget him. After a thorough scrubbing, it would be as if they had never been there, all smell of them and their weapons and their leather leg coverings and their bloody seaxes would be washed away. It would be as if they had never been, as if he had never come.

Except that her father's grave could not be washed away.

Tears stabbed, hot as coals, behind her eyes. These stupid, melancholy thoughts accomplished nothing. Melania brushed a hand across her eyes, pushing the tears away, daring them to come and challenge her authority. They wouldn't dare. Better to think of something else. She didn't want Wulfred to leave too quickly, not when she had just come to understand something of him and his almost blatant desire for her. After all, she did not want the Saxons to leave until she had killed Wulfred. He couldn't possibly leave until she had achieved her vengeance. Autumn was only a month or so away; she had better not delay or he might escape her.

Was it desire she had glimpsed in him? He was so guarded with her. Hardly the way Cenred was with Dorcas. How could she get him to relax with her? She could hardly stab him to death if he wasn't completely relaxed.

Leaning back on her elbows and closing her eyes, Melania dangled her feet in the water. It felt good on her bare feet, clean and smooth and cool. Refreshing. Relaxing. Peaceful.

"I thought you didn't bathe in the river, Roman."

Her feeling of relaxation slid from her into the river at her feet, leaving only agitation and a sick rolling in her belly.

"I'm not bathing, Saxon, and must you follow me everywhere I go? Can't you find your own entertainments without intruding on mine?"

Her words came out more harshly than she should have allowed, but his constant proximity was putting her on edge. Could she not have a few moments to herself, a few isolated moments without being forced to look at a half-naked man? Melania turned her head back for a quick glance at Wulfred, hoping he had found a tunic somewhere. He had not. He was glistening gold and rippling muscle. He was clean. He was combed. He was close to smiling. Smiling? What did he have to smile about?

"It is too hot to seek entertainment, unless it involves water." He walked straight through her glare of annoyance and seated himself on the grass next to her, the length of his legs dwarfing hers. "I knew you were young by your stunted size, but I had thought you too old to splash in the water like a child. Shall I make you a ball of wood to play with?"

Again the reference to her being childlike; did he not act on his desire for her because he thought her still a girl? "I am perfectly formed by civilized standards, barbarian, with no defect, as any educated man would know."

"And you are always trying to educate me."

"With no success."

"No?" He smiled and looked out over the water, the light from the moving river reflecting and sparkling in his eyes. "You have forgotten my conversion to the Roman bath."

"A small victory, but one my nose appreciates."

"And your eyes?"

"My eyes?" she asked, pulling her knees to her chin in a gesture of unconscious protection, leaving the water to drip from her feet back into the twisting river.

"Yes, have you not noticed a change in my look? I have noticed a change in yours."

He had? He had certainly not shown it. What deviousness did he practice now? Would he not appreciate her beauty if she did not note his first? Not that he was beautiful; he was merely tall and golden and banded with muscle. Melania shook off the uneasiness in her belly; he was a typical Saxon, except that he was clean.

"Well?" he prompted, turning to look at her.

"Well," she hedged, distrusting him, "your hair is longer than it was, though I would not have thought it possible. You almost could be taken for a horse, but you lack the whiteness of teeth for it." It was not true; his teeth were very white and surprisingly even, but he could not know that and he would definitely not hear it from her.

"Well," he repeated, "I had thought the water and soap of a Roman bath would wash the spite from a nasty Roman child and reveal a woman, but no water in the world can change childish spite into a woman's warmth."

What made his insult so cutting was that he said it casually; he didn't even look at her.

"You want warmth from this woman's body, Saxon?" She smiled coldly. "Why, I have given you the heat of my hatred since I first saw your dirty face in a place where it should never have been! My home!"

"Only a child bleats always of home," he said dismissively.

"Or a woman who has been robbed of hers! I am a woman, Saxon oaf, as any of your men will swear. If you doubt, ask them." It was a vicious taunt, but she didn't care; she wanted only to strike and hurt him. As he had hurt her with his cool dismissal of her womanhood.

Now he looked at her, and it fed her fire to see the smothered anger burning in the depths of intense blue.

"What will they tell me, little Roman?" He leaned over her, and she forced herself not to lower her torso to escape him. If blue could burn, his eyes burned into hers, but she held herself rigid. She would not avoid and she would not run and she would not yield. Not to him.

"Will they tell me that you have a woman's breasts, full and soft?" His breath, scented with wine and yeasty bread, fanned her face. His lashes were long and curled and the color of wheat.

"Will they tell me that your hip is smooth and curved?" His teeth were very white against the pink of his mouth, and his lower lip was very, very full.

"Will they tell me that your hair is as thick and soft and black as fine wool?" She felt the grass under her feet and the sun on her hair as if in a dream; it was a hot summer day, yet all was frigid next to the blaze of his eyes.

"Will they tell me how soft and small your mouth is and how easily it could be devoured?" Was he saying that he would destroy her or was he saying that he desired her?

"Will they tell me anything that I don't already know?" he whispered, his lips a finger span from hers.

He was so close. She could see herself reflected in odd distortion in his eyes; eyes so blue, so completely blue that the hot summer sky seemed pale and weak in comparison. He blinked slowly, his lashes dropping down to cover that blue for just an instant, a languorous instant, and it seemed to her that he had fanned the flame in his hot blue eyes.

He desired her; she could see it, hear it, even feel it.

It was all she needed of him. All she wanted. She wanted his desire; she did not want his touch. His kiss would scorch her lungs and his touch scald her. She could not let him touch her. It must never come to that. She would not allow it. Now that she knew he desired her, she had but to pick her moment and he would lie dead at her feet.

Melania smiled into the face of his hot desire. "You want me," she stated bluntly, not damping the glow of her victory.

Wulfred pulled away sharply and mumbled something in his barbaric language under his breath. Melania smiled more fully in the face of his embarrassment. His shame at being caught desiring her was food she could eat daily.

"I do not mock you, Saxon. You show a scrap of intelligence in doing so and should not be ashamed. Truly, this does you credit." She couldn't help grinning as she said it.

Now he studied her and she tried to control the flaring joy that flashed out of her smile. Really, she did not want to be obnoxious in her victory, because she did not want him to know how much this news pleased her. But it was so very hard not to smile.

"You declare that I want you," he said, stroking the angle of his jaw with the knuckles of his left hand, his eyes not leaving her grinning face. "And you smile with pleasure . . . or is it victory?" Wulfred leaned forward and brushed his knuckles against the line of her own jaw, and her smile faltered under the heat of even so casual a touch. "Will you still smile in arrogant Roman fashion when I tell you that I mean to have you?"

Melania's grin vanished as her stomach tumbled. Anger rose up to protect her against the image of his body heavy upon hers.

"You mean to *have* me?" she asked under her breath, giving air to the fire of her anger, shielding herself from the seduction of his words. "Is that some sordid Saxon metaphor?" Lurching to her feet and towering over him—and *that* was a glorious feeling—she shouted, "I said you showed a scrap of intelligence in wanting me, but you will never *have* me. I am far beyond your grubby Saxon reach!"

Wulfred jumped to his feet with far more agility than she had and grabbed her by the upper arms. His touch was bruising but she said nothing, showed nothing. She would not give him that. As long as he touched her in anger, she was safe. He said nothing, but his eyes were violent and expressive, blazing with the blue intensity of flame. Beyond his reach? He was showing her just how easily he could take her, hold her, subdue her. She read all the power of him in his eyes, more power than the strength of his hands, though they came close to breaking her. So much angry power in him, so much turbulent emotion in those eyes, and all of it directed at her. It was enough to frighten anyone, but not her. His anger was her ally. His desire for her was her ally. It was the growing knowledge that she saw him as a man that was her enemy. He was Saxon, she Roman; never could they forget that. She could not allow either one of them to forget.

"I will agree to nothing," she said with cold precision, though her skin burned where he held her.

He smiled. "I do not need your agreement."

"And you most definitely will not have my cooperation."

"It also is not needed," he responded, releasing her slowly.

She would not rub her aching arms with him standing right there; that would give him nothing but perverse pleasure. But then, he always seemed to want what would cause her the most distress. It had been his purpose from their first meeting, and certainly nothing had changed between them. Except that he had admitted to desiring her. Did he *want* her violent refusal? By taking her against her will, the idea of which seemed to please him inordinately, he would be torturing her spirit. It would be a case of her punishment and his pleasure: an ideal situation for him. But she didn't think she could take their contest of wills that far. It would be better to die than to endure the claiming he was promising. Her stomach heaved at the thought and flopped around under her ribs. She could hardly catch her breath.

She had wanted him to desire her because she had wanted him groveling. He was not groveling. He was not weak with love for her. In fact, scowling up into his set face, she didn't think she'd ever seen him look stronger or more indomitable.

"I had forgotten, for a moment, that you take what you want, even though it is not given," she offered, trying to sound placid. There had to be a way out of this; there had to be a weapon, an advantage, for her. "Now you will add me to your list of destruction." Into his pleased face, she added on inspiration, "You must want me very much."

Such overwhelming desire must surely give her some power. If he was caught in the throes of passion and she stood free of it, that would give her the advantage over him. It was a very definite weapon.

"You have not such power," he said flatly, reading her thoughts too accurately.

Turning his back to her and again facing the rushing water, he said, "I will take you. As wife."

There was numbness rushing through her mind and a tingling in her fingers and toes . . . her vision was black in spots . . . she would not faint in front of a barbarian! There would be too much victory for him in that.

No, she had to think of this calmly and clearly, and she would see a way out. There had to be a way out. She most definitely would not—could not—marry a Saxon!

Of course! She almost laughed in relief. *Of course.* It would be a Saxon marriage, pagan; not binding on her. It would be an empty ritual. Meaningless. And even if someone, somewhere, believed in its meaning, divorces were easily obtained within the bounds of Rome, and Britannia was certainly within the legal bounds of Rome. In fact, slavery was more permanent than marriage in the Roman Empire. He obviously didn't know that.

When she said nothing, Wulfred cocked his head and looked at her over his shoulder. She wiped the smile from her face just in time. Let him think he had her cowed by this pronouncement, the latest of many; his defeat would be the sweeter for its being unexpected.

"Did you have a day planned for this momentous event or is that the bride's province?" she said evenly.

Claudia Dain

Wulfred frowned at her and shook his head. "It will be when I choose."

Melania tilted her head and smiled wickedly. "And that is . . . ?"

"Not yet." He grunted, clearly upset by her composure.

"Soon?" she trilled, edging closer, crowding him.

"You will know when I tell you."

"Obviously," she said with as much sarcasm as she could, which was considerable. "Well," she said, turning away from the river, "be certain to let me know. A girl likes to prepare for such a day. In fact," she drawled, "I can hardly wait."

That should cause him to delay for a while, if only to spite her. In fact, she *could* hardly wait. There would hardly be a better day to kill him.

Chapter Fifteen

"She won't go through with it."

"But how will she escape it? He hasn't shown himself to be a man who changes his mind."

"Especially not with her."

"Why marriage, though? He cannot mean to honor her—"

"Honor me?" Melania interrupted. The people of her household jumped and turned to face her, guilt and embarrassment revealed in their eyes. "How can marriage to him honor me? It is my humiliation he wants and my death he plans; marriage is but the latest means."

"Will you marry him?" Finn asked nervously.

"Certainly," she answered easily. "It will mean nothing. I do not believe in whatever pagan deity the ceremony will invoke."

Theras was not in the room, so there was no one to argue with her on that point. It could have been said that a marriage was a marriage, no matter the differences in culture. It could have been said that vows spoken carried legal and spiritual weight. But only Theras would have dared say such things to her. And Theras was checking the grain stores. She knew: she had checked on his whereabouts before coming to the kitchen.

"But after," Dorcas said softly. "What of what comes after?"

Melania's stomach tumbled end over end at the words. Of course Dorcas would ask that; her nights were full of what came after.

Melania turned quickly to Dorcas, the end of her stola swinging wildly with the movement. "What comes after also means nothing." And when Dorcas raised her brows in surprise and mild disbelief, Melania repeated hotly, "Nothing."

She would not explain to her, to any of them, that it was because the only "after" on that day would be Wulfred lying in a bloody heap on the floor. It would be perfect. He would expect to avail himself of the marriage bed; he would be vulnerable, unsuspecting, and so very close. She had often worried how to get close enough to him. The bridal night and the marriage bed would get her very close, as close as she would need to be.

"He won't go through with it."

"When have you known him not to follow through on his stated word?"

"Especially with a woman."

"Balduff, for the sake of all that's sacred, can you not once stop talking of women?"

"We *are* talking of marriage? And you suggest that I do not speak of women?" Balduff shook his silver-blond head and sipped his wine. "You are in a sad state, Cynric. Worse than even I would have thought. Time you put down that shiny sword and raised up one of a different hue before you forget what it's for."

"*By all the gods!* Can you not for *once* stop thinking with your best and dearest companion and begin to think of what this marriage will mean for Wulfred!" Cynric shouted, his fists balled and ready to swing at the head of his most irritating comrade.

"His best companion?" Cenred smiled. "Why, Cynric, that was actually very funny."

"He's very upset," Cuthred offered in explanation.

"Aren't we all?" Balduff huffed indignantly. "But at least I can still see the good that will come of this marriage—"

"What good when he can have her at any time?" Cynric interrupted, shouting.

"He doesn't seem to want her; not like that," Cuthred said slowly.

"Well, he'll have to take her or it will be no marriage," Balduff said with authority, taking a long swallow of wine for emphasis.

"He'll take her. He wants this marriage," Ceolmund said quietly, his eyes not on his comrades but

189

on the flickering light cast by the lamps mounted on the walls of the triclinium. As was becoming the norm, his thoughtfully spoken words caused a hush to fall.

"What a strange thing to say . . ." Cenred began.

"Strange how?" Balduff roared amiably. "It was his idea, wasn't it? Certainly not hers!"

"No. Certainly not hers," Wulfred echoed as he entered the room.

"Did she fight you long over your decision, Wulfred?" Cenred chuckled, looking Wulfred over for teeth marks.

Wulfred smiled abstractedly and held up his arms for inspection. They were clean of wounds. "No, she resisted the urge to follow her natural bloodletting inclinations."

"When will you marry her?" Cuthred asked, eager to leave this place of no battles.

"When I choose," Wulfred answered bluntly, telling them something of the latest torture he had devised for Melania. The waiting in blind ignorance would eat away at her like poison.

"That will not please her," Cenred said with a smile.

"That's the idea." Wulfred smiled in return, his earlier misgivings about Melania's calm reaction waning.

"Then you had better be very careful in your bed, Wulfred," Balduff advised, "or she will not think herself tortured at all."

"No"—Cenred grinned—"she may even torture you with her demands for satisfaction." Stroking his chin, Cenred asked slyly, "What was the name of the woman who screamed your name as if in torment of the worst sort . . . ?"

"Bekia," came the single reply from five throats, Wulfred's the loudest of them all.

"Melania is hardly the same type of woman as Bekia," Cynric said.

"Hardly," said Balduff in mock solemnity. "Melania is far more passionate."

The laughter continued unchecked, and Wulfred pointed to his knee and the teeth marks Melania had left at her first passionate attack.

"Take care you do nothing to inspire her to score your back or you will have a most contented wife and defeat your purpose in marrying her."

"You do not want her to *like* her new position in life, lying flat on her back."

"Never leave her with a smile on her face."

"Never leave her with a scream in her throat."

"Never leave her with your back exposed," said Ceolmund into the raucous mix.

The mood dampened immediately. True, Ceolmund had never been boisterous, but when had he turned so sour? Balduff wiped the tears from his eyes and drank deeply of his cup. Cynric did not hesitate to launch again into his favorite theme: the deathly mistake it would be to marry the Roman snake.

"The torture you devise for her will be your own," he reiterated hopelessly, tirelessly. "You will be bound to a Roman for life."

"For her life, certainly," Cenred interjected.

"It will not be torture to have her under my complete control and miserable for the rest of her days. It will be a pleasure," Wulfred answered before drinking deeply of his beer.

"You look forward to this marriage with pleasure," Ceolmund paraphrased. "You do not find that strange?"

Wulfred drank again, enjoying the yeasty tang of the beer. Wiping his mouth with the back of his hand, he answered easily, "No."

Before Ceolmund could respond to that, Balduff joked, "Then why wait to have her, and I know you have waited, because none of us has heard her screams of rage. Or of pleasure."

Wulfred paused before answering, staring into the golden swirl of his drink. They had been together for years, these men of his. They knew of his rage against Rome and they knew why. They had fought and killed and plundered together. They had wenched together. They all had known of Bekia, and the laughter her memory aroused had been shared and good. But Melania was different. Melania was effortlessly and eternally different. He did not want her name so casually on their tongues. He did not want to talk like this about her, not with anyone. And the thought, which seemed so traitorous, disturbed him. Troubled, Wulfred said nothing.

"Her appeal is as recent as her first bath and her first combing," Balduff said, "though I could see the beauty of her beneath the rags."

"Could you?" Wulfred said, reentering the con-

versation. "I see her no differently. Clean or dirty, smiling or snarling, she is the same woman."

"Roman," Ceolmund supplied into the momentary silence.

"Yes," said Wulfred with a slight jerk of his head and a flexing of his hand around the mug. "Roman."

But he had not been thinking of that. She was beautiful in her dark, Roman way, and passionate in her intensity. He had not thought a woman of Rome would have so much passion; he had not thought any Roman could have her courage. She, with her reckless hatred and her unflinching aggression, was the sort of woman Saxons admired. She was ferocious, tenacious, and fearless; at least she appeared so. If she struggled against fear and overcame it with angry defiance, he could but admire her for her determination.

Wulfred drank again from his cup. These thoughts were wrong; she was Roman and nothing else mattered. He had waited too long for his vengeance against Rome to be distracted from it now by a beautiful woman with a warrior's heart.

"Since you feel that way," Cenred said, "she would be easier faced as a slave than as a wife in the marriage bed. Maybe you should force yourself to sample her before the bond is made, to see if you can face a lifetime of her. Or perhaps someone could do the service for you."

Wulfred said nothing at first, but his eyes grew flat and his mouth tightened. Cenred clamped his

Claudia Dain

mouth shut and moved away, caught off guard by the censure in Wulfred's eyes.

"You will watch your words and your actions concerning Melania, Cenred. She is not your woman. She is mine. Remember that when next you see her."

Into the sudden and heavy silence Cynric intoned, "Your sons will have a Roman mother."

"And a Saxon father," was Wulfred's quick reply.

"You go far in your vengeance," Cuthred said.

Wulfred slammed his beer down onto the low Roman table. The contents spewed up and slapped down on the smooth surface of the table, sounding like heavy rain—or the crackle of a fire newly lit.

"I can never go far enough."

They said little after that. What was there to say? Melania would be crushed under the wheels of Wulfred's revenge. It was why they had stayed as long as they had.

Theras, watching and listening from the shadows of the columns that fronted the triclinium, studied Wulfred. Little had been revealed that he had not already understood, yet . . .

There was in Wulfred's manner toward Melania . . . something . . . something that told him that Melania was not as repugnant to Wulfred as the Saxon liked to think. After a long, hot summer, Theras had some understanding of Wulfred, and he would almost swear that Wulfred was coming to value Melania for her fighting spirit alone. Of course, there was much more to her than that.

194

Theras was becoming more certain with each passing day that Wulfred knew it.

"Will you really marry her?"

Wulfred looked down at the group of boys clustered around his legs and smiled. They were practicing their swordplay with hewn tree limbs and fallen sticks—little boys of Rome working so diligently to become good Saxon warriors. A good revenge, if he chose to see it that way. Strangely, he could not. Whether Roman or Briton or Saxon or Frisian, these boys would become men, and men must fight. To fight and win was to survive. Looking down at them, their faces dirty and their eyes bright, he hoped that each one would survive and win.

"Will you?" Flavius asked again. He was the one who spoke for them all. Wulfred knew it was because of the bond that had been forged between them that day in the courtyard.

"Yes."

"Melania said she would marry you?" Petras asked.

"Yes." Wulfred smiled.

"Did she say it like she meant it?" Aquilas asked.

Wulfred crossed his arms and looked down upon the troop. "Does not Melania always say what she means?"

"Well, yes," Flavius said, frowning in concentration.

"Then . . . ?"

"Do you always do what you say?" he asked,

chewing his lip. "I mean, I remember . . . we all know . . . we all heard you say that you . . ."

Wulfred stopped smiling. They had all heard him say that he would kill her. He had said it. He had shouted it. He had even dreamed it. But not recently.

"I will marry her," Wulfred repeated.

"Why?"

The question was asked with as much innocence as could be summoned from a boy who had seen his world plundered and torched. The man who had held the torch had no answer to give.

"Do you think she'll go through with it?"

"Will he?" Dorcas whispered against her lover's neck.

Cenred smiled and answered, "Yes. Wulfred has stated it, and he is not one to deviate from his purpose."

Dorcas leaned back against the circle of his arms. "And what is his purpose? To kill her in the marriage bed?"

Cenred lost his smile and released his hold on Dorcas. "His purposes are his own. I would caution you not to stand in his way."

Dorcas took a step away from this Saxon who had so easily charmed her. And bedded her. Perhaps it had all been a little too easy for Cenred; not so for Wulfred.

"Because I would find myself with a seax in my back, Cenred? Is that what Wulfred plans as Melania's husband?"

"His plans are his own," he repeated, turning from her to face the ancient avenue of vines.

Dorcas adjusted the fall of her stola as she studied the back of Cenred's blond head. The Saxons were fanatical in their devotion to Wulfred; trying to pry into the motives of their leader was like peering into a rainstorm—all was obscured. But she did know one thing, something that was certainly no secret: Wulfred hated Romans, Melania in particular. Therefore it was certain that this marriage was not in Melania's best interests.

"As are Melania's," she said with some bite.

Cenred turned to face her, his smile pleasant while his eyes were clouded. "But she will marry him."

"Her plans are her own," she said with acidic sweetness.

Cenred's smile froze for a moment, and then he forced a laugh. "She has no choice, Dorcas. She will marry him; Wulfred has decided it."

"There are always choices, Cenred, and you know Melania."

It was not a statement that inspired easy confidence.

"Yes," he said, pulling at his chin. "She is very . . . proud, very difficult."

"Don't you mean to say that she is very Roman?"

Cenred smiled warmly and reached out to take Dorcas into his arms. Dorcas took only half a step back before he was embracing her. She had not tried to elude him with any diligence; certainly Wulfred would not have subdued Melania as easily.

Claudia Dain

And Melania had received a proposal of marriage.

"Very Roman," Cenred agreed, trailing a finger down her spine. "Very proud, very arrogant, and very stubborn."

"You could be describing Wulfred," she said, still thinking of Melania, soon to be married.

"Wulfred?" Cenred chuckled. "No, he is a great Saxon warrior—"

"And very proud, very arrogant, and very stubborn. I could also add vindictive."

"With reason."

"There is always a reason, but only vindictive people feed it."

Cenred dropped his mouth to the top of her head and said under his breath, "You do not know the reason."

"Then tell me," she whispered against his chest.

"It is just," he said as he kissed her brow.

"Is it kind? Will he treat his wife kindly?"

Cenred pulled Dorcas back by the arms and stared into her eyes. "Why do you ask what will happen to her? She is nothing like you. . . ."

"Why do you say so? I am as Roman as she!" Dorcas flared. Melania was beautiful, intelligent, eloquent. What was she?

Cenred kissed her softly on the lips, saying, "Because she is teeth and claws, rattle and fangs. You are soft and warm and . . ."

"And?"

"Mine."

But only for now. She was not to be married. Melania was. Wrapping her arms around Cenred

198

and returning his kiss, Dorcas considered that it was, perhaps, time to show Cenred her claws.

"I'm quite sure he means to go through with it, if only to harass me," Melania answered, fiddling with the shoulder folds of her stola.

Flavius ran his hand over the stick Wulfred had given him, smoothing the bumps with the friction of his movements. "And you will? You will marry him?"

Melania looked down at Flavius, covered in dust from his battle play and with at least ten bruises on his shins. A forthright boy who had, strangely, come to no harm from the Saxon horde. The memory of Wulfred rushing to the boy's defense rose with the familiarity of the sun in her mind. How many times had she relived that moment? Wulfred had touched a vulnerability in her heart with his act that all the scoldings of her father had failed to harden. And therein lay her failure. To be soft, sentimental, was to be weak. She could not be weak and be Roman.

She could not admire a Saxon. She could not yearn for such tenderness to wrap itself around her as Wulfred's arms had wrapped themselves around Flavius. If she did, if she gave in to her growing desire for laughter and tenderness and respect from the man who was responsible for the death of her world, she would kill the very essence of her father's life as surely as the Saxons had taken his breath. She could not kill the memory of her father and the legacy he had striven for. She could not be

Claudia Dain

such a weak and emotional Roman daughter.

"Will you?" he asked again, his brown eyes solemn.

Melania smiled and crossed her arms over her chest playfully. "Have I not told him I would? Does he not believe that I will?"

"I think . . . I don't think he believes that anyone can defy him, especially a Roman," Flavius murmured, his stick making a hole in the dirt.

"How well you know him," Melania murmured in reply, her smile rueful. "But what do you think, Flavius? Do *you* think that I will be a docile Saxon wife?"

"No." Flavius smiled suddenly, tossing his stick in the air so that it tumbled end over end until it fell back into his hand. "I don't think anyone thinks that."

"Not even the oaf?"

"Especially not him."

"Yet he will marry me." She shrugged, losing her lightness of mood though she struggled to keep it wrapped around her. "Or so he says."

Flavius said nothing. Poor child—the world was as confused for him as for her, yet he bore all bravely and with little show of fear. Initially, all had feared the worst of the Saxon conquerors, most especially the children. But time had eased such worry. The Saxons had been temperate, even kind . . . loving, toward the children of her villa. The image of Wulfred holding Flavius in his arms, gently stroking, assuring the boy of his protection, comforting his tears, assaulted her again. Her father would never

200

condone such a memory or the confused longing that accompanied it.

"Tell me, Flavius," she said, throwing off her melancholy, "how should a proud and fearless Roman—"

"He says you are not fearless," Flavius burst out, and then bit his lip in embarrassment.

"Proof that he does not know me at all," she answered quickly, stung by the indictment.

Flavius looked up at her, his stick twitching at his side, his lip caught between his teeth.

"Tell me all he said and I will negate each point with proper Roman logic," Melania prodded, eager to defend herself and ease the boy's fears.

"It was when I told him that you were never afraid, right after the sword missed me. He told me it was all right to fear. I told him that you were never afraid and he told me . . . he told me . . ."

She remembered the moment, that whispered moment. She had wondered what crudity the oaf had whispered to the child. Now she would know.

"Yes, he told you . . . ?" she prompted.

"He told me that you were more afraid than anybody, but mastered it better than anybody and so you were the bravest person he had ever known."

Proper Roman logic collapsed. She did not know if she'd been insulted or complimented. Remembering the source, she decided it had to be an insult. And a lie. She was not afraid, not of any of them, and certainly not of him.

He thought her brave?

There was no logic in that, just as there was no

201

logic in the warmth those words generated in her. Did she expect logic of a Saxon? Did she expect praise from Wulfred?

"Melania?"

She jerked her thoughts back to Flavius and gave him a weak smile.

"*Are* you afraid?"

"Not of him." It was the stark truth.

"Then . . . you will marry him?"

"I've said I will." A marriage that would not last an hour.

"Do you think . . . do you think he might . . . like you?"

"Absolutely not." A logical answer, deeply rooted in evidence. Her training dictated that she allow no other impressions to cast seed in her mind.

Her father would have been proud.

Chapter Sixteen

Time passes slowly to those who wait, but the summer was waning fast, and Wulfred had still not said one word as to when this mock marriage would occur. How long had she been made to wait? Two weeks? Three? And how much longer would she be forced to wait in ignorance? Until he had enjoyed her frustration to the fullest, of course. Not that she wanted to marry him, but this waiting for him to pronounce that today or tomorrow would be the day, as if he were God himself, directing the fate of all mankind . . . it was so very typical of him.

Oafish pagan.
Drooling imbecile.
Murder victim.

Oh, yes, that was truly what he was. Though it would not actually be a murder, but an execution, and she the happy executioner. It was so difficult to wait for him to tire of making her wait; she had so much true eagerness for the day to come, and yet she knew that if she displayed even the smallest part of her impatience, he would spin the waiting out even longer, happy in his torture, delighting in her defeat. And so she waited. Patiently.

Well, as patiently as she knew how. Unfortunately, patience was not one of her gifts and, also unfortunately, she was not getting any better at it with practice.

Still, he was such a barbarian, how would she even know if the thing had been done? Saxon ways, hardly above the animal, were inexplicable to her. Perhaps she was already married!

Impossible. He would have forced her to bed, if only to humiliate her. In fact, she couldn't help wondering why he hadn't forced himself upon her already. It was amazing that a barbarian could show such restraint. Unless it wasn't restraint. Indifference? She ran her hands up the nape of her neck, smoothing her hair. *Impossible.* He had all but admitted that he desired her, and she had felt his heat herself that day by the river. But since that day, he had kept his distance from her—for which she was grateful, certainly. It was not as if she wanted the oaf near, spouting words of seduction and desire, touching her, perhaps even kissing her. . . . *Ridiculous!* She was profoundly grateful that he was keeping the distance that she demanded.

She had asked Theras days ago for information

about the ritual of Saxon bonding, and he had promised to find out what he could. Obviously he had found nothing yet. Perhaps there was nothing to know. It was probably based on something as primitive and improbable as the color of the moon or the pattern in a stone toss. Dorcas had known nothing either, claiming no Saxon had said anything to *her* about marriage. A sharp enough answer for a simple question, Melania had thought. *Someone* had to know about Saxon marriage rituals. Oh, yes, *someone* did, but she wasn't asking him.

Melania sat up straighter on her stool and consciously eased the tension in her shoulders and across the top of her back. The Saxon was to blame for that. She had never had a moment of tension until his appearance in her life; at least none that she would admit to.

She had taken refuge in her favorite pastime: jewelry making. It was fine work and required total concentration. An excellent method for forcing thoughts of a blond, near-naked barbarian from her mind—a barbarian too big to be physically managed, too ignorant to be reasoned with, and too naked to be comfortably ignored.

Obviously, jewelry making was not a perfect method of controlling her thoughts.

A hand on the back of her neck almost sent her vaulting off her stool. Only one hand, one touch, one man caused such a violent response in her.

"Oaf! Can't you see I'm working?"

"I see you playing with bits of gold. Hardly work."

She would not look at him. She would ignore him. She would patiently hold her tongue until he left her alone.

Patience was not one of her gifts.

"It takes great skill, not to mention creativity, and it is also one of the few tasks you have authorized as acceptable for me. Or had you forgotten?"

"Only a lazy Roman would call this work. It is pointless."

She ignored him, or tried to. His hand still lay lightly on her nape. His legs pressed gently against her stiffly erect back. She could hardly breathe for his nearness.

"Only a stupid barbarian would demean artistic effort."

"Perhaps that is because I see nothing artistic about it."

An insult? He was insulting her creative ability? Her skill as an artisan?

"You would have me believe that you Saxons have none among you who fashion articles of adornment for the dual sake of beauty and function? Are you truly so bestial? And let me hasten to add that I would have no difficulty in believing it."

She looked up at him as she said it, unable to resist the desire to insult him to his face. It might have been a mistake.

He towered over her, his loins at her eye level as she sat upon the stool; she couldn't help staring at the tiny golden hairs that swirled in flowing precision below his navel. A lump rose from her chest to fill the small space at the top of her throat. With effort, she forced her eyes to his face. That might also have been a mistake.

The Saxon smiled down at her with sickening superiority before idly contemplating her efforts. He stepped even nearer to do so and bent down so that his broad chest was a handspan from her face. Surely that had not been necessary. The lump in her throat began throbbing in rhythm with her heartbeat.

"No," he answered. "We also have jewelers among our people. Skilled artisans."

"Workers of gold?" she asked skeptically, closing her eyes against the sight of him.

"Workers of gold. Of bronze. Of copper. Of steel."

He straightened and moved slightly away. She thanked God.

"Stolen metals, I would guess," she managed.

"And where did you come by your tiny hoard of gold? Dig it yourself?"

"We traded for it."

She kept her eyes on her work. She would not look at him again. She was heating the golden circle so that the tiny balls would fuse to it. He was trying to distract her; he wouldn't.

"Ah, yes, the famous Roman trade. 'Give us what we want and we'll let you live on the land of your ancestors.' "

She looked up at him swiftly, her eyes alight and golden, her concentration broken. She set aside the gold, removing it from the heat.

Claudia Dain

"And what of the Saxon trade? 'Give us what we demand and you may live another day.' "

"But Roman," he said under his breath, running his hand through the coils of her hair, "you have not given me what I want."

"And I do not want to live another day." It was not exactly true anymore, but she had said it so often that she could think of no other reply to his taunts. "I also do not want you depositing your fleas in my hair! What took an hour to achieve, you have destroyed with a single touch! How very Saxon of you."

"I like your hair better the old way: loose and dusty." He smiled, pulling and tugging until her careful coiffure hung in a tangle down her back.

The very nearness of him jolted her. His touch almost brought her to her knees in a spasm of what she could only identify as nausea.

"Stupid, *stupid* barbarian!" she said in a snarl, backing away from him. "You have no culture and certainly no taste!"

"I follow my own tastes," he said, watching the distance she was putting between them, learning from it. "I like a woman's hair down her back, either loose or braided, but not twisted and tortured to sit atop her head."

"Uncivilized," she spat.

"Beautiful," he said softly.

Beautiful? Tickles of nervous fire swirled in her belly and her mind shouted alarm. This was not a word she wanted of him. This word, *beautiful,* was not adversarial, and he was her adversary. He would always be her adversary. She did not want to hear *beautiful* on his lips. She did not want to see his gaze of intense and impossible blue skim her body and pierce her eyes as surely as his sword had pierced her ordered Roman world. She did not want to see him close the distance between them. Did not want him to ease the tangles from her hair with his battle-roughened hands. Did not want him to run a gentle finger down the length of her left arm. Did not want him—God what was he doing?—to touch the tip of her breast.

And she did not want to feel the fiery shiver that ran like a wild flame through her core as her nipple hardened in response.

She reacted instinctively. She hit him.

He reacted as always. He did not move.

She hit him again, a ringing blow across the face.

He did not move. He smiled. Slowly and confidently. Knowingly.

God, God, God, how she hated him.

"You never disappoint me," she said coldly, pulling away from the scorching nearness of him. The hauteur of Rome clung to every word. She walked away, leaving him, since he was so obstinately immovable.

"And you, little Roman, never disappoint me."

The worst of it was that he said it on a laugh.

Oaf.

Animal.

Imbecile.

Saxon.

Melania made her way as straight as the arrow

flies to the kitchen. No more pretense. No more subtlety. Oh, yes, she had held herself in check with him. None could have done better. She had tried to get along with him, stupid savage that he was, but he was impossible. Untrainable. Wild. Savage. There was only one response to such a beast. Without a word to anyone, without a thought for the strange looks she was receiving, without heeding the gasps of dismay, she took a knife from the table. Let him touch her again. Let him touch her and he'd feel his own blood before he choked on it. Let him touch her again. Just let him.

Hiding the knife in the folds of her palla as she walked across the sunlit courtyard, she smiled her own smile, and her laugh more than matched his.

Later, at dinner, Melania stroked the cold reassurance of the knife hidden within her clothing. She had spent what remained of the afternoon sewing a small pocket into the vivid yellow stola she wore. By tomorrow each of her stolas would be graced with a hidden pocket. She would never be unprepared for his assault again. And how happy she was that she had a weapon. His comitatus, never warm toward her unless under the charm of her seduction, was positively frigid now. What lie had the oaf told to provoke such a response? It was true that she didn't want their friendship, if the barbarians possessed the loyalty required for true friendship, but she did want their ease in her presence, and she had achieved it—until recently. Daily their reception of her grew more chill. It went against her plans. She did not want a suspicious, snarling band of barbarians prowling her villa when she killed their leader; better that they should be relaxed and pacified than armed and growling. They were all but growling now.

Obstinate, contrary savages.

The fact that Wulfred was behaving as usual, as relaxed in a hostile environment as only a barbarian could be, made it worse. What did he have to be so pleasant about? And if he said one word about touching her . . . well, his blood would flavor the wine.

Where to stick him? The throat was oh so appealing: such a lot of blood in the neck, such a lot of deceitful Saxon blood. But then the breast was closer. His back she had to discount because it was much too muscular; what could be worse than a flesh wound that would only aggravate him? Besides, she wanted him to see who wielded the knife. There would be immense satisfaction in that.

Melania stroked her knife and smiled. She would achieve satisfaction from the Saxon, and he would know he had given it to her. She would win. Rome would defeat the Saxons. She would defeat *this* Saxon.

If only he would proceed with his ridiculous marriage. Once married, they would be alone, in the dark, with her knife. Oh, yes, she was very eager for this mock marriage, because on that day he would die, as her father had died. But no longer would she content herself with killing him and letting his mob murder her in angry vengeance. No.

Now she wanted to live more than she wanted to die. He had given her that. If she killed him in the dark, in the quiet of their bridal night, she had a chance of escape.

Melania smiled coldly as Wulfred handed her the tray of meats. He had no idea what she planned. He had no idea what she was capable of.

But he would.

Yes, it would be in the dark. He would lie bleeding out his miserable life on the couch where he had planned to humiliate her, and she would flee west. Marcus had gone west to find Artos, the bear, rumored to be urging all men of Rome and Britannia to fight in concert against the barbarians invading their world of order. Marcus would have found Artos, heir to Ambrosius, son of Utha, and he would have joined with him because Marcus needed no urging to fight the Saxons. If Marcus could go west and find Artos, she could go, too, after she had killed her own Saxon.

She was no fool; it would not be easy to kill the Saxon beast. But she would kill him. She could even die happily if she beat the oaf at his own game, and he died knowing it.

"You are thoughtful tonight," he said, interrupting her contemplations.

"I am thinking of the future. Yours. Mine." She smiled and sipped her wine.

She had the great satisfaction of seeing his brows lower in a sudden frown.

Chapter Seventeen

It was at the close of the meal when Theras began to cross the triclinium floor toward her. Since it was inconceivable that Theras would have voluntarily approached Wulfred, Melania rose to her feet in a graceful manner to join him. It was in the act of rising that Wulfred magnanimously announced, "You may go, but only so far as your bedchamber."

Melania looked down onto the top of his head, fighting the impulse to crack a dish over it. She reverted to the weapon of words, a cleaner weapon and one less apt to stain her palla.

"Are you, in your oafish way, attempting to give me permission? Permission to travel from one room in my home to another? Did I ask you anything?"

"No, you did not." He looked down into the

murky liquid of his cup before adding, "But still, you may go. To your bedchamber only."

He was baiting her, and, because he was looking for a fight, she decided not to give him one. Whatever he wanted, that was what she would withhold. It was with great difficulty that Melania held her tongue, but she was learning to bide her time. After all, it would not be too much longer. The nights were cooler now, summer's heat was on the wane, and with the change of season, the Saxon horde would creep homeward to huddle into whatever caves they called home. Until the earth warmed again. Then they would return, a summer pestilence: deadly, swift, and inescapable. But they would not return to her. There was nothing left here to destroy.

Theras watched as Melania approached him. It was probably obvious that she was furious, but at least she had said nothing provocative. She didn't want Wulfred to suspect her of being any less than pleased that they were to marry. It would be a very short marriage for him, since he would be dead within hours of it. It was with that vivid thought that Melania reached Theras.

"I have listened to them," he said without preamble. She had been waiting for this information for days. "It has not been difficult; it is all they speak of."

"How very flattering," she said, sounding not at all flattered.

"Perhaps it is," Theras said seriously, his eyes dark in the shadowed light of the broad portico.

"As a race, they take their marriage vows seriously. This is not lightly done for them."

"I can assure you that this is not lightly done on my side either!"

"Of course not," he softly agreed. "Yet they speak of this bonding as a permanent state. It seems that Saxons marry for life."

It was in her mind that Wulfred's married life would be extremely short, but she said nothing aloud. Theras would most likely try to talk her out of her plan. He had become quite conservative in his advancing years. Why, he must be all of forty.

"Just how long do Saxons live? I would think they would die like flies since they live off the destruction of others," she said breezily, looking over Theras's shoulder into the triclinium. The Saxons were a golden mosaic in the flickering light of the triclinium lamps: golden and large and solid. As she looked at them, for just a moment it seemed that they would last forever and that her beautiful Roman world would be crushed under their ponderous weight, but that was impossible, inconceivable; Rome would live forever.

"He will live long enough to make you his wife. And he makes you his wife for life. Think on that, Melania. He must feel something for you to make a lifelong commitment."

A lifelong commitment. A binding marriage. To be his wife. To have his children. Melania chewed her lip gently and tentatively touched her belly as the words took hold. Wulfred was not one to act on impulse, so it was logical to believe that he had considered the weight Saxons put on the marriage vow. He must have realized that, once married, she could conceive his child. Melania ran her hands across the narrow span of her hips and the flatness of her belly; would any man kill the woman who might be carrying his child? Would Wulfred? Wulfred had the adoration of every boy in the villa and treated each with a kindness and gentleness she would never have attributed to a Saxon warrior. Would such a man kill his unborn child in an act of revenge against the mother?

Perhaps . . . it was possible . . . he might want more from her than the pleasure of torture. Perhaps he did see something in her, something more than an enemy. Perhaps that was what she felt when she was near him. It was possible that it was not disgust. It was possible that he was a handsome man who had enough civility to be gentle and enough intelligence to be humorous. And enough virility to make her lose her breath. It was possible that he was worthy of the leadership his men granted him. It was possible that he possessed some admirable traits and that he had seen that there was more to her than her hatred. It was possible . . . perhaps. And if so, if he did actually have a fondness for her, even an attraction for her . . . perhaps . . . perhaps she should not be planning to kill him on their wedding night. That was rather harsh.

Harsh? Melania closed her eyes against compassion and mercy and hope, forcing herself to remember just how this Saxon had hacked his way into her life. Was it not harsh when he raged into her life like a sweeping fire? Had he not demolished her home? Had he not been responsible for the death of her father? Had he not burned away all her dreams so that not even ash remained? Had he not told her repeatedly that he meant to kill her?

What would her father have said if he knew she was considering showing mercy to a Saxon? This was not the way of Romans. Her father had taught her better.

Melania shivered like a dry leaf in a scorching wind and opened her eyes. Truth faced her. There was no room for mercy in such a light. Yes to all of her questions about Wulfred. If he had tender feelings for her, so much the better; he would be easier to manipulate onto the point of a knife. He would find no mercy at her hand, as he had shown her none. The mercy her father had received stood only on the tombstone his killers had allowed. Wulfred was Saxon, and Saxons were the enemy. There was no other truth.

"You will not soften toward them, toward him," Theras said, observing her closely.

She closed her eyes briefly before answering.

"No."

"He will be your husband."

"No!" she flared.

"Even for a Roman, marriage is a serious thing."

"It was not my idea."

"But you will be married nonetheless."

"Only until he dies," she said with as much lightness as she could manage.

"Melania," Theras urged, "you follow Christus,

as do I. You know the teachings on marriage."

"He is no Christ follower." She snorted. "He worships the air."

"But you do not," he reminded her sternly.

No, she did not. How much easier if she did. If she did, she could kill him without a thought, husband though he be. Would Christus smile on her as she killed her husband of an hour? She knew the answer. It was a hard answer. She walked away from Theras, thinking hard on what she planned, thinking more deeply about what she had imagined doing than she had yet done. To kill, to murder, was forbidden.

But it would be justice, not murder, to kill the murderer of her father; even Jesus . . . even Jesus wouldn't object in such a righteous cause . . . Jesus who had let himself be killed by unrighteous men. Yet Wulfred had said that he hadn't killed Melanius; he had no reason to lie to her. He had never lied. Melania twisted the end of her stola as her mind twisted on too many truths that had nothing in common except that each one increased her unhappiness.

Why couldn't everything be clear and uncomplicated, the way life had been before the Saxon descended? She hated all these confusions and shadings; things should be clear and straight, casting no shadow in one direction or another. That was the world her father had taught her; that was the world she struggled to regain. The Saxon should die, and it should be right to kill him. He should not have muddied the issue by not killing her father and by not being a liar, or a rapist. He should not have saved Flavius. He should not have treated her people with consideration. He should not be so . . . beautiful.

Melania grimaced in irritation so fierce it was almost painful. Saxons were not supposed to be like this. They were wild and uncontrollable, like untamed animals with no ability to reason. They were nothing like Romans, just as fish were nothing like flies. Except that one was food for the other, and the Saxons had been nibbling at the corners of Rome for decades. Wulfred was nothing like what she had been taught, yet her father could not have been wrong. Could Wulfred never help her by doing what she expected?

Still, he was ultimately responsible for everything that had happened. And she would have vengeance. There would be justice. That had to be right.

But . . . but perhaps it would be safer not to kill her husband. Jesus probably wouldn't forgive that. Better to do it before they were married. If Theras had accomplished anything, it was to convince her that she should kill Wulfred before the marriage ceremony and not after. The sooner the better. Tonight.

The decision made, she felt immediately better. It was excitement that made her hands shake and her mouth go dry, not dread. Melania slipped into the shadows and left the noise of the triclinium behind. Crossing the deserted courtyard, the dirt hard-packed and dry under her sandaled feet, she made her way to the stable. It was empty except for her father's horse, Optio. Optio was her horse now and would go with her. Of course, Optio did not cooperate and it took much longer than it should have for her to get the mare saddled and ready. Unnatural animal to prefer the Saxon's touch to civilized Roman hands. By the time she left the stable her hands were shaking with both anxiety and fatigue—or perhaps it was only excited anticipation. The Saxon would die tonight. She would win the battle that he had begun with her.

The kitchen was her next destination, and though it was quiet, it was not deserted. However, because she had spent so much time in the kitchen in the past weeks, little notice was paid her. She found a large leather sack to hold bread, cheese, wine, and oil. It would be enough. It would get her to Marcus. It had to.

Melania walked quietly back to the stable, the sack held like a babe in her arms. Optio, true to form, tried to step on her foot as she positioned the sack behind the saddle. Moving away from the snorting animal Melania stood in the stable doorway and listened. The wind rustled the forest treetops, brushing branch against branch in enforced intimacy, and the leaves moaned in whispered response. The wind was cool and wet. Rain. Autumn. The ending of one season and the beginning of another. The ending of one life and the beginning of another.

One more preparation and she would be ready. Melania once again crossed the empty and dark courtyard, saying a silent farewell as she did so. Good-bye to the safety of the villa walls. Good-bye to the rustle of manuscripts in the library. Good-bye to the familiar and ordered routine of a Roman household. Good-bye to all she knew and all she had known. And good-bye to the girl Melania; she would be a new person after tonight, a better person. A woman who had demanded justice and won.

In the room that had become hers with the coming of the Saxons, Melania opened a weathered wooden trunk and removed a stola of pale blue. Into this she wrapped a golden pin, a circular pin covered with tiny balls of gold. She had finished it. This would be her currency, should she need it. For this she had made it. She would not leave her home unprepared.

Melania stood in the dark of her chamber, stood with her hands idle and her mind oddly empty. Stood feeling the blood run through her veins, listening to the hammer of her heart and the moan of the rising wind; stood feeling time stop. There was nothing left to do. No more preparations to make. No arguments to voice. There was only . . . only . . . her mind flailed in frigid darkness, grasping and for a moment lost . . . only the deed. And only she could perform it.

And she would. She had to. Didn't she?

And now there was only one more preparation to make, only one more deed before the final deed: she must get Wulfred alone and on his back and ready for the knife.

She left the womblike dark of her chamber almost reluctantly and entered the relative brightness of the portico. She could see him with his men at the table; her table. They blended together, those yellow heads bent over their cups, all except Wulfred. He watched the doorway, almost as if he could see her in the darkness. Almost as if he expected her to come. Almost as if he waited for her. But that was impossible.

Melania edged into the room. It was quite unlike any entry she had ever made into a room, and she was instantly furious with herself for behaving so out of character. Why not just wear a sign proclaiming herself a skulking assassin?

Swallowing the fear that threatened to drown her, Melania raised her hand and beckoned Wulfred to come to her. This was the Melania he would expect. This was the Melania whom he would not beware.

This was the Melania whom he ignored.

Her anger rose and enveloped her, and it was a welcome friend indeed. Fear fled, and she motioned toward him again, this time her movements jerky and abrupt and edged with violence.

Wulfred watched her, raised his cup to his lips, and took a casual sip. His disregarding of her wishes was completely intentional and completely predictable. *Oaf.* Could he not do one simple thing? Could he not walk calmly and in an orderly and timely manner to his own execution?

"Saxon!" she barked.

He raised his brows in silent inquiry, the lamps

behind his head throwing the hollows of his face
into deep shadow. She could not read the expression in his eyes.

"If you have finished," she said stiffly, "come to
me."

"And if I have not finished?" he said pleasantly,
taking another sip.

"Come anyway," Cenred said to a burst of general laughter.

If she had had any doubts, any twinges of guilt,
that barbaric laughter burned it to cold ash. It
would be with laughter—her own—that she
plunged the knife into him. If he would only come
and present himself.

In a softer tone, she said, "I would like to speak
with you."

"I can hear you very well."

"Privately."

The moaning catcalls and lewd remarks of his
men bounced against the plastered ceiling of the
triclinium and off the marble tile floor and out to
where she stood with her back to the portico. Given
the chance, she would kill them all. But she would
begin with Wulfred, who now rose grinning and,
winking at Balduff, walked toward her.

At last.

His stride was long as he moved through the
room, closing the distance between them. The flickering lamplight lit strands of his hair to molten gold
that moved around his face as he walked. Of
course, he was naked from the waist up. With all
the pillaging the Saxons did, shouldn't they have

found at least one tunic? He was a powerful man, this Wulfred of the Saxons; killing him would not be easy. Pray God that it was quick, because she would never be able to best him in a struggle.

He was almost upon her now; it was foolish to have thoughts of killing him on the surface of her mind, where he might be able to read them in her eyes. It was an aura of seduction that she wished to exude, not an aura of death. For no matter that he was a Saxon, he had proven to be intelligent.

She backed toward the broad portico as he approached, not giving ground, merely leading him where she wanted him to be. He followed her, the darkness of that late-summer night almost swallowing them both. She could see nothing of his face, only the sheer size of him and the dull yellow halo of his hair. It hardly seemed possible, but he looked even bigger in the dark, and he kept closing the distance between them. The moon was hidden by thick clouds, and the wind gushed down to swirl within the confines of the courtyard. It was a cool wind and heavy with water. That sharp pulse of wind pressed against the long drape of her stola for just a moment, but it chilled her and she shivered.

"Why do you shiver, Melania?" he said in a soft rumble. "It is only a summer wind. The winter is far off." When she said nothing, he said, "Or do you tremble in anticipation?"

She turned to face him at the door to her chamber, thankful that there was no light to show her face, thankful that the moon was hidden so completely in the night. "Anticipation? What is there to anticipate? Other than our nuptials."

"Is that what you wish to discuss with me in such privacy?"

He was so close to her now that she could feel his breath on her hair. He smelled of smoke and beer and cool night air. And her soap. Yes, he was close—close enough for the knife, but all she could see were the knots of muscle encasing his chest and the ridges of muscle lined up upon his abdomen. She swallowed hard. He was a massive man, bounded by muscle and golden skin. He seemed too huge to fit into her tiny room; she couldn't get enough air into her lungs with him so close. He was a fire, stealing air and leaving only heat. Her father's stern voice sounded in her head, scolding her for her wild and uncontrolled thinking and the intensity of her emotions. She was Roman and must behave as such. Wulfred was a man and vulnerable. Mortal. She needed him prone and relaxed so that she could reach his throat or his eye—soft targets and fatal.

"There is little to discuss," she said, backing into the room, silently urging him to follow her. She could still easily hear the noise of conversation in the triclinium. Across the courtyard someone clanged a pot in the kitchen. She needed more privacy—and more secrecy—for her act of justice. "You are making whatever arrangements there are to be made, isn't that right?"

"You are right," he said, accepting her silent invitation and entering fully the small space of her chamber. He had not been here since he had carried her in kicking every step of the way. "But you are unnaturally calm in your response, isn't that right?"

She felt the hair rise on the back of her neck at that too casual and too pointed observation. He was right. She was too polite and too calm; she had never been so with him before and it was a mistake to act that way now. But it was difficult to summon anger when fear and caution had their fingers around her throat.

"I choose my battles, Saxon, but if you are looking for one, you will find one here."

"I am here for battle?"

She could see his head turn in the darkness in mock bewilderment and his arms spread wide in question. She ran her hands, shockingly moist, down the sides of her stola. The heft and shape of the knife gave her solid comfort.

"What else have you done here?" she answered a bit sharply, thankful that her words could bite and thereby mask her ultimate purpose. "Yes, I have said little on the issue of this marriage that you have announced in godlike fashion, but I will say that I will not be bound to a man who . . . whom . . . whom . . . I do not know more intimately."

There. She had said it. The words tumbled from her mouth like pebbles, and she felt her heart pound convulsively, but she concealed it all. She was truly becoming a master of self-control.

He said nothing. She wiped her hands again and squeezed the knife for reassurance, thankful that the dark hid her from his scrutiny.

"Is that why the lamps are dark?" he said.

By all under heaven, he was too close on the mark to her thoughts.

"Of course. Do Saxons . . . fondle . . . with torches blazing?"

"Do Romans . . . fondle . . . before being joined?" He said it abruptly, sarcastically.

"I thought only to spend time alone with you," she snapped, turning her back to him. Of course, he would make it all so difficult. He was so predictably obstinate. "Do not try to convince me that Saxons who are to be married do not . . . know each other to a certain degree, because I won't believe it. One has only to look at Balduff and Cenred to know that for a lie."

"But Balduff and Cenred are not joined. And are not about to be."

She could hear the laughter in his voice. Oh, how she longed for the moment when she could pull loose the knife.

"Fine. Leave. Go back to your beer and your band of murderers and rapists and arsonists—"

She got no farther. She could feel his hand in her hair. If she hadn't been so nervous, she would have seen it: tell him to come, and he would want to remain; tell him to go, and he would choose to stay. He was the most contrary and irritating man she had ever met.

His hand snagged a looped braid and she winced, moving away from his clumsiness instinctively.

"I told you that I liked your hair down."

"And I told you . . ." No, she must not forget her

purpose. "Fine." She licked her lips and swallowed heavily. There was no way out. She must say it. "Then take it down."

He did not answer her, but turned her within his arms until she could feel his chest almost touching her back. She could physically feel the rise and fall of his breathing just beyond her touch. Surprisingly, he was gentle. He was as gentle with her as he had been after rescuing Flavius from the flying sword; she was just as afraid now as Flavius had been then. Section by section, he released her hair so that it fell down her back. She was glad for the extra layer of something, anything, between his hands and her body. What to do now? She didn't like that he was behind her; it left her feeling vulnerable. But facing him would hardly be better.

He took the choice from her.

Her hair swung free, the waved ends just above the curve of her bottom. His hands cupped her there, one firm hand on each globe.

She jumped, jerked, whirled to face him, drew a fast breath to scream at him, and found herself choking on her own spittle.

"Did you not say that you sought fondling from your future husband?"

He said it calmly but even with her coughing fit, she could hear his suspicion.

"You—" she started to shout, and then breathed deeply to control her ire. "You do not have to grab. I am not a joint of pork."

Had he laughed? Was that choked laughter from the darkness?

"Then come to me, Melania, and I will not need to grab," he said softly, the humor still evident in his voice.

Yes, she should go to him. There would be no relaxed intimacy, there would be no relaxed Saxon lying helpless beneath her knife if she did not go to him. Yes, she would need to touch him. Touch the bulging muscle that had assaulted her eyes all summer. Touch the golden hair that hung down his back in rippling waves. Touch the throbbing column of his throat. Touch the hard planes of his face. Touch his mouth. Kiss his mouth.

"Come to me, Melania," he said softly in warm command.

The space between them was not great, not in so small a room and not with him so close. He rose up, a darker mass against the dark of night, huge and immovable. She could not see his eyes. She could not read him in this darkness. Yet that was why it was so purposefully dark: so that he could not read her. She would control her body and make it go to him, but she could never control the thoughts that would besiege her as she did so. She did not want him to see her eyes.

She felt movement in the air and saw his hand stretch out to her, palm up. He was giving her this last measure of control. Somehow she had known he would never force her. Allowing herself to think no more, she placed her hand resolutely in his . . . and allowed him to pull her gently to him. Strange that he could be so gentle.

The oddly pleasing combined smell of soap and

smoke came to her. And the heat of him. His body heat washed her like a bath.

"Touch me, Melania. Know the man who claims you as wife."

"You're always telling me what to do," she blurted out without thinking. She couldn't think. She felt sick to her stomach.

How much worse it would have been if she could have clearly seen him as she had seen him all summer: blue eyes heating the air between them as he stood unmoved by her taunts and dares, hands sometimes clenched in anger but never striking, shoulders that could carry laughing boys, and the light sweep of yellow hair—all before her eyes. Her father's face was fading and Wulfred's had taken its place.

"I only remind you of what you told me. Is this not to be a session of fondling?"

Her stomach heaved and her breath came out in a sickly rattle. Could she not have picked a better word?

"Fondling is not groping," she answered.

"And keeping your distance is not fondling," he replied easily. How could he be so calm? "Would you prefer me to begin it?"

"No! I'll do it!"

"Then do it. Here I am. Or can't you find me in the dark?"

"Oh, I can find you. My nose will lead me." He could not know that she did not mean it as an insult. This time.

She had meant to seduce him, to flirt with him

as she had seen Dorcas flirt with Cenred; instead
she found him daring her to touch him. Daring her,
as if it were a contest of wills.

Worse, she responded more easily to his challenge and his voice than to the dictates of her own
reasoning.

"Lost?" he prodded.

Only my reason, she thought. "Of course not.
You're a difficult target to miss."

There was no point in delaying the inevitable any
longer than she already had: she would have to
touch him. He was only a step away, one step that
was both unnaturally large and uncomfortably
close. Taking a breath to steady her fraying nerves,
she took that step.

Now the smell of soap mingled with another,
nameless scent, and the heat she had felt emanating
from him intensified. How to begin? What had she
seen Dorcas do?

Oh, yes.

Raising a hand that trembled only slightly, Melania ran the fingertips of her right hand down the
uneven planes of his chest. Could skin burn? He
was so hot to the touch . . . and smooth. And hard.
And bare.

Wulfred said nothing.

Both hands now, from collarbone past chest to
ringed abdomen until her hands brushed the
leather that bound his hips. He was so hot. No wonder he never wore a tunic. She had wondered how
he would feel under her hand. She had wondered
if skin could be smooth that sheathed such rippling

power. She had wanted to touch him. It truly was better that her father had died; he could not have lived and known that his daughter was touching a Saxon, alone and in the dark.

Wulfred did not move.

Her hands skimmed up his torso, rubbing the muscles she had seen so often. Hard. Smooth. Hot.

His throat was a massive column, with a pulse that seemed very fast and strong. *So hot here.*

His hair hung down around his shoulders and she brushed it back; it was so very soft and thick. Capping his shoulders with her hands, she felt the muscle knotted there; Flavius and Petras had ridden on these shoulders. His arms were long, the muscle fiber lying in rippled twists and creating hills and valleys on his arms that did not exist on hers.

She ran her fingers over his right hand, noting the calluses, feeling the bulge of muscle at the base of his thumb, touching the hard edge of his fingernails. Lifting his hand, she unknowingly caressed it and mindlessly brought that warrior hand to her mouth.

She kissed the palm.

She felt him jump.

Heard the sharp intake of breath.

Felt him move.

And then his hands were in her hair and her body was in his arms and his hands cupped her bottom and his breath covered her face.

Until his mouth touched hers, and then his

breath became a part of her. His breath and hers, breathing together, one.

His hands slid in a firm caress up her body, over round buttocks and slim hip and narrow waist and flaring rib cage to slender neck, and he held her there, one hand at her hip and the other at her throat, holding her against the length of him, the hard, hot length of him, while his mouth learned hers and his breath poured heat into her bones and blood.

Her feet dangled over the tile floor.

Her hands tangled in his thick hair.

Her mouth was hot against his and wet, and there was nothing in her mind but that she wanted to be hotter and wetter still.

More of this.

More of him.

More.

She wanted more.

He let her slide down the length of him, her breasts hot and hard at the friction, her legs weak, her hands clutching his hair, pulling him down to her, keeping his mouth on hers. She needed his breath to breathe. She needed his heat to keep her alive. Without this contact, she would grow cold and die.

His tongue was between her teeth, in her mouth. She tasted beer for a moment and then the taste was in her mouth, was on her breath, and there was no distinguishing between his mouth and hers.

His hands spanned her ribs and moved upward. Her breasts were on fire and tingled, each nerve alive and clamoring, wanting his touch, wanting to feel his hands on her. She arched into him with a throaty whimper and wondered where the sound came from. Her nipples were hard and distended, ready for him, ready for whatever he would do. She wanted his hands upon them, upon her, mindless of any other need.

He did not make her wait. His thumbs brushed across the rigid peaks in firm ownership and she almost lost her footing, moaning as she collapsed against him. She wanted more immediately.

More.

His hands slid down. Anger flared at his stupidity—until his fingers brushed the apex of her thighs. Fire scorched her. She throbbed and ached. He traced her there, and if he had not held her around the waist with his other hand she would have fallen at his feet.

She lurched against him, throwing her arms around his neck to hold him to her and continue the hot, wet kiss he had begun an eternity ago.

And as she did so, as she threw herself more firmly against him, she felt the knife shift in her pocket.

The knife.

To kill him.

The knife to kill the Saxon.

Saxon.

Reason fought for life in the blazing heat. She could not think; her brain was on fire. She could not see. What was wrong with her eyes? She could not breathe.

There would be no better time. He was close, he was relaxed, or at least his guard was down, and she had a knife.

Her right arm slid down as her left held him close. The kiss continued, confusing her, distracting her. But he would never be closer. She clumsily found the knife and gripped it. It was hard and cold; it helped to anchor her to her plan. The kiss lightened, changing, and he kissed the corners of her mouth and the spot just below her lower lip. A tingle ran down between her breasts and landed in her belly, where it sparked.

He was so close.

She had the knife.

He was a Saxon.

The Saxon.

Justice was due.

Overdue.

She pulled the knife free, thankful again for the darkness, and leaned away from his kiss. She had to strike for the face, the eye. It had to be a mortal strike. Perhaps the throat so that he could make no cry and she could run to the west. To Marcus.

She did not make the mistake of pulling back to add strength to the blow. This was not a blow of strength; this was all placement. She did not make the mistake of shouting her intent to raise her bloodlust. Her bloodlust was high enough. She did not make the mistake of hesitating. The Saxon was quick, too quick for her to falter.

No, her mistake was in choosing her opponent.

235

The knife was out of her hand and in his before the kiss had truly ended.

His holding her knife in his fist effectually ended the kiss.

"Do Romans use knives when they fondle?" he asked in a growl. "It is no wonder the population dwindles."

For perhaps the first time in her life, she could think of nothing to say.

"Come, Roman. We have lingered in the dark long enough," he said, anger edging into his voice. But she had heard him angrier.

Gentleness gone, he dragged her by the back of her stola, propelling her ahead of him. She blinked in the mild light of the torches lining the portico and was momentarily blinded by the whiter light of the triclinium. Was this where he would kill her? It was late. The triclinium would be deserted.

Or so she had thought.

The triclinium was filled. Every person who lived within the confines of the villa was present. And all were staring at her.

Wulfred held the knife, her knife, in his fist and raised it high for all to see. He would kill her with it. She knew it. In just a moment her earthly life would end, and end in defeat. She would die by his hand, at a time of his choosing, having failed to kill him first. But at least she would die. At least this misery would be behind her.

And she would die proudly.

Standing straight, head erect, she looked out over them all. No tears marred her vision. No hands begged for leniency. No knees collapsed with fear. She would face her execution bravely and would shame them all with her courage. He would get no satisfaction from her.

"The knife is Melania's," he said into the silence. "She has given it to me. A gift of arms."

A gift? It was no gift. . . .

Blond Saxon heads nodded in affirmation.

A snort and a rattle of harness was her only warning before Optio was brought into the triclinium and right up to her. She had to sidestep or the beast would have knocked her over. *Unnatural animal.*

A single shout and she jerked instinctively. Then the room erupted in shouts, the Saxon horde banging sword and seax to shield until she thought the plaster would crumble off the walls. Stupid Saxon pigs; could they not even kill someone with dignity?

"Do I have to lose my hearing as well as my life?" she barked, trying to jerk free of Wulfred's hold.

"You will lose neither your hearing nor your life, Roman," he said, grabbing her firmly by the elbow. "You have just gained something."

"A headache?"

"A husband."

Chapter Eighteen

"Impossible!" she exploded, pulling free of his touch. "You hold a knife to my throat and tell me that by some hideous miracle we are now married? When did this miraculous transformation occur? And when will you kill me, for surely you must know that . . . that what I did . . . what we did . . . that it was not real? I was but maneuvering you onto the point of my knife!"

He smiled down at her with his eyes of brightest blue and clasped her gently by the nape. "And look how close you came to maneuvering yourself onto the point of mine."

"You're disgusting." She tried to wrench herself free of him, but he held her fast.

"How changeable you Romans are." He smiled, fingering the knife. "Unless I am not translating you correctly. You did say disgust? Or was it lust?"

"Will I prove my point if I throw up all over your dusty feet?"

"Is that how Romans show their desire? Or is it only you?"

Melania pried his fingers off her neck and clenched her fists, mutely daring him to touch her again. "Will you kindly tell your murderous friends to stop banging away on their toys! I can hardly think!"

"They only show their approval of our bonding," he said as he tucked the knife—her knife—into the waist of his pants.

"We can't be married," she stated, crossing her arms over her chest, willing it not to be so. "There has been no ritual to bind us."

He obviously thought otherwise.

"You gave me a gift of arms. I gave you a horse. It was witnessed. We are one."

"That's . . . that's not a marriage ceremony," she stammered. It was as she had feared: a Saxon marriage ceremony was as flimsy as cloud trails across the face of the moon. She should have wagered gold that a Saxon bonding ceremony would include a knife. "And Optio is *my* horse!"

"My horse, by conquest, given to you as a gift. *Now* Optio is yours."

"This farce of a ceremony is not binding by Roman law, the most just law ever—"

"You live in Saxon-controlled land now, Melania," he said, turning her to face him, holding her by the arms when she tried to move away from him.

239

"Saxon law rules this land. By Saxon law you are my wife."

"I am Roman. I know nothing and care nothing about Saxon law. This"—she waved her hand all around her—"means nothing."

Wulfred let her go and stood looking down at her. His expression was solemn, almost rigid, and she found herself trapped by his look more than by anything his hands could have achieved.

"You accepted my intention to marry you. You gave me a gift of arms. You are on Saxon land ruled by Saxon law. Will you stand by the bond or ignore it because it does not match your own customs?"

There was far more subtlety to this barbari than she had at first thought. She could see no honorable way out.

The noise of the barbarians had stopped. Their drinking had not. Balduff toasted her loudly, his light blue eyes gleaming in amusement. Cenred and Cuthred and Cynric drank to his toast, but their faces were wiped clean of emotion, any emotion, and they regarded her with a look that spoke clearly of distrust. Only Ceolmund, of that group, eyed her warmly. He said little, but he seemed almost to respect her. Of them all, she considered him the least offensive. And the most intelligent.

Standing behind the barbarian group were her own people, dark-haired and silent—a grim contrast to the boisterous Saxons. Theras watched her, and she could feel the weight of his expectation. Would she honor the bond or would she fight? The decision she must now make would affect the precarious peace that time had established in her villa.

There was no help for her in this room. There never had been. In her fight against the Saxons she had fought alone; if only Marcus . . . But Marcus was gone. She was alone, and with a Saxon for a husband.

The world was not running the way it should. What to do when all the laws of nature and order were cast into the fire to burn away and leave only smoke? What to do with a Saxon warrior claiming he was now a husband?

"I ask you again, Melania," Wulfred said, his voice rumbling over the tumult of the triclinium. "Will you stand by your vow?"

She turned abruptly away from the chaos of her orderly triclinium and faced the man who had tilted the foundation of her world by his very existence. "Leave me alone, Saxon! I don't know what I'm going to do! *I don't know!*" she shouted, her fists clenched in impotent fury.

Impotent, yes; there was little she could do. Saxons had outnumbered and outarmed Romans, and outfought them, too, on this desirable isle. He watched the emotions whirl behind her eyes: anger, panic, frustration. She screamed that she did not know what to do. It was the best answer she could have given him, because it told him many things. It told him that the answer she gave him would be a serious one. It told him that she would tell him the truth. She was devious, but she was not a liar.

As he had told her the truth. She was his wife now. She had performed her part in the Saxon bonding ritual, albeit unwittingly. He had suspected her motive in leading him to her chamber; he had also suspected her methods. But what he had not suspected, what he never could have guessed, was the passion that had fired between them. Unless she had deceived him in that. It was possible—she had proven her duplicitous nature more than once—but he couldn't convince himself that her responses hadn't been genuine. He didn't want to. Yes, she was sly, but she was also passionate and fiery of temperament; he had the scars to prove it.

And she was his wife. He would claim her. Now.

Her hands were still fisted at her sides, and she looked blindly at the tile floor at her feet, deep in thought. He knew the direction of her thoughts. And knew his own. He reached out and ran his hand down the length of her hair. So black, so smooth, and so straight. She turned to him, distracted, irritated, the spark that never slept in her eyes flaming again. Strange eyes, strangely alive and volatile. Eyes like sun, trees, and earth mingling, fighting for dominance.

"What!" she snapped, brushing her hand over her hair, wiping away his touch. "Can't you leave me alone for a moment? Haven't you done enough to me this day?"

Wulfred smiled, tracing his finger down her arm from elbow to wrist and catching firm hold of her hand. "No. Not nearly enough."

She would have said more, but he pulled her from the triclinium, out into the portico, and then into her chamber. She had to know what was coming next; she had to understand what would happen now that she was his wife. He must lay his claim on her, but she could not know that he wanted to possess her as a lover. He wondered if she recognized the desire he felt for her and the small power it gave her over him. He would never admit such weakness to her. He would never hand her the club with which to beat him.

He had not wanted her at first. She was Roman; that was all. She could have value to him only in her downfall. But he had seen her fire and he had watched her odd Roman honor enacted throughout the summer. There was something about her that defied his hatred. He could look at her now and see a woman, a beautiful and passionate woman, and because of that he could take her—and he would. She would be his in a way that even a Roman could understand.

He did not want the darkness now; he did not want her to have the protection of it. He wanted to see her in her passion. He would watch desire contort her features. He would watch her yield to him.

Wulfred had brought a torch from the portico with him into the chamber and now used it to light the wall-mounted lamp. The room was immediately cast in a warm, golden glow that masked the flaking plaster and the missing floor tiles. The couch stood out in bold relief in the far corner of the room, a dark presence in all the warmth of tinted plaster. He had lain with her on that couch once before when he had held her while she slept, learning her shape and her texture. He would lie with her there again. They would not sleep.

There were two windows in the room and they were black rectangles set in muted gold. The wind was rising, an autumn wind with the smell of water and ripening wheat. It blew softly into the chamber, freshening the air and cooling the temperature. The days were still hot, but the nights were mild. There had been no rain.

"Autumn comes," he said into the unnatural silence.

Melania jerked out of her introspection to glare at him. She seemed almost surprised to find herself in her chamber again. "Yes, autumn comes, and when it does you will go, if God is merciful."

"The gods are rarely merciful," he answered mildly.

"With such a people as you, it is hardly surprising," she said with a spiteful smile.

"And when I go," he said, continuing her earlier observation, "you will go with me. You are mine now."

"I haven't yet decided if that is so."

"I have decided. It is so."

"Go back to your pack, Saxon," she said in a snarl. "Leave me to my thoughts. I will tell you what I decide."

"You tell me to go and sleep with my men? Tonight? You have made many pronouncements and many judgments, Roman, but none so wrong as this. I will not sleep with my men tonight. I will not sleep with my men again. Not when I have a woman to warm me. Not when I have you."

Melania stared at him in surprise; shock quickly followed and was capped by anger. Always she had her anger. "You think to sleep here? By the Christ, you show me that you do not think at all, as if I needed a demonstration, which I most certainly did not. No Saxon oaf will touch me or share my couch. Especially the imbecilic oaf who has tried to find devious ways to kill me for the past weeks. That's what this is about, isn't it? This is just another way to torture me! Find another method, Saxon dog, because—"

"I have touched you, Roman snake," he said softly, closing the scant distance between them, ignoring her anger, understanding the shield that it was to her. Her anger blazed away all other emotion. She could defeat fear and grief and shame with her anger; he would not allow her to kill her desire with it. Her eyes glowed yellow in the small room. "I have touched you and tasted you. And you have tasted me." She backed away from him, her strange eyes wide and burning bright, her lips snarling; she backed from him until she was framed in the open window, the wind lifting the ends of her heavy hair. "Taste me again."

He bent to her mouth, holding her face between his hands so that she could not turn from him. She could not turn, but she did resist. Her lips were firm and tight against his mouth, and her hands pried at his. It was a futile struggle. He would not release her—not tonight, not when he had already tasted the fire within her. He would ignite her again, and this time they would not stop. She was now his wife. And he had disarmed her.

Her kiss was cold but he was still hot from their earlier fondling; mere coldness on her part would not stop him or even slow him. He burned for her. He would have her burn again for him. It would be a part of her defeat at his hands. It would do much for his pride to have a Roman aristocrat whimper for his touch, and it would be a blow against Rome that would salve old wounds.

Compelling her to participate by the very urgency of his mouth, Wulfred moved one hand behind her head and held it stationary while the other fondled her breast. Small it was, but round and full and large of nipple. She was responding, though her mouth was still hard against his. Where was the woman of moments ago?

She was thinking of her anger and her newly married state. Melania would never respond to him unless her body overtook her mind. For that to happen, as it had earlier, he would have to outpace her. No idle and slow-paced tarrying would do; she required a quick and hard assault. Only speed and ferocity would drive her intellect to ground and allow her passion to rise up.

As he had already risen for her.

Breaking the kiss, he lifted her in his arms and carried her to the couch. He sank with her to it, her body prone and he kneeling on the floor at her side. Of course, she was not silent during this shifting of position.

"I have no desire to taste you, Saxon, which you may have noticed, if my reactions mean anything to you. While I understand that you have the base desires common to all barbari, I do not, and I have no wish to share yours. Surely anyone, any breathing, rutting animal, would do."

"As long as you keep breathing, Roman snake, you'll do," he said, grinning.

Again he kissed her, silencing her, assaulting her, seducing her. It was a kiss of pure passion with no restraint, and he heard her expel her breath with a gasp. Her breasts, nipples hard, jutted upward, and he fondled her with a firm hand, thumbing her in determined circles. She lay on her couch like a platter on a table; so small and so easily accessible. One of his hands moved to her legs, rubbing the fabric that covered her thighs and then brushing it out of the way. Her hair was black and soft. She kept her legs closed against him until he wedged her apart with his hand. And when he touched the seat of her womanhood, his fingers were instantly covered in her milk.

She burned.

He dared now to move his mouth, testing her desire by her lack of speech. She was quiet as his lips caressed her shoulder. She bucked beneath him when he licked her erect nipple. She swallowed a moan when his fingers played with the source of her woman's milk, milk made for a man and not a babe. His mouth moved down and he plunged his tongue into her navel, tasting her sweat, smelling her passion, feeding off her desire for him. She groaned and sat up, shaking her wild black hair around her.

"Pagan," she croaked.

"Husband," he corrected, pushing her down with the flat of his hand. He knew where he would go. He would taste all of her.

His tongue traced a line over the soft swell of her belly and then abruptly plunged into the well of her desire. She tasted of salt and fiery passion.

"No!" she cried, clawing at his head, tangling her fingers in his hair, trying to wrench him free of her.

"Yes," he murmured against her heat, taking her hands in his and holding them down at her sides. He would have all of her, and she would not stop him.

He nipped her gently and her legs jerked in spasm. He moved his mouth to her breasts and she thrashed her head back and forth, a low, keening moan building in her throat. His fingers roved over her like the wind on the sea. His mouth tasted her; he blew air onto the fire he built in her.

When all she could do was moan, when she lay limp and tossing in her sexual distress, when she did not react to his dominating touch other than to turn in to it, he slid her off the couch and onto the floor. He was not certain that she even noticed. Her arms reached for him, pulling him atop her so that her high-pitched crying moan was in his ear. She spread herself for him, her legs wrapping around his hips, pulling him down to her, wanting him.

"What do you want, Melania?" he said, his hips lifted away from hers, resisting her pull.

"Do it," she panted, tightening her legs against his obstinacy.

"Do what?" he pressed.

"I don't know!" She moaned, reaching for him, touching him, stroking him.

Wulfred smiled, believing her. "I do," he whispered against her hair as he plunged into her.

She bucked against him, but not in pain or sudden regret or fear. She met him fully, eagerly, with only a grunt to mark the loss of her virginity. She held him to her and lifted her hips to meet his assault. He forgot his plan of vengeance. He forgot that she was a hated Roman. He forgot that he was a Saxon. He knew only the blazing red fire of her. He had wanted to set her on fire, and he had, and in her fire she consumed him.

He burned.

Melania's face was a grimace of concentration. A sheen of sweat covered her, dampening the fine hairs around her face and neck. Wulfred watched as she pursued the fire he had ignited in her. She scored his back with her nails as her groaning escalated to wailing and ended on a high and wild scream. Her eyes flew open; they were as gold as flame and as hot. He pumped her hard and fast and she matched him, digging into his back for purchase in the inferno they shared. Harder, deeper, while she shuddered wildly and he groaned in his own release and collapsed down on her, his nose buried in the subtle scent of her hair.

For a moment they lay still, victims of the fire. It did not last.

"Get off me, Saxon," she demanded, her fists beating against his back for emphasis. Did he hear tears in her voice?

He raised his torso off hers, his arms bracketing her head. Her face was as cold as he had ever seen it, though her eyes were shimmering with a teary glaze. She behaved as if she had forgotten they were still joined. He had not forgotten.

"Are you deaf as well as stupid? Get off!"

He slid out of her and stood, looking down at her lying in rampant sexuality on the floor. Something of his thoughts must have shown on his face, because she hastily stood to face him, arranging her clothing as she did so. Arranging her Roman armor.

"Given your limited intelligence," she began, her voice betraying the merest tremor, "you will no doubt suppose that conditions between us have changed. They have not." She took a deep breath and smoothed her hair, which tumbled wildly down her back. She obviously was not pleased with its appearance. He had never seen her look better. "In fact," she continued, her voice gaining strength, "I hate you now more than ever. Of course, I will endeavor not to let this influence my decision; I am a Roman and just. Now get out."

He said nothing. He readjusted his leggings, retrieved the knife, which had lain within easy reach of her on the floor, and saluted her with it. And then he left.

He understood exactly what had happened to her on that floor, as did she.

Chapter Nineteen

"The little snake has fangs after all, Wulfred, if I can judge by the condition of your back," Balduff said with a laugh the next morning.

Wulfred paused in his arms practice to stare at Balduff.

"She has claws, not fangs," Cenred joked, coming up behind Balduff as they left the triclinium. "She is a vixen, not a viper."

Wulfred hefted his seax and swung it before him ominously. He was not smiling; his eyes were the cold blue of sea ice. The smiles on Cenred's and Balduff's faces disappeared like summer mist.

"You are speaking of my wife," Wulfred said, his voice low and vibrating from deep within his chest.

"Yes, but—" Cenred began.

Balduff elbowed Cenred in the gut as he lowered

his head in submission to Wulfred. "Words spoken without thought, Wulfred. Your pardon."

Another elbow jab and Cenred followed Balduff's form. "Your pardon, Wulfred. No offense was meant."

Wulfred considered them for a few moments in silence and then nodded his acceptance. His look was still somewhat severe when he turned his back on them and left the courtyard. Clearly he was not in the mood for companionship. When he was out of sight, Cenred felt free to speak.

"By the welts on his back, he had a good time last night with his Roman wife. Dorcas does not leave the signs of her pleasure so boldly on me."

"Dorcas?" Balduff grinned. "The woman who has thrown you from her couch?"

"Leave off, Balduff." Cenred scowled in distraction. "I do not need you to instruct me on the ways of women."

"That's not what Dorcas said."

"You've spoken with her?" The wounded eagerness in his voice was painfully clear.

"You've not?" Balduff asked, twisting the emotional knife.

Cenred scowled more deeply and backed up a pace; he would not be a toy for Balduff's wit.

"We were speaking of Melania. What harm—"

"What harm?" Cynric said. He had followed them from the triclinium and had heard the exchange.

"It was wrong to speak of his wife in that way," Balduff said softly.

"Worse has been said of Melania," Cenred argued.

"Melania is now his wife," Cynric snapped. "Did you not understand that when he married her, she became his? And once his, then one of us? We serve Wulfred, and now Wulfred has a wife. A Roman wife."

Cenred's eyes widened in the beginning of awareness. "Ahhh."

"Ahhh," Cynric mimicked. "Now you begin to see what has been done. She is the wife of the man we have sworn to follow into death." Adjusting his belt, Cynric said, "Think on that, brothers." Cynric walked on toward the kitchen.

Standing in the weak sunlight of the courtyard, Cenred and Balduff said nothing. They stared at each other with something like shock. Cynric would have been very gratified.

Wulfred had not given the two men a second thought; his thoughts were all for Melania. He had not seen her since she had evicted him from her chamber last night, but he knew that she had not left the villa enclosure; she was still too well monitored for that. He understood her need to be alone. Losing a maidenhead was a momentous event; she needed to come to terms with it. She also needed to come to terms with her blatant enjoyment of it. With a Saxon. He was a little stunned by her performance himself—happily stunned. It was a passionate woman he had married, but then he had known of her passion all along. She was usually passionately angry and always passionately proud;

he should not have found her sexual passion surprising.

A blowing and stomping in the stable alerted him to her presence. The stable smelled of warm hay and fresh dung. The last flies of the season hovered and buzzed in the slanting morning light, drowning the sound of the larks in the treetops. She stood in the shadows, the warm brown of her clothing blending into the worn wood of the room. Her hair hung in two long black braids down her back, Saxon fashion. He read her mood instantly: Melania was morose. Optio was agitated.

She turned as he entered, facing him, challenging him.

"You knew what I intended last night." It was a statement.

He crossed his arms over his chest and leaned against the wall and nodded his answer.

"How?"

"I followed you. Also, I know you."

She turned away, picking at a strand of straw on her skirt.

"The stupid animal would probably have run off without me anyway. She hates me."

Wulfred uncrossed his arms and walked across the dirt floor toward his wife. Never had he seen her so defeated. Why wasn't she railing at him for ruining her plans of escape? Where were her caustic words of contempt? Where was her passion?

"Hate is a strong word."

"She's a strong animal," she mumbled, toying with the end of one braid.

"And so are you." He turned her toward him by tugging on that braid and then gave her a quick view of his back. It was crisscrossed with bright red welts and two or three hairline scabs. She turned away, appalled. Or was she ashamed?

"Can't you find a tunic?" she yelped. "You haven't been walking around like that, with those, with that . . . Oh, of course you have!"

"I thought you'd be pleased that you managed to draw a little blood."

"Pleased? Why, it's obvious how . . . when . . . and now everyone will know what I did. What I allowed to happen."

"What you allowed to happen?" He understood now the source of her mood. As much as he had wanted to defeat her, this pathetic creature would bring him no pleasure. No, he wanted a fighting adversary, one who would challenge him before she was vanquished. "You hardly had a choice, little Roman." His voice was harsh, intentionally so. "You tried to kill me, with your pathetic Roman knife. And did you come at me in honor? No, it was in stealth and in secrecy and in subterfuge. I disarmed you easily, bent you to my will easily, and will continue to have the pleasure of doing so for the rest of your life, because now you are my wife and there is no law that can protect you from me."

Wulfred lifted her up by the waist until her feet dangled, and shook her once before lowering her to the floor. He ignored the feel of her under his hands and the trimness of her waist as she brushed against his body on her way to the ground. He ignored it because he did not want to seduce her; he wanted to anger her. He didn't believe he'd have any trouble.

"Now do you understand what happened last night? Have I explained it so that even your devious Roman mind can grasp it?"

"Yes, you hideous oaf, I understand. I understand that I hate you. You are the source of all the misery in my life. Before you came I had a father who loved me and a life worth living; now all I have is a shaggy beast dropping fleas all over my home! I hate you!"

Melania had closed the distance between them, stalking him. Wulfred only raised an eyebrow at her aggression.

"I want you to hate me!" he thundered back.

"You do, don't you?"

"Of course, or what is the point of all this?" he boomed, flinging his arms wide.

"Exactly," she snapped, holding her ground and raising her own eyebrow. "And I do hate you; you have managed to succeed at something. You're a monster, a plague, a pestilence. I don't know what was wrong with me, but it will never happen again."

Wulfred watched her stomp away, swinging her arms furiously as she went. Melania was herself again; better that her anger flare up than smolder within her. And he did want her to hate him. Obviously. Why else would he have married her?

Hateful, odious man. Melania burned with excess energy—energy of mind, body, and emotion—and she had no way to release any of it. She was sick to death of the courtyard, sick to death of the sight of all those hairy Saxons clanging their weapons within the confines of her home, sick to the point of physical revulsion of the Saxon who was her chief enemy. His voice was too low and guttural. His hair was too light and too long and too . . . everywhere. His body was too big. His eyes were too blue. His mind was too quick, certainly too quick for a stupid barbari. And his hands . . . his hands . . . and then there was his mouth . . .

She was filled with vile thoughts, and a dishonor to her race! What would her father have thought of her if he could have seen her behavior last night? Would she never learn to control her thoughts and her passions as he had trained her to do? She was a disgrace to her heritage; certainly no other member of her family had experienced such trouble in disciplining the mind as she seemed to have. No wonder her father had so often been exasperated with her. She tried so diligently to be the Roman he expected her to be, and she so often felt that she failed. Especially since Wulfred's coming.

She had to get away from all of these half-naked men! With a determined stride, a stride that just begged to be stopped, Melania marched out of the villa. No one stopped her. She felt more at ease immediately. Even breathing was easier away from Wulfred. She wandered up a ragged flagstone footpath to the old vineyard. The large leaves were heavily rippled and shot with yellow; it was the end of the growing season. The vines were old and heavy, contorted around their supports with the comforting look of things well established. Only a few vines were left now; her father had not had the skill for grapes, and the vintner had died before she was born. Still, it was a lovely spot and very quiet. Quiet was good. Peace would be better, but she wondered if she'd ever have a peaceful moment again for as long as she lived.

Last night had certainly not been peaceful.

Melania felt her face heat at the memory and wondered if her cheeks were pink. She hoped not. She didn't want to give him a blush on top of all else.

Last night had been . . . unexpected, certainly. He had been so ardent, so passionate. So accepting of her responses.

She walked a row, her feet scuffing the dirt and sending up tiny clouds of dust. The sky was leaden and heavy with rain; every breath of wind announced that rain was coming. When would it finally rain?

When would she ever understand Wulfred?

The vineyard was bordered by forest, forest that became denser with foliage every year. She remembered that, as a girl, she had run among the trees in play, but there were too many wolves for that now. Still, the cool quiet of the forest beckoned her, but she had learned to listen to the calm voice of reason, even when her heart shouted another message. At least usually. Her father had taught her that, but not as successfully as he had hoped.

He had been even less successful in teaching her to control her tongue. Not that she needed to now, not with a houseful of Saxons. Still, he had stressed that her volatile nature coupled with her emotional explosions had been most un-Roman. She had tried to be more reasonable and cool in her manner and she was often successful. Perhaps sometimes successful, but never without conscious effort.

Wulfred hadn't seemed to mind her extremes. It was even possible that he preferred them. Of course, he was very uneducated and hopelessly uncivilized.

The wind gusted and she felt the delicate beginnings of rain. *Please, God, let it rain.* The trees swayed and groaned in the wind, their leaves blowing to show the paler undersides. A drop hit her on the cheek, evaporating before she could wipe it away. Would Wulfred leave before the weather turned foul?

If he did, he would have a reason. She had learned that he did nothing without purpose, which was why she knew that his latest provocation had been deliberate. Not without truth, but deliberate. As to his purpose, did she hate him more? *Impossible.* But she did hate herself less. Could that have been his goal? But why? He couldn't care that she felt overwhelmed with guilt for the responses he'd called forth from her last night; in fact, he should be thrilled that she had cause to feel such shame and that he was the author of the cause.

Melania shivered and crossed her arms over her

Claudia Dain

chest. The truth was not as easy to see as she had been taught. Wulfred was a Saxon; that meant he was undisciplined, wild, uncivilized, blood-mad. Wulfred was also her husband by Saxon law, and her husband was perceptive, tender, intelligent, passionate. In order for the truth to be true, Wulfred could be no Saxon. But Wulfred was most definitely Saxon. Melania ran her hands into her hair and massaged her scalp. Again the trouble was with Wulfred; he never cooperated.

But he accepted her without condition.

Melania's hands froze in her hair as a new realization struck: Wulfred, the same man who matched her shout for shout, the man who ran his hands possessively and tenderly over her body, the man who declared her his enemy and with calm acceptance understood that he was an adversary to be thwarted by her in turn, accepted her. He accepted her as she was, for what she was. He had never tried to change her. He had never judged her and found her wanting.

Why? She had never experienced such complete acceptance from anyone. Why would she have it from a Saxon warrior?

There was no reasonable answer, no answer that would mesh with what she understood of the world from her father's careful instruction.

The forest was very near. She had walked slowly, deep in thought, and without direction, yet the order of the rows had led her to the heavy shade of the wood. It was not safe here; the area had gone wild since people rarely came to it. Melania turned back toward the villa lying in its snug valley, and as she did, the crunch of crushed leaves and twigs behind her spun her around again.

The sky was darkening rapidly, the clouds thick and gray; the forest was in black shadow. If there was a wolf, she could not see it. If there was a man . . .

Melania turned to run, angry that she had wandered so far from the relative safety of the villa. As barbaric as the Saxons were, she didn't think they would eat her alive. . . .

"Melania!"

She knew that voice. She would know that voice forever.

"Marcus!"

Chapter Twenty

She would have run to him, was in the act of running to him, when he stopped her.

"Do not come! Do not show that you have heard anything, Melania. You are followed."

Of course. She was always followed. She had grown so accustomed to it that she had forgotten, but she must not lead the Saxons to Marcus. Marcus must remain free.

She turned back to face the villa, toying with a grape leaf, pretending to be idle. She was far from idle. Marcus was here. Marcus would help her. Her blood pounded just knowing he was near.

"Marcus," she said to the grape leaf, trying to keep herself from smiling like a fool. "Marcus, you are well? Where have you been?"

"I am well," came the voice, that beloved voice,

from the shadows. "Uninjured. Footsore. Hungry."

"I'll get you something, a bag full of food."

"But I can't come with you to the villa, can I?"

Melania responded to the angry pain she heard in his voice. "No, it's crawling with barbarians. I'm sorry, Marcus. It's better if you stay hidden. I will provide for you."

"But what of you, Melania? How have you survived this invasion?"

She did not want him to know what had happened to her, the world she had inhabited for the length of the summer. "It won't be any trouble. I'll come after dark, in full dark, and give you whatever you need. Clothing? How are your shoes? I'll bring you extra shoes—"

"Melania," he interrupted harshly, "have they harmed you? Have they—"

"You can see me, Marcus. Do I look battered? No, the Saxon oafs have not harmed me. I . . . have learned to adjust."

"You do look good to me. The same girl, unchanged. Would I could say the same of Britannia."

He thought her unchanged? Strange, for she did not feel the same. "You have seen other barbarians? In other places?"

"They overrun us; from the east, south, and north they come and drive all before them. They leave burned towns and villas and fields behind them. They are a pestilence."

She had thought the same, felt the same, but it was strange to hear it from Marcus's lips. "What of the west? Have you been to the west?"

"I . . ."

Ceolmund climbed the hill, his long hair swaying and blowing in the wind. He stood in clear view at a distance, giving her her privacy, but watching her all the same.

"Go, Melania. Come to me here when the moon is high and I will hold you in my arms while you feed me to your heart's content. I will even let you put new shoes on my sore feet."

"I'll come," she said, walking away from his beautiful voice, still trying not to grin like a fool. "But you can put on your own shoes."

Ceolmund waited for her. He did not speak to her as she neared him, not unusual for him, but she was unusually grateful for his silence. She had much to think on.

Marcus was here! At last, at last he had come for her. Marcus would make everything right. Oh, he could not defeat all the Saxons who had invaded Britannia, but he could take her away from here, away from one particular Saxon. If she were only away from here, her marriage vow would mean nothing. If Wulfred were not always in front of her, she could forget him and his ridiculous talk of vows and laws and honor. Away from him, she could forget passion.

She was still high above the villa when she saw the men come. *Barbari. More barbari.* Her heart sank as her temper soared. More? Was she expected to adjust herself to more? More pillage? More death?

Never.

Melania stormed down the hill, hardly noticing that Ceolmund followed at her heels. Hardly caring that Dorcas came running up to meet her. All she could see were barbarians streaming through her gates and into her courtyard, dropping their filthy belongings on her tiled portico, drinking from her cistern with their dirty cupped hands. It was more than any civilized woman could be expected to tolerate.

"Melania," Dorcas huffed, having finally climbed the hill from the villa. Melania did not break stride, and Dorcas fell into step behind her, bumping into a grim-faced Ceolmund as she did so. "Melania," she repeated. "Important Saxon leaders have come. Wulfred wants you. Immediately."

"He'll get me immediately, as will all of his dusty friends, though I don't think he'll be cheered by my presence."

Dorcas cast a worried look at Ceolmund. He did not return her glance. He merely unsheathed his short sword and stayed a half step behind Melania.

What this would mean for Marcus she could only guess, and all her guesses were unpleasant. Why did there have to be so many more of them right now? Couldn't they have stayed in their holes until she had left with Marcus? Whatever happened to her or the villa, she had to make sure that Marcus escaped them. Marcus must survive.

The courtyard was almost empty by the time she reached it; they had all swarmed into the triclinium to eat her food and drink her wine and drop lice on her floor. Entering the triclinium, hot with rage at

Claudia Dain

this latest and unexpected affront, she saw Wulfred at the far end of the room with his men fanned out behind him. The new horde, filthy to a man, were fanned out in direct opposition. Pushing through them, she had one target: Wulfred. Someone reached out and patted her bottom as she surged through; she turned in righteous anger, but Ceolmund was there before her. The man, a redhead, fell to the floor.

Elbowing her way into them, a most revolting endeavor, she felt a pinch on her breast and spun in the direction of the attack, filled with fury and fear. Ceolmund sliced the man's finger and he howled before putting the grimy thing into his mouth and sucking on it. Before another of them could touch her, Wulfred was there at her side, filling her eyes and crowding out her vision of the horde in her home. He surrounded her, his huge body a shield that encompassed her completely as he walked her to the front of the room, one hand firmly on her shoulder and the other on her waist. He declared his possession of her and his decision to protect with every step they shared. None dared touch her with Wulfred at her side, and she was ashamed at the thankfulness she felt at being so clearly rescued. He was a Saxon, one of them. She was a Roman, able to take care of herself. Yet she had needed him and he had come to her defense without a word having been spoken between them. There had been no need for words.

"Is this why you have been so absent during our forays?"

"She's not much, is she?"

"Let me have at her and I'll let you know!"

"Have you all been doing her or—"

Melania whirled within the shelter of Wulfred's arms, fire on her tongue, but Wulfred spoke first.

"Enough!" he said abruptly, his voice the throaty rumble of a wolf's. The room slowly became silent and still. Wulfred, taller than most of them, scanned the room with his eyes full of challenge and command. Melania knew the look well. "This woman will receive respect from you and nothing less. She is my wife."

Wulfred pulled her tightly to his side, his body a vibrating fortress as they faced the Saxons together; she watched their faces register shock and even horror. Standing beside him, strangely allied with him, she faced this new threat to her home; more Saxons, more strangers. Invaders.

One stood out from the rest. His clothing was richer than any she had yet seen, far richer than the plain leather garb Wulfred wore. His cloak was dyed red and lined with fur, and his boots were well-tanned leather. A leader of sorts. Wulfred's leader? A man in mastery over Wulfred; it was difficult to imagine.

"A wife," the stranger said. "Now it is clear why you kept your distance this summer. But was it profitable?" He looked her up and down. She held herself erect and stared back. She had unwillingly absorbed enough Saxon to understand the gist of what he said. If he wanted to take her measure, she would use the opportunity to take his. He would find much to commend Rome in her.

"She is a beauty, Hensa," Wulfred answered, "with enough spirit for ten warriors. She is a worthy wife."

Melania reeled privately; Wulfred thought her beautiful, spirited, worthy. He had said little enough of such admiration to her, not that she needed praise from a Saxon warrior.

"The villa was hers?" Hensa asked pragmatically.

"Mine then, mine now, mine stay," Melania spat out, staking her claim with her limited Saxon vocabulary. She eyed Hensa in return, evaluating his worth as an adversary. He was a large man, taller and thicker than Wulfred, and older. Were no Saxons of normal proportions? His hair was grayed brown and just past shoulder length, and his eyes were thin slices of grayish blue. He had the look of a man who was comfortably in command and one who was uncommonly observant. That was unfortunate for her and for Marcus.

Wulfred stood at her side in silence. He did not speak for her. He did not apologize for her. He did not try to overshadow her. He stood stalwart and immovable at her side and he lifted his brows in silent comment: she was a woman of great spirit and fire, a wife of whom to be proud. He was proud of her. Melania felt the breath go out of her and had to remind herself to breathe again.

Hensa laughed in reluctant approval and said to Wulfred, "She will give you strong sons."

Wulfred crossed his arms and nodded, his smile pleasant if not warm.

Melania understood the difference. Hensa was a Saxon, but Wulfred was not at ease. She did not understand the nuances of the interaction between the pair, but she understood enough to be wary. Also she understood that Wulfred had not belittled her in front of his kind, but had shown her respect and demanded that all others respect her. Without hesitation, she aligned herself with Wulfred.

She would not disgrace him in front of Hensa and his men, not when he had done his best by his Saxon honor. She would show him that her Roman honor was more than a match for his and twice as just. Whatever battles they fought were between them; it would hardly be right to make their battles public, especially in front of one who had authority over Wulfred. Shaming him in front of his leader would hardly classify as a victory, not to her logical and unemotional Roman mind. She stepped nearer to Wulfred so that her shoulder pressed against his arm in an unemotional show of support.

Wulfred's men had watched the encounter with hands on weapons; they would have killed to save Wulfred's honor. Because of Melania's loyalty they would not have to. She had proven herself a stalwart wife, if only this once.

Now that possible conflict had been avoided, manners dictated that the visitors—she would not refer to them even in her own mind as guests—be served a meal. These barbarians would not find Roman hospitality lacking, not in her home. Deftly

Melania directed Theras in the choice of foods and in their presentation. Their resources would be stretched to the limits, but they would never show a lack to this rabble. Never would she show weakness to a Saxon.

Her servants, whom Wulfred had declared slaves, moved among these new pagans, hiding their uneasiness in exemplary service. Melania sat in her usual place and monitored everything, her eyes missing nothing, including the scrutiny with which Hensa regarded her. Wulfred sat between them, a welcome and, she suspected, intentional barrier.

The second course had been served when Hensa spoke. Melania had the uneasy sensation that he spoke to her as well as to Wulfred.

"You found rich and fertile land, Wulfred. It needs only strong men to make it produce as it should. Saxon men."

Wulfred set down his cup and picked up a chunk of bread soaked in spiced olive oil. The oil ran over his fingers. He did not seem to notice.

"I agree. The land is good. It will take much work and many years, but it could flourish again."

"Perhaps not as many years as you imply," Hensa argued pleasantly. "And there are many slaves here to help."

"The destruction and decay of years takes years to correct," Wulfred said, abandoning his bread to the table.

When Melania leaned forward to argue that her home had not been in decay for years, that the lack of anything in her home was the result of Saxon mischief, Wulfred quietly reached out and placed his hand on her knee. It was a plainly conciliatory gesture. She was plainly puzzled by it. She decided to hold her tongue. For now.

"The buildings," Hensa continued, "are in sound condition. A rare thing, these days, to find anything still intact that is of Roman construction."

And whose fault was that? But she said nothing; the pressure on her knee increased before his hand slid up to her thigh. His hand was a warm weight that held what was left of her world in place; his touch soothed her.

"All of the rooms have damage," Wulfred softly argued, "some more than others. The walls are useless, the location indefensible—a poor strategic choice. The place smells of Rome."

Perhaps because the place was Roman? Her anger shot upward in silence and she literally bit her lip to keep it that way. Wulfred had a reason for his disparaging words, she was certain, but . . .

It was when she turned away from Hensa, turned away to try to control her anger, that she looked out over her "guests" and understood. They looked with greedy eyes upon all they saw; fingering the plates, rubbing the goblets, breaking off into groups of two and three to explore the rooms of her home. And the way they looked at her people, as if they were standing gold. The Saxons were famous for their love of slavery and the profit to be made by it. Hensa was talking about her home as if he were ready to carve it up for his pleasure. Was Wulfred just going to let this dirty barbarian snatch it away from him?

"You are a gracious and efficient hostess, wife," he said quietly in Latin, his eyes studying her and apparently reading her outrage. "You have added honor to my name."

Praise? From the Saxon oaf? And even stranger, she felt herself flushing with pleasure at his words, as if his approval meant something to her. Oddly, her anger all but disappeared beneath his approval. Melania frowned in panicked confusion. This was weakness, weakness as her father had explained it. The need for approval was the evidence of weakness; the need for comfort and loving words of kindness, the measure of a damaging loss of control. Romans did not lose control. Romans were ruled by logic, not emotion. Melania was Roman. Wulfred was Saxon. His approval should mean nothing.

"He caught me unawares," she mumbled, troubled by her own response. "I fell back on my training without thinking. Don't get used to it."

Wulfred smiled briefly and picked up his goblet to cover his own loss of control. "I won't."

But Hensa had noticed.

"Speaking Latin, Wulfred? And smiling as you do so? That shocks me more than your sitting in one poor spot all the summer long."

Now her land was poor? The man would say anything to make his point. Or to cause trouble. No wonder Wulfred was so cautious.

"It is a skill I needed to revive," Wulfred said simply.

"Yes, because you found a place populated by Romans, but I do not understand why any were left alive after the first encounter. And I would never have gambled that you would take a Roman wife. She *is* your wife?"

Wulfred set down his goblet as he answered. "Yes. And I have witnesses."

"Your men would lie for you."

"But hers would not. Ask them."

Hensa chuckled and drank again. "No need. I know you would not lie to me."

Wulfred said nothing, but his hand tightened on her leg. She put her hand over his and squeezed his fingers. It was *not* to comfort him. She could just barely make out what the two men were saying; the Saxon tongue came at her so fast, too fast. But she knew that Hensa was challenging Wulfred in some way and that it concerned her. She stopped eating and tried to concentrate more on their garbled and uncivilized tongue.

"Why did you marry her?" he asked.

"Did I not already answer that?" Wulfred said.

"But there are spirited Saxon women, women who understand our customs, women who speak our language." Hensa leaned forward to look intently at Wulfred and bring Melania into his line of vision. "There are many women. She is a Roman above all else."

"She is a woman first."

"Spoken like a man who has been long from

home." Hensa laughed. It was not a pleasant laugh. "Look at her. She smells of Rome. Her Roman pride radiates from her like a fire. You, of all men, to have mated with a Roman . . ."

Why "of all men"? Was it her imagination, or was Hensa slowing his speech so that she could keep up with the conversation and the insults?

"She becomes less of Rome with each passing day."

Even Wulfred insulted her? And with such a lie? It had to be a lie. *Lord God, let it be a lie.*

"But still of Rome," Hensa argued. "Always of Rome."

"She will bear Saxon sons."

Hensa paused in his attack, if for nothing else to eat and drink. Wulfred did not relax. Melania sensed his tension and trusted it. Clearly the subject was not ended.

The third course was served. Wulfred ate and drank sparingly. Melania matched him. For once he did not make an issue of her portions.

"Did you ever think that you would one day choose to marry a Roman?" Hensa said suddenly. Melania could feel the tension in Wulfred escalate. There was something more, something coming that Wulfred could feel and she could not. She reached out a tentative hand and placed it lightly on his shoulder; the muscles bunched beneath her fingers and then quieted. He quieted, for the moment. "Would you ever have thought that you, a slave of Rome, would marry a Roman landowner? And by choice?" Hensa laughed loud, his men joining him.

Wulfred's men did not. "The gods play with us, do they not, Wulfred? The gods play and laugh."

A slave. Wulfred had been a slave. Of Rome.

Her hand did not move. She could feel his breathing quicken, could feel the quivering heat and tension of his muscles; she could feel his rage. And she understood it. So much explained by just that one bit of information.

"How long was it, Wulfred?" Hensa prodded. "How many years were you enslaved by the mighty, crumbling Roman Empire?"

"Long enough," Wulfred answered tersely.

Perverse and destructive man, would he never stop? He obviously thought to cause friction or an open argument; he would get no such cooperation from her. Never would she give a Saxon warlord what he wanted; never would she attack Wulfred for another's spiteful pleasure. Never had that been the way between them. He poked at Wulfred with the spear of bad memories; he prodded her in slowly communicating that she had married a Roman slave. She did not care; she cared only that Hensa be denied his perverse pleasure. He had caused trouble enough; since he was little more than a beast, food would distract him.

"Theras! Bring Hensa a joint of pork and a cup of beer; he has traveled far today and is hungry."

If she could just keep him busy putting food in his mouth, he might leave the topic of Wulfred's Roman slavery in the past, where Wulfred obviously wanted it. But there were a few things she wanted to know, and a few more that she had to say on the subject of Wulfred's slavery.

"You could have told me!" she whispered in angry Latin while Hensa guzzled his beer.

"Why?" Wulfred mumbled, pausing in the drinking of his own beer. "So that you would know why I hate all things Roman?"

She was Roman. It was all he called her. Every insult he threw had the hatred of Rome at its core. It was not shame at his slave state that Wulfred had hidden from her; it was his motive.

"It was for revenge, wasn't it?" she asked in a hiss, crushing a crust of bread into a moist ball. "It was all revenge."

He paused and put his cup down. Looking at her out of the corners of his eyes, he said softly, "It was."

Of course it was. She had known it. He had made no secret of it. And she had made no secret of her hatred; she was ready to take whatever revenge she could on him, too. He had killed her father, made her a slave, destroyed her way of life. She hated him with every drop of her blood. She hated him with every breath she took. She hated him with every glance and every word and every touch. . . . Such passion was hatred, could only be hatred; she could not allow it to be anything else.

"I can't sit here for one moment more and watch that beast fill his face. Tell him what you will. I'm leaving." She rose and walked out, walked out on all the Saxons, every single one. It was the happiest exit she had ever made.

Her bedchamber was her only refuge, and she

walked straight to it. And then she walked all around it. She couldn't be still. She couldn't sit and she couldn't sleep. She couldn't stop thinking.

It was difficult to fault him, although there were many slaves in the world and few reacted so violently to that state. Of course, she had. Didn't she hate him and want to take revenge because he had robbed her of everything, most especially her freedom? But they weren't the same: he was Saxon; she was Roman. There could be nothing that they shared. He was an animal, as all Saxons were; she was a product of the highest culture the world had known. Saxons were savage, lawless, while Rome was the seat of reasoned justice and impartial philosophy. She had known this all her life. She had been told this all her life.

So many of his statements made sense now. He had told her that he wanted her hatred and that he understood it. A hate to match his own. Melania snorted softly in bitter amusement; they were well matched in that.

He had known better than anyone how death would have released her and, knowing, had withheld it. How long had he yearned for death? How long had he remained captive to Rome's will?

Wulfred slipped into the room as the sun dropped below the treeline. The wind was still, unnaturally still, and the air charged and thick. The air in her chamber was charged and thick as well. Melania whirled on him, her eyes angry and her posture rigid with suppressed energy.

"Were you ever going to tell me?" she demanded.

"No."

He didn't even have the grace to look apologetic. *Oaf.*

"Why did your fellow murderer want me to know? He certainly made a point of it."

Wulfred walked across the room and stood by the window, looking out at the sunset.

"So you would know that I hate Rome," he finally said when she was on the point of pushing him out the window, "and . . ."

"Me," she supplied in a furious undertone. It was so difficult to give in to a truly magnificent rage conducted in whispers. "The imbecile did not know that I already understood that perfectly."

Wulfred said nothing. He stared out the window as if he had never seen a sunset before. Wouldn't he tell her anything unless she pried it out of him?

"Are you going to tell me about it now?"

"What more do you need to know?" he said with some bitterness. "I was a slave of your glorious Rome. I am a slave no longer."

"Was it . . . was it very bad?" She felt a fool for asking, but she could think of no other way to get him to talk of it.

Wulfred chuckled and turned away from the window to look at her. He was in shadow, a silhouette against the fading light. "Is being a slave ever good? Tell me, slave of a Saxon warrior?"

She ignored his question and asked another: "How long?"

"Too long."

"Can't you give me a simple answer?" she flared.

"I only want to know . . . to understand what—"

"A year," he said abruptly. "A year that stretched out to touch your Christian hell."

"A year," she repeated. It wasn't such a long time, yet she had been a "slave" to him for only a season, and that had seemed more than long enough. "It could have been worse. . . ." Slaves were usually slaves for life; a year was hardly—

"As a galley slave," he said, his voice vibrating in intensity.

A galley slave. Merciful God, a galley slave. Melania felt her stomach tighten and cramp, and she wrapped her arms around herself. They rarely lasted a year, and often died still in shackles. Worked to death. It was the worst thing that could happen to a man; it was a slow and agonizing death sentence.

"How . . . ?" she whispered.

"How did they catch me or how did I escape?" Wulfred asked with an empty laugh.

"Catch you . . . ?" she stammered in open-mouthed stupefaction.

"Little Melania, who knows so much of Rome," he said softly, and turned again to the window, turning away from the sight of her. "I was . . . I am a Saxon. An animal, by Roman measure. When the legions defeated us, as we defended our own land, they offered us the famous Roman peace. We were to trade self-rule for Roman rule, and pay the Roman tax. I did not want peace with Rome. I fought. I lost. I was enslaved, chained at foot and hand and throat. An animal, to be worked. Dragged from my

279

land, from my home, from my people, to work and starve and die on a Roman boat."

He said it tersely, in a choked recital that was bare of detail, but it rocked her with its very spareness. He sought neither pity nor understanding. Why, then, did both rise up in her to flood her eyes? Melania watched him. His back was broad, his arms long, and every inch of him was bound by muscle. It took time and much labor to build such muscle on a man. He was no animal.

"But you did not die," she whispered into the silence.

"No," he answered softly. "But they thought I had. I should have," he said softly into the night air. "Whipped if slow, whipped if weak, whipped if asleep when ordered to be awake, whipped if awake when ordered—" He turned to face her. "And never fed enough. Starved as punishment. Given watered wine and beer as a reward for living another hour."

Melania had closed the space between them without realizing it. She wanted to touch him, to comfort him, to reassure them both that he had survived. He was alive. He was free.

But she could not touch him. She was Roman. The enemy.

"I collapsed. It was at night. We had just come through a storm, rowing for our very lives to keep the boat from swamping. They lashed me. It did nothing; it was like a dream. And then they unlocked the chains that had kept me bound to that wooden seat for a year and threw me over. Garbage. Like garbage."

"They threw you . . . into the sea? But how . . . ?"

Wulfred smiled—he actually smiled—and said, "I am Saxon. Water is my ally, not my foe. I will not die by water."

He turned again to the window. The sun was gone completely. Stars struggled against the heavy clouds and lost; even the trees were swallowed in the totality of the darkness.

She lit the lamp. There was too much darkness in this room. It was suffocating.

His back, the back that was ever bare, glistened golden in the wavering light of the flame. She had never really studied his back before; she had seen only his nakedness. She studied him now. Lines, ragged and broken, covered him—covered him so completely that at first she did not understand what she was seeing. These ridges were not muscle but scar tissue, old and thick. And over all, the slim, bloodied scabs of her nail marks.

"I have scarred you again, bringing up blood," she whispered, her breath on his back. She thought she would be sick and gulped in air to ease her nausea. So many scars . . . so many lashings. So much pain. So much rage.

Wulfred turned to face her and she wanted to hide her face. "It was the only Roman lashing I did not mind," he said softly, his voice hoarse in his whisper.

"The pain . . ." she murmured, guilt riding her hard—the guilt of a whole empire.

Claudia Dain

"I feel little there now."

She met his eyes, an act of moral courage, and read his lack of anger. *Impossible.* He had every reason to hate. He had every motive for revenge. And he had the means. He had her.

There was nothing of hatred in his eyes.

"You have not had much of a revenge on me, have you?" she whispered softly.

"You have not been very cooperative," he whispered back.

He stood out like a golden flame against the dark and empty window. No wind ruffled his golden hair, no cloth covered his bronzed chest, no veil of distrust clouded his blue, blue eyes.

"Even making me your wife . . . those bonds were supposed to hurt, I suppose."

He lifted his brows and said, "Have they?"

"Not very much." She slowly shook her head. She did not offer that it was because she had been very little tempted to honor those bonds. Now everything had changed. Yet everything was the same.

He reached for her, his authority as her husband clear in his manner. But it was not as clear to her. Too much had she learned; there was too much to think on. She had to reason it all out and come to a conclusion that made sense. But he wasn't going to give her time to think, to reason. Perhaps he did not want her to think. Perhaps this was his revenge.

His kiss was hot, as hot as his anger should have been. Hotter. He devoured her and his wet heat inflamed her, igniting not her anger, but her passion. He could so easily touch her passion; her reason ran before its fire.

Hands pulled at her clothes, freeing her of their bondage. She realized that some of those hands were hers. She had to touch him and had to feel him touch her. Skin to skin. Mouth to mouth.

Her breath came in pants and gasps. The single light of the lamp was too intense for her suddenly sensitive eyes and she closed them, intensifying the impact of his touch. He stroked her and laid her down, his kiss never ending. The tile was rough on her back. She didn't care. His hands were on her breasts and his weight pressed her down; that was all that mattered. All she wanted. She did not want to think that he was her enemy and she his. She did not want to think that he had just cause for his hatred of Rome and what Roman law could do. She did not want to think that he had as much hatred in him as she had in her.

But she could not find any hatred in her now; she felt only passion. And, at her core, empathy.

She opened for him, knowing what he would give her. Wanting it. Wanting the smooth length of him. He lay between her legs and she savored the hard thrust of his manhood against her belly.

He moved his mouth from hers and nipped her neck. She arched into his bite. He took her breast into his mouth and sucked; she held his head to her, imprisoning him. She moaned and he grunted his pleasure as he moved to her other breast. She bent her head and pulled him up to her by his hair, attacking him with her mouth. He was so hot. She needed his heat. She craved this fire he lit with every touch.

He controlled the kiss she had started, and she was content to allow it. He spread her legs with his, poised himself above her, and attacked her breasts. He wrung a cry from her of pure sensual pleasure.

"Come to me," she said softly in command. She wrapped her legs around his hips and urged him down to her, down to that place of melting heat. Down to that place only he knew of, that only he seemed able to find.

He broke the kiss and stared down at her as she lay spread and eager. His hands spanned her waist and he lifted her, showing her how easily he could control her. "I am no slave to command, Roman. I take you at my pleasure."

He turned her on her stomach, and her breasts almost cried aloud their loss; until his hands stroked the round globes of her cheeks, finding the folds that held her milk. She lifted her hips toward him, unmindful of the tiles against her face, wanting his touch above all else.

One hand drifted down and under her, rubbing the soft skin of her belly before finding a distended nipple to roll between thumb and finger; she moaned, lifting herself to her hands so that he could give her more. He did. He ran his hand across both breasts simultaneously while fondling her below; she rose to her knees at his prompting, so that he could reach her, pleasure her, fire her.

On hands and knees she quivered before him. She could feel his manhood throbbing against her hip. His mouth bit her lightly on her left cheek and she jerked, moaning. And then his mouth moved down and his hands parted her from behind. She fell forward, her arms useless, so that her head rested on the floor. He took her in his mouth from behind and she lurched forward at the contact. Pulling her back, a hand on each hip, he held her while his mouth nibbled.

She was burning. The fire roared all around her. No, it flamed within her and sprang to greater heights wherever he touched. Wherever he kissed.

When he sucked on the nub of her desire, she screamed in a ragged whisper.

It was then that he took her. Kneeling behind her, he plunged in, his arm wrapped around her hips to hold her to him in an unbreakable hold while his hand plucked her nipples.

Fire sprang up and scorched her, consuming her, licking her.

She was dying, throbbing with death, convulsing with death.

He had taken her from behind, like an animal.

She didn't care.

He withdrew and turned her quickly onto her back and spread her to accept him. She did. He plunged in and out, his full weight on her. She wanted it. If this was his revenge, let him take it.

It was a poor revenge.

She held him to her, gripping him with legs and arms, his ear between her teeth.

Again, the roar of fire and the sound of flames. Again, the throbbing of near death. Again, his strangled shout of achievement.

When they cooled, she did not release her hold on him. She did not push him from her. A small part of her argued that by this action, he would know that his revenge had missed the mark; by enjoying his sensual attack, she had negated his vengeance in it.

She knew she lied—to herself. Defeating him had had no part in this mating.

He stroked her hair and eased his weight from her. She cradled him between her legs and rubbed his back. They held each other almost tenderly while their heartbeats slowed and calmed. Melania buried her face in the angle of his neck and shoulder; he smelled of sweat and spent desire. It was a smell that made her smile.

"You smile," he said, his voice a throaty whisper. "As I said, you are not very cooperative."

She smiled more fully and retorted, "You will have to try harder in your acts of revenge, Saxon. You are failing miserably."

"I do not know if it is in me to try harder," he said, smiling with her.

"Is it in you to try again?"

"Is that what you want?"

"Ummm, how to answer that? We have walked this road before, haven't we? You always seem to do whatever it is I do not wish you to do, and do it most enthusiastically. And what I want, you will always refuse to do."

"Always?"

"There is the matter of my death."

"You are not dead."

"Thanks to you."

"Do you still want to die?" He kissed her face gently, his breath a caress. "Because there are ways. . . ."

"I have tried them."

"Not this one. This one you have just learned." He grinned and kissed her neck, his teeth grazing her skin. He left a bruise, certainly.

"And would this kill me?" she asked, letting her hands drift down in a flickering caress.

"Just a little," he said softly before outlining her ear with his tongue.

She shivered in pure anticipation.

And remembered Marcus.

Marcus, waiting for her in the dark. Marcus, relying on her for food and clothing. Marcus, trusting her.

"I . . . I . . ." she stammered, pushing at his chest, raising her knees to dislodge him. "I have to . . . Would you get off me?"

Wulfred allowed her to rise, his expression plainly perplexed. And suspicious? He watched as she hurriedly arranged her stola and palla, watched as she strapped on her shoes, watched as she ran shaking fingers over her hair.

"Where are you going?" he finally asked.

She looked at him, sitting comfortably naked on the floor of her chamber, his hair a hopeless blond tangle and his eyes fathomless blue and inscrutable.

"I have to . . . empty my bladder!"

Chapter Twenty-one

It had begun to rain.

She hadn't had time to collect anything at all for Marcus, not even a crust, and there was certainly no opportunity to do so now. Wulfred was in the chamber behind her, strange Saxons were in the triclinium to her right, and the courtyard was turning to mud; she had to go now, empty-handed as she was.

Crossing the courtyard, thankful for the obscuring clouds, Melania raced out into the night. No one would be watching her; all Saxon eyes had seen her go to her chamber and then seen Wulfred follow not long after. There would be no Saxon shadow to follow her tonight. The hill to the vineyards was steeper in the dark and more slippery in the rain, but she knew well the path and was not

daunted. Finding Marcus might prove more difficult in the rainy darkness of the early autumn night.
She hoped she would not have to penetrate the
wood. She hoped he would be watching for her.

He was, thank God.

He came out of the deeper black of the forest and
held out his arms to her. Without hesitation she ran
into his embrace. Marcus, beloved man!

He held her close, his face buried in the tumble
of her streaming hair; he held her high off the
ground, letting her feet dangle above his. If they
could have fused, they would have chosen to. This
was what she had not dared to dream when the
Saxons had descended. Marcus, alive. Marcus,
strong and fit and—

He dropped her as suddenly as he had taken
her up.

"You've been with a man."

It was not a question, and his voice was hard as
stone. She fussed for a moment with her clothing,
and her hand reached for the havoc that was her
hair.

"Don't bother," he snapped, watching her outline in the murky light. "I can smell his seed on
you."

"Marcus, I—" she began hesitantly.

"Again, don't bother." He turned his back on
her, crossing his arms against his chest, crossing
them against her. "You have found some solace in
the Saxon destruction, it would seem. I would wish
you joy, but can't over my bile."

Anger rose up at his judgment, pushing tender

feelings down into the mud. "You don't know what's happened! You don't understand anything! You ran off—"

He spun to face her, his anger obvious even in the dark. "I didn't run off! I left you safe! We both agreed that it was safe here, so far inland, and you encouraged me to go!"

"Yes, you went," she shouted against the storm, thankful that the rain hid her unbidden tears of fury and rejection. "You went and I stayed and the Saxons came. Do you have any conception of how I yearned for death? Of how I pursued it?"

"You seem healthy enough," he grumbled.

Melania laughed almost hysterically, "Oh, yes, very healthy. But not by choice! Do you think he would let me die when he knew how desperately I wanted death? I could teach you many things about the perversity of Saxons."

This was not what she had wanted; this was not what she had dreamed when she had dreamed of Marcus coming to her. The rain lightened and clouds broke into tatters across the face of the moon, so white and distant, so far from the conflict that was embedded in her heart. She loved Marcus, but how could he find her guilty when she had fought so long against the Saxon who was now her husband? Marcus was here and she had a Saxon husband; no, this was not like anything that she had dreamed.

Marcus must have felt something of the same disappointment, for his face drained of angry passion and his eyes softened. "Melania," Marcus soothed, reaching out for her. "I'm sorry. I spoke with passion and not with reason. I have been taught better."

As had she. Melania refused his touch at first, but soon gave in to him. He offered her comfort in a world gone wild. She needed him. She had always needed him.

"Tell me what happened," Marcus said softly, rubbing her back. "I will listen and not judge. Or try not to," he added with a smile.

She buried her head beneath his chin and wrapped her arms around his waist, thankful for the familiar feel of him, feeling safe even in this unsafe place.

"They came. They killed." She gulped back a sob. "They killed Melanius. He is buried and his place marked. He is at peace. Then they stayed."

"I find I am not surprised," Marcus whispered, tightening his hold on her. She relished his strength. "He fought them, didn't he?"

"Yes. He died in battle."

"When?"

"At the start of summer."

"Why have they stayed? It is not their way."

"No." She smiled grimly, turning her head to look into the blackness that was the forest. "It is not their way, but their leader wanted something of me."

When Marcus began to curse, she stopped him with a hand to his mouth. "It is not as you think. He wanted to defeat me in a way that would give me the greatest pain; he wanted me to live and watch him live, a Saxon in a Roman home. He has a great need of vengeance against all things of Rome." After a pause, she said softly, "With reason."

"Has he used you . . . in the way of a man? He is the one . . . ?"

Melania turned her face up to the sky, feeling the solid strength of Marcus, feeling the scratch of his chin against her forehead.

"Yes."

Marcus said nothing, but his arms tensed. She knew he yearned for a weapon; he had found his target.

"Even that is not as you think," she said. "According to Saxon law, we are married. Of course, I did not know what he was about, not knowing their barbaric customs, but, by their law, I am his wife."

"It is their law, the law of animals. It is not binding."

"I will not argue it, but I was untouched until he believed us one by his law. By his own code he did not abuse me." By his own code he was honorable; what other code was there for a Saxon than Saxon law? What law for Roman but Roman law? Strange thoughts to have tumble inside her when she was held safe in the arms of Marcus.

Marcus swallowed hard. She could feel the movement in his throat. She knew what his next question would be. She had asked it once herself.

"Was he the one who . . . ?"

"No. He saw him buried according to our rituals.

The Saxon swore to me he was not the one. And I have found, barbarian though he is, he does not lie."

"For your sake, I am grateful."

"I also," she murmured. "But there is more. More Saxons have come with a barbarian called Hensa as their leader. They came as I left you, and they are a horde. It is why I could not bring you what I promised. Oh, Marcus, I have not even a handful of bread to ease your hunger!"

Marcus ignored her apology. He ignored her distress. He had heard one word, and that word had captured him: Hensa. Hensa was one of the most well known of Saxon leaders. Hensa made decisions. Hensa was in a position of power. Hensa would know what the Saxons would do next.

"This Hensa, did he seem capable?"

Melania answered the question with a snort of derision. "He is as devious as all Saxons, and a troublemaker besides." She would never forget what he had put Wulfred through at the meal, and she would never forgive.

"But a warrior? A man of power?"

"I'm certain he thinks so; he has the arrogance of ten Saxons."

"Melania, think," Marcus urged, gripping her arms and searching her face in the drizzling rain. "Do not let your emotions rule your head—"

"You did not have to eat with him—"

"He is the leader of the Saxon raiding force. He is the mind behind their attacks on this island. What did he say of his force? Of his plans?"

Honor. The word rang in her mind like a bell. Marcus was safety, a familiar and beloved man in a raging world. Marcus wanted her to tell him of Hensa's plans. Hensa was ally to Wulfred. And Wulfred was her husband, or claimed to be. What they had just done was the province of the married; he believed them married. Did she?

"Did he say nothing? Is there nothing you can tell me?" Marcus pressed.

"It's not as if I am fluent in Saxon, and you can be assured that he spoke no Latin," she answered, evading him.

And he knew it. His hands dropped from her arms and he stepped away from her, his eyes cold and measuring.

"You're right, Melania. I don't understand you. Do you give your loyalty to the murderers you shelter from the rain? Have you forgotten who you are?"

"You don't understand anything at all!" she flared, furious with him for questioning her loyalty to him and for constructing a loyalty for the Saxons that did not—could not—exist. . . .

"I want to," he said softly, maintaining the gap between them. "I want Melania the way I remember her. Melania before the Saxons."

Now she turned her back on him, needing the space he had given her. Melania before the Saxons had been a girl, both proud and naive; that girl was retreating into the mists of dreams with every day the Saxons lingered. But even if . . . even when they left, she would never be the same. She could not return to that arrogant and innocent girl. That girl had died on the same day as her father. Couldn't Marcus see that?

"I am the wife of a Saxon warrior," she said bluntly. "How can I ever again be the same?"

"You are Roman," he answered just as bluntly. "How can a barbaric ritual have any meaning for you? You owe this Saxon nothing. Nothing but a blade in the back."

But there *was* meaning between them. There was . . . something. Something more than the hatred they both vowed and the vengeance they both hungered for. When he looked at her, sometimes there was reluctant approval in his eyes, even respect. Sometimes . . . it almost seemed that he understood what her honor demanded, and she could half believe that he would not ask her to cross that line of personal honor because, in his way, he had honor of his own. Did Marcus understand her system of personal honor as well as Wulfred did? At the moment it did not seem so. He urged her to act against her own inclination, using guilt to persuade her; when had Wulfred ever done that?

Yet wasn't Marcus merely telling her what she had so often told herself? What meaning was there for her in empty Saxon ritual? None. But there was Wulfred, and he was not so easily dismissed. It was Wulfred they spoke of, not some nameless Saxon warrior. And because it was Wulfred . . .

"Easily said, Marcus," she said, turning aside from her twisting thoughts, "and not so easily accomplished. I have tried. Repeatedly. Saxon hides are tough."

"Like the oxen they are," he said.

But Wulfred was no animal, and she bristled to hear Marcus refer to him so.

"Give me a day to prepare. I will come to you at the break of dawn on the day that follows this and I will bring you food and clothing."

"And information?"

"I will bring whatever I can to help you, Marcus," she hedged. She didn't know what she would do; her thoughts were a muddle.

"I will wait," he said. "Come to me again in the apple orchard. I will wait behind the far fence for you." He paused and studied her, taking one of her hands in his. "I will leave with the dawn, Melania; staying here is too dangerous. Bring enough food for two."

"I will bring enough for ten."

"Use the day to think over what you will do. I need you, Melania."

"As I need you," she choked out, her voice full of tears. "Now go. I must return . . . I have been gone too long."

He melted into the misty forest before she had quite finished. She stared at the place where he had been and sighed. It would have been so simple, if only he had come before . . . If only he had come before Wulfred had touched her.

Things were no longer simple.

Walking gingerly through the wet brush to a leafy bush, Melania squatted and emptied her bladder. That, at least, would be the truth.

She was becoming more barbaric each hour, to squat out in the open to relieve herself as she had just done. Lord God of all, what was happening to her?

Melania hurried down the path to the villa, muttering under her breath.

Chapter Twenty-two

Melania awoke to the sound of birdsong. The rain had stopped. Wulfred was gone.

She had returned last night, soaked, and endured Wulfred's attentions while the memory of Marcus was very strong within her. He had stripped her of her clothing—it was amazing how quickly he had mastered the complicated workings of the stola and palla—and wrapped his arms around her as they lay entwined on the small couch. She was warm and dry very quickly. Very, very quickly.

She needed a bigger couch.

But not too much bigger.

Remembering the sensation of his huge hands on her bare flesh caused her skin to burn and tingle. Was she blushing? She hoped not. How hopelessly unsophisticated.

And how very uncomfortable it was to remember the wonderful feeling of lying in his arms, the long length of him a solid force that pulsed with energy and strength. It was embarrassing to admit, even to herself, how safe she had felt with him. Safe. With a Saxon.

Unbelievable.

Unadmittable.

Luckily, no one was asking her to admit anything, and she would certainly not dwell on it herself. Last night was best forgotten and, if not forgotten—for how could she truly forget the passion that he had scorched her with?—then at least pushed to the darkest shadows of her thoughts, where they would die for lack of light.

But, given the strength of her memories, it would be a full fifty years before she forgot the passion he had elicited in her last night.

Melania sighed and rose from her couch. It was best to be up and face the day. Even fifty years must start with a single day.

She ached, deliciously so, and it took her far longer to dress than usual. What had he done to her to make her skin so sensitive? Her nipples rose up at the slightest friction of cloth, so that she wanted to rip off her clothing and stand naked. With Wulfred in the room. At just the thought of him the throbbing began, throbbing for which she now knew the remedy. Curse the man, where had he gone?

With such a start to the day, it was understandable that she would be a little on edge. Actually she was flatly irritable. The sweating, lice-ridden horde in her triclinium did nothing to soothe her. She had forgotten in the warm darkness of Wulfred's arms how they had multiplied yesterday.

She avoided them and made her way to the kitchen. Perhaps Wulfred was in the courtyard, or loitering around the kitchen. . . .

He wasn't.

Adjusting the drape of her stola, Melania ate the morning meal. Even without Wulfred watching her, she ate. She was being very reasonable today, and he wasn't even around to notice. Where was he?

Dorcas all but flew into the kitchen just as Melania had finished eating. She was wild-eyed and breathing hard, like a hare on the run.

"What is wrong, Dorcas?" Melania asked, rising to her feet.

"Oh, Melania," she said in a gasp, "I was . . . they were . . . and I didn't do anything . . . but then I . . . it was . . ."

"Calm yourself, Dorcas, so that I may understand you. I know already that only Saxons provoke such a response in reasonable people. Now, where have you been?"

"The triclinium," she said on a shaky breath.

"Which Saxon did this to you?"

Dorcas's face lost some of its healthy color and she bit her lower lip. "I don't know their names, and it was not just one, and they—"

"How many?" Melania could feel her own color rise.

"Three." She trembled, ready to cry.

"Did they touch you?"

"Yes," Dorcas whispered, twisting the ends of her stola.

"Did they hurt you?" Melania asked, her voice rising as Dorcas's dropped in volume.

"No, not really."

"But they frightened you? Yes, of course they did," Melania said with a snarl. "Did they threaten you? Can you gather your wits about you enough to tell me what they said? What they did?"

Dorcas kept looking over her shoulder and twisting her stola, but she did speak.

"They cornered me near the portico. Cenred, all of Wulfred's men, were out of the room. One of them, with red hair and silver on his wrists, grabbed me . . . touched me . . . between the legs."

Melania kept listening as she began to search the kitchen for a nice big knife.

"The other two," Dorcas continued, "held my arms and told me what they would do to me when they had the time."

When they had the time. Pigs. Arrogant pigs.

"I didn't know what to do." Dorcas began to cry. "They are Saxon; they have the power. What can I do to stop them? What can I do?"

"Avoid them; that is all you can do. But I think what I will do is set a Saxon against a Saxon. And if that is not enough, I have a knife."

A good knife. Bigger than the last one.

"We will set Cenred on their tails," Melania explained. "He should care that you have been molested by his brothers in arms. And if he doesn't care, I'll teach him to."

Dorcas's head jerked up at the mention of Cenred and she gulped a sob.

"Things are not as they were with Cenred," she said, crying harder. "I . . . I am pregnant."

Melania narrowed her eyes and fingered the blade; it was satisfyingly sharp.

"You told Cenred, of course," she said.

"Yes, and things have not been the same."

"I would think not. He is now to be a father. And a husband."

Yes, the blade was wondrously sharp, as was her anger.

"He—" She cried, dabbing at her face with her stola. "He has not offered for me."

"He will." Melania smiled coldly. "You stay here in the kitchen and keep the door closed. If any of the Saxon vermin enter, start screaming."

When she left the kitchen, with the door closed firmly behind her, Melania had the happy task of finding Cenred. She couldn't wait; she had a nice, smoldering anger and he was going to feel its heat. It would be entirely deserved. What did he think he was doing to leave Dorcas, who plainly adored him, in the grasp of his littermates? Did he not have any care for her at all? If not, he should never have bedded her. He should have exercised a little civilized self-control, though how a savage could do anything tinged with civilization was a mystery. Still, he should have attempted it.

She marched across the courtyard, her stola flapping violently against her legs. The sun struggled against the thick clouds that all but blanketed the sky. It was an autumn sky; summer was almost a memory.

It was truly past time for the Saxons to go.

Crossing under the portico, she entered the triclinium. It was seething with Saxon bodies. Melania paused in the doorway, scanning the room, looking for one particular Saxon: a Saxon with red hair and silver on his wrists. And she was looking for Cenred. Unfortunately, she found neither.

The Saxon warriors rose up around her like a flood, but it was not in respect. The motion was predatory. Melania clutched her knife and faced them, uncertain of their actions, but knowing their intent. They hated her.

She hated them.

It was a fair balance, except for one thing: she was outnumbered.

"What do you want here, Roman?" one of them asked in a snarl. He had light brown hair and pale blue eyes and food embedded between his teeth. *Revolting.*

"What do I want?" she blazed. "In my own home? In my own triclinium? Perhaps I want you out. Perhaps I want you to return to the sty you normally habituate and to take your fleas with you! Yes," she said with a return snarl, "that is exactly what I want."

Of course, she had reverted to Latin in her rage, so he understood none of it. But he understood her intent and that was enough.

"Do you want to feel my hand between your thighs?" another one said, edging close to her.

In answer, she raised her knife meaningfully, her eyes communicating the seriousness of her intent.

"No?" he said. "Then perhaps it is my blade against your breast you ask for. I will cut you slowly so that I may enjoy you as your blood runs out."

Melania backed toward the arched doorway to the portico. She was no coward, but she was outnumbered and they were closing on her, like wolves on a stag. She had but one knife. One knife would not go far against so many.

"You speak of thighs and breasts and knives to the wife of Wulfred?" came a deep voice from behind her, a voice she knew. She looked over her shoulder to see Cynric holding his seax. She had never known him to look so good. "You are thirsty for death, it seems."

"You are a fool," Cuthred said simply.

She looked again. Now they all stood behind her, fanned out and holding weapons: Wulfred's comitatus, defending her against their own.

"I am no fool if I kill a Roman when I find one," a Saxon with white-blond hair said.

"Wulfred has claimed her. She is under his protection. She is his wife. Think on that before you bray about killing," Cynric said coldly.

"And she has you to protect her?" one asked.

"Of course," Cynric said. "We are pledged to Wulfred. Wulfred is pledged to her."

"By the gods, Cynric," the first said, "you protect a Roman against your own?"

"She is wife to Wulfred. That is all I see," Balduff said.

Ceolmund had edged in front of her, blocking her vision, but protecting her from them. Cenred stood behind. Wulfred's comitatus bristled with weapons and they brandished them in her defense. Against their own. Humiliating tears of thankfulness built up in her eyes so forcefully that it was a struggle to blink them away; she would show no such weakness as tears to any Saxon.

Balduff's remark was the excuse they needed to retreat, and Hensa's men took it.

"Ho, Balduff," she heard, "I knew you would see a woman as a woman only."

"And why not? There is no race between warm thighs and round breasts," Balduff answered pleasantly, still holding his weapon.

"But when did you start marking the difference between women and wives? You have never done that before."

"Since Wulfred took a wife," he huffed. "I have my loyalty."

"I thought your first loyalty was to the little warrior between your legs—"

"You ox, Cynfrid," Baldruff roared goodnaturedly. "My warrior is a giant. Do not judge me by your own stunted standards."

Slowly, gradually, the confrontation ended. The Saxons, bickering in their typically vulgar fashion, drifted back into the triclinium. Ceolmund and Cynric stayed with her, moving her like a dumb animal out into the courtyard. They obviously

didn't want to take any chances with the changeable mood of the mob, but she had something to
say to Cenred; Cenred would not disappear into the
triclinium to drink her beer with his unwashed
brethren.

"Cenred!" she said firmly. "Do not think to slink
away with your brother wolves!"

He stopped and turned to look at her over his
bare shoulder. What was wrong with these Saxons
that they went about nearly naked day upon day?
If he had been clothed, perhaps Dorcas would not
have become enamored of him and had her heart
bruised. But then again, perhaps not. Clothing, or
lack of it, seemed to have little to do with the attraction Dorcas felt for him. The ignorant lout—
did he not have even the slightest feeling for her?

"Do you call me back to thank me, Melania?"

"You are a fool, aren't you?" she spat, angry that
he might be correct. Gratitude for their interference was probably in order. But to thank a Saxon?
She couldn't do it; besides, they had defended her
because of Wulfred, not because of her. Wulfred
should thank them.

"You're welcome." He smiled, turning again
to go.

"And do you thank Dorcas when you pleasure
yourself on her? Or is it the men you claim broth-
erhood with who get your thanks . . . when they assault her?" *There*. That stopped him.

Cenred turned and faced her fully, his warm
brown eyes suddenly stormy. Ceolmund had not
left her side, and Cynric, although distancing him-

self, remained near. She did not care if she had an audience. Cenred would do the right thing, or . . . well, she still held the knife.

"What did you say?" Cenred asked, his voice low and tight.

"I said," she said clearly, "that Dorcas has been threatened with rape by the men you run with. The woman who carries your child. Is that clear enough for you? Of course, since you practically raped her yourself, you might not object if more of you Saxons avail yourselves of her body. Still, she does carry your child, and such rough work might dislodge the babe. I don't suppose you care. But whether you care or not, you will marry her, Cenred." Holding up her blade so that it pointed at his throat, she added, "I'll even supply the matrimonial knife."

Cenred hardly heard her. His face was a mask of astonishment and fury.

"But why? Why Dorcas?"

"Why not?" she returned bluntly, pleased to see the fury building behind his eyes. "Did you not use her in the same way? And are you not all Saxons? She has no husband to protect her, Cenred. What do you think will happen to her every time a band of barbarians decides to descend upon us? Will they leave her untouched because you have been there first?"

He answered none of her biting questions. He hardly could. Melania smiled her pleasure.

"Where is she?" he asked.

"She is in the kitchen, waiting for a proposal of marriage."

After watching him walk toward the kitchen to assure herself that he wasn't going to miss it or become waylaid, Melania turned to Cynric. For a man who had just defended her, he looked less than pleasant. *Poor Cynric.* That must have been hard duty, defending a Roman for the sake of honor. Melania caught her breath at the direction of her thoughts—again, this notion of honor. Saxon honor. Where had she acquired such aberrant thinking?

"Cynric?" she asked. "Where is he?"

Cynric hesitated. Perhaps he thought that Wulfred had disappeared to escape her. Perhaps he had. Still, he would be found. She wanted to talk to him about the matter of Dorcas and Cenred. It was a good excuse.

"I'll leave the knife with you, if that's what worries you," she chided, trying to shame him.

"He is on the rock that overlooks this place. Take the knife, if it suits you," he said, turning from her. Apparently he was unshamed.

Glad for a destination, Melania left the villa courtyard and Cynric and all others behind as she climbed the hill to the rock. Ceolmund was not left behind, however. He stayed with her, at a discreet distance, obviously having decided that she needed a personal guard of sorts. After her experience in the triclinium, she was disinclined to walk alone.

Wulfred sat on the large, flat rock wedged into the hillside like a king on his throne surveying his holdings—in this case, her villa. The sun had overcome the heavy bank of gray clouds for the moment and shone down on the hillside in golden splendor, shimmering on rain-covered leaves and sparkling in puddles. Below, the valley remained in shadow under the advancing cloud front.

Wulfred did not welcome her by gesture or word. Melania was highly aggravated. Had he not held her in his arms all night? Had he not kissed her so passionately her lips were all but seared? Had he not claimed to be her husband?

Had he not disappeared, effectively avoiding her?

"If you had bothered to stay within the walls of the villa, you would be aware that those animals you call allies assaulted Dorcas this morning." When he did not react except to look up at her as she glared down at him, she added, "And when I went to condemn them for it, they all but attacked me!"

Again he said nothing, merely looked toward Ceolmund, who confirmed her words with a slow nod.

"And now I have . . . strongly advised Cenred to do the decent thing and marry the girl he impregnated so casually, and I want you to add your voice to mine. He is your man and should do as you tell him. Cenred must marry Dorcas!"

Wulfred looked up into her face for a moment longer and then, saying nothing, looked out over the valley again. How could he act with such blatant superiority when she was standing over him?

"Did you hear me?" she snapped.

"Of course, who does not hear Melania when she speaks?" he said with a chuckle. "But I know you did not climb this slippery hill to talk to me about Cenred. Or about Dorcas."

"What are you babbling about? Of course I did. Why else—"

He turned to look at her, and the sun lit his hair to molten gold and his eyes to lapis. "I think you wanted to find me. I think you wanted to be with me." Turning away again, he added, "I thought you more direct."

How had he known? Regardless, she would never admit it. She could hardly admit it to herself.

"Direct?" she countered. "Wasn't it you who always accused me of being devious? Are you so ignorant that you do not understand that the two words are in direct opposition?"

"You have always been very direct . . . in your deviousness." He smiled.

Now he was amused. He was not going to be amused at her expense.

"You are a complete oaf. Do you know that?" she said in a soft snarl.

"I've been told," he said just as softly, looking at her over his shoulder. Which, of course, was as bare as the day he was born. And rippling with muscle in the strong sunlight. And gleaming gold in color. And . . .

"I can read it in your eyes, you know," he said, his voice low and throbbing. Just as she was throbbing.

"What?" She licked her lips, distracted.

"Your desire, Melania. It's as blatant as a fire in the night. And just as beckoning."

"This is . . . hardly polite conversation," she said.

Wulfred smiled slowly. He reached for her hand and held it to his mouth. Gently he traced the line of her veins with his tongue. She couldn't even think to pull her hand away.

"When have I ever been polite?"

Never. He had never been polite.

Was it important?

"Wulfred."

Who had said that? Oh, Ceolmund. Melania pulled her hand away and rubbed it, but his touch would not leave her.

Wulfred stood, placing her just behind him while keeping her in view. Saxons, strange Saxons, were coming out of the trees behind them.

One of them had red hair and silver bracelets.

Melania stepped forward, standing shoulder-to-shoulder with Wulfred while Ceolmund closed the distance he had left between them. Wulfred pushed her firmly behind him; the expression on his face kept her there. Three Saxons walked through the brush. Melania rubbed her hand on the hilt of the knife, thankful she had kept it.

"Ho, Wulfred," Red Hair saluted. "Ho, Ceolmund."

"Does not my wife deserve a greeting, Sigred?" Wulfred asked coldly.

Sigred smiled tolerantly and saluted Melania, Roman fashion. "Hail, Roman."

Claudia Dain

"You seem preoccupied with her origins." Wulfred smiled in return. "She is my wife. She is Saxon now."

Under different circumstances, Melania would have howled her objections to that statement. Now she held her tongue—nearly bit it off.

"If you say so—"

"I do," Wulfred interrupted.

"What are you doing up here?" Sigred asked, changing the subject, coming to the point. "Your people are below in fellowship. Why do you seek to be alone?"

"I am not alone," Wulfred said. "Or have you no eyes to see?" He gestured to both Melania and Ceolmund.

"But they have just come,"one of the others said.

"Yes"—Wulfred eyed him coolly—"and you would know that only if you had been in the triclinium, while my wife was there. Was Walfric there, Ceolmund?"

"He was," Ceolmund answered evenly.

"I hope you were not one of the men who was rude to my wife. She puts great store in manners." Wulfred barely breathed, "As I have learned to do."

"Wulfred, we did not come to discuss this," Sigred said, drawing closer. "We came to bring you down with us. It is not our way to seek solitude." He eyed Melania with open suspicion. "Saxons do not leave the company of Saxons."

"Even when they are newly joined?" Wulfred smiled. "You know that is not true. Here is my wife. I choose to be with her in a more private place than

312

the rooms below. Understandable, is it not?"

"She was below—"

"Because she was required to comfort a woman who had been abused by Saxon hands and Saxon words." Wulfred walked to Sigred and stood a handbreadth from his face. "I have won this place by conquest. I have won the people in it. I will not hand it over to you. Not one small part of it. Understood?" When Sigred nodded in curt answer, Wulfred said, "Now return to my holding and enjoy my hospitality, while you may."

Effectually dismissed, Sigred, Walfric, and the other men brushed past Wulfred and walked down the steep hill toward the villa, anger and frustrated defiance showing in every movement. Melania stopped stroking her knife when they disappeared from view.

"Is this the amity shared between Saxon allies?" she asked. "Your world is peopled by enemies."

Ceolmund faded away into the brush, giving them a modicum of privacy; she had no doubt that he could still see them. Wulfred looked down at her, his manner strangely hesitant. This was altogether a new behavior for him. She had seen him angry, passionate, disgusted, and vengeful; this was . . . sorrow? Tenderness?

"What is it?" she asked, disturbed more than she cared to admit.

"It is not I who has their suspicion. But you are right; my bond with them is strained. It will heal. In time."

Melania looked into his eyes, so blue and suddenly so soft. "Is it because of me?"

Wulfred took her into his arms. The wind brushed her hair and pushed the dark clouds across the sky, cheating the sun of its day. It would rain again and soon.

"You are Roman and among us. It troubles them," he said against her hair.

He had trouble with his own kind? Because of her? Because of a hated Roman? Of them all, Wulfred had the most reason to hate Rome and all who sprang from her; of them all, Wulfred stood with her, against them. She had not forgotten that his comitatus had stood to defend her, but only because of Wulfred. Because of Wulfred, she was safe. Because of her, he battled his own.

Regret surged through her powerfully. Regret that someone was hurt because of her and sorrow that she could not mend it. She could not stop being Roman even had she wanted to. Strangely, in this world of ravaging Saxons, she was more effortlessly Roman than she had ever been. But for the first time in her life, her Roman birth brought her no satisfaction.

"I am sorry," she whispered against his chest.

She apologized for being a Roman.

Wulfred, savage, uncivilized, and uneducated, understood.

How had she come to this? How had the barbarian holding her so tenderly learned compassion? Or was it she who had learned understanding? Her world had been a simple place of simple and straightforward principles; Romans were the apex of civilization and the epitome of all man could achieve on earth. Saxons were, of course, the nadir. Yet the Saxon holding her now would stand tall in any culture, and his own was not as degraded as she had once believed. He had an honor from which he never wavered. He had the courage to stand against his own and the compassion to see the need. He inspired loyalty and dogged devotion. He was not the animal she had named him.

Her father died a little more at that moment as her arms wound around a half-naked Saxon warrior and her lips pressed against his thudding heart. Melania quietly let her father go. *Peace, Melanius.*

She shifted in his arms so that she could look up at him as he held her. His jaw was strong and sculpted, his mouth wide, his nose straight. He was a well-featured man, and strong. And he was gold all over. She had never known a man could be so golden. On impulse, she stood on tiptoe and kissed his throat.

"Planning where next to set your knife?" he asked, holding her close.

She smiled against his chest and answered, "Too difficult to reach. I had considered it."

"You obviously thought it through. Unusual for you."

"I'm still thinking, still considering."

"I can see I've taught you caution."

She reached her arms around his chest and nuzzled her face against his width. She loved the smell of him.

315

"It would be much more fair if I could only get you down on the ground."

"I don't think you'll have a problem with that." He smiled, running his hands down her back to cup her bottom.

"Good. You have been something of a problem in the past. I don't suppose you can help it, being a Saxon."

Wulfred lifted her so that her legs straddled his thigh. The friction was exquisite torture, and she clung to his shoulders, closing her eyes to the world around her.

"I don't suppose *you* will admit to being a problem? Not even once in your short life?"

"Romans are not problems; they are challenges," she murmured, seeking his mouth with hers.

He kissed her. She felt the wind against her skin, and Wulfred's hands against her body, and his tongue hot against hers. She was all sensation, and reason was buried. He was a Saxon and she had been taught to hate him, but all she wanted was to feel him, be with him, talk to him. Could this fire that burned with every touch be the reason that she saw him differently? He was no longer Saxon to her. He was Wulfred.

And what of Marcus? Her father was gone—she had released him to the eternal—but Marcus was here.

That name tortured her more than the blaze of Wulfred's touch. She had again forgotten Marcus in the heat of Wulfred's arms. Marcus was depending on her for his very life. The area swarmed with

Saxons, and Marcus waited in hiding, waited for her. And she stood on an open hilltop with her arms around a Saxon warrior. What had she become during the passage of this summer?

Pushing herself away from his kiss, she said, "I must go."

"You must not." He smiled, reaching for her again. Why was his grin so engaging, his manner so light, his lower lip so full? He had been easier to hate when he kept pushing her in the dirt.

"Because I have things to do, and so should you."

"Do what calls you. I will go with you."

"You don't have to do that!" How was she going to supply Marcus if Wulfred dogged her steps?

"But I will."

She walked down the hill, hoping to put some distance between them with every step. Of course, it didn't work; his stride far outpaced hers. Did he feel he had to protect her? Certainly he had cause, but if he stayed by her all day, she would never be able to meet her obligation to Marcus—an obligation rooted in love.

They reached the villa walls and walked into the courtyard, Ceolmund not far behind. She still had thought of no way to remove Wulfred from her side, until she saw Cenred's back outlined in the kitchen doorway. Inspiration hit.

"Wulfred, why don't you go to the baths? And take Ceolmund with you. I want to speak to Cenred privately."

Wulfred looked at her speculatively, seeming to measure her motives. She had told him the truth, and she let that shine from her eyes. She did want to speak with Cenred again about Dorcas . . . and Cenred would be so much easier to evade than either Ceolmund or Wulfred.

"I did not know you were so generous with your baths," Wulfred remarked, stroking his jaw.

"I am very generous where my nose is concerned."

"You will be in the kitchen?" So he had seen Cenred's back, too.

"That is where I am going," she said truthfully. The food for Marcus was in the kitchen.

"Then I will be in the baths, should you need me," he said, and he playfully pulled her hair in passing.

"There are Saxons enough to drown in. I won't need another," she called after him.

"There are Saxons enough to drown in," he repeated. "Stay in the kitchen." He didn't even look back as he said it. *Arrogant oaf.*

She entered the kitchen without giving in to the urge to watch him until he was lost to her sight. Cenred was there, as was Dorcas. Cenred was flirting outrageously. Dorcas was ignoring him, her earlier vulnerability buried. Melania watched, fascinated and a little mystified. Watching Cenred cringe, Melania saw that Dorcas clearly knew more of men than she did. *What mastery.*

"I would have been there, had I known, but I did not know," he explained pitifully. Stroking the length of her arm, he said, "You are too beautiful a woman to wander without an escort—"

Dorcas rapped his hand with a wooden spoon. "It was safe enough to walk from the triclinium to the kitchen before you Saxons came."

Cenred pulled his hand back and rubbed his knuckles. A nice red welt was developing. Melania smiled.

"These men have been long without a woman, and you, with your dark beauty . . . your smooth skin and sparkling eyes, have driven them wild with desire."

"Is that what happened to you?" Dorcas asked as she stirred the pot.

"I? Well, I . . . yes," Cenred scrambled, "you are so beautiful—"

"Because I am the only woman available."

"No! Because—"

"Because you traveled far and saw no one else."

"Dorcas! That is not what I said!"

"That is what I heard, didn't you, Melania?"

"You did say that your . . . friends couldn't control themselves enough to keep their hands off Dorcas because they hadn't lain with a woman in a while," Melania supplied happily, completely enjoying the green look that seemed to come over Cenred's face.

Cenred shot Melania a glance that clearly told her to close her interfering mouth and then gave all his attention to Dorcas.

"You are special to me, Dorcas. You know you are. I don't want anything to happen to you."

"Like rape?" She slammed her spoon on the table, just missing his fingers.

Claudia Dain

"It wouldn't be rape!" he burst out, defending his Saxon brothers instinctively.

"No? You think I'd be willing? As willing as I was with you?" Dorcas snapped, and then she smiled. "Perhaps I would." And she ran a light hand over her belly.

For the barest moment, Melania thought Cenred wanted to strike Dorcas. Or throw up.

"You'd better leave, Cenred," Melania offered. "Don't come back until you know the right words to say."

"Yes, Cenred, you run along back to your comrades," Dorcas called out breezily. "No need to worry about me. I won't be lonely." Her smile as she said it was pure wickedness, and Melania bit the pad of her thumb to keep from laughing out loud.

Cenred looked pleadingly at Dorcas once more before he walked out of the kitchen.

Melania studied Dorcas. She was a shrewd woman, and resilient. And she had been right about Wulfred being attracted to her. Dorcas seemed to have an unusual understanding of the male mind.

"Do you want to marry him?" Melania asked without preamble.

"Yes," Dorcas answered calmly, her playfulness gone, "but only if he asks. I think he wants me to ask him, to trap him into marriage by some female fit so that he can give in. I won't have him holding his reluctance over my head for the rest of my life."

"I think you're right. He's a proud man. Marriage was not on his mind when he came here."

320

"And it was on Wulfred's?" Dorcas laughed wryly. "No. I have my pride, too. And I have his child."

"I would think that, above all else, would sway him toward you, but I don't understand Saxon customs. They could feel very differently about children." Melania's hand crept to her own belly; she could very well be pregnant as well.

"They could," Dorcas agreed, "but I think it is unlikely. I pray so."

"I will pray, too," Melania said. "Your child will need a father."

Dorcas smiled and pointed to the doorway. Cenred's broad back and blond hair could be seen just beyond the threshold. It was obvious he was listening. And just as obvious that Dorcas would take full advantage of it.

"There are many Saxons," she said cheerily.

Both women laughed silently as Cenred cursed fluidly in Saxon.

Chapter Twenty-three

It had taken her the better part of the day, but she had done it. Now all that was left was to hide her bundle somewhere until she could get to it. At dawn tomorrow she would give it to Marcus.

It hadn't been simple. It had been much easier before Hensa had come; now her world seethed and swirled with Saxons. But since the ordeal in the triclinium and then the smaller confrontation on the rock, no one had bothered her. They hadn't been cordial, but she was far from wanting courtesy from filthy barbari.

Melania edged along the rear wall of the villa, near the furnace. The vegetation was closer to the house there and offered her some cover against curious eyes. She had wrapped her bundle of clothing and food in the folds of her palla, and with her arms around it, she melted into the woods. Brush snagged her stola and scratched her legs until she reached the deeper shadows of the forest. She cut through, aiming for the old apple orchard. She hadn't been there in years, but she had played in it often as a child and so was certain of finding the path.

How wild everything had become in the years since her childhood. This path had once been wide and clear all the way to the orchard; the orchard itself had been clear of tall grass and weeds, the trees pruned of crossing limbs once a year. The orchard was too far from the villa for that now, the servants too few.

Eventually she found it. She didn't dare step into the open upon reaching the orchard, so she tucked the bundle into a tight space between two rocks. One rock was covered with lichen and the other was deeply embedded with reflective crystals. She would find this spot again.

Preparing the bundle, hiding it, planning an escape; it was too reminiscent of her own attempt to flee the villa. Pray God, Marcus would be more successful than she had been. And pray God, she would know how to answer Marcus about the escape from Wulfred that he offered her.

Marcus wanted her with him. He loved her. He wanted her to be safe, and safety meant being as far away from the Saxons as possible. She could not argue against any of that; she had argued for it all of her life. She had sat at her father's feet and listened to him expound upon civilization's curse:

the Saxons. The legions would not have left Britannia if not for the need to fight the Saxons on the continent. Taxes would not be so high if not for the damage incurred by the Saxon raids. Travel would be possible if not for the danger of the Saxons. If not for the Saxons, it would be a perfect world, a world populated and controlled by Romans. Marcus shared the same beliefs, as had she—until Wulfred.

Wulfred had been made a slave of Rome when he fought to protect his own land. Rome had invaded his homeland, as Rome had once invaded Britannia, changing her, renaming her. It had been hundreds of years ago, but still, it was true. Rome had a history of enlarging itself and, in the process, conquering. Perhaps she could understand Wulfred's rage; she could certainly understand his need for vengeance, since she shared it. Or she had.

Wulfred had taken her to wife by Saxon custom. Wulfred protected her. Wulfred reminded her of the binding force of a vow and of honor, be it Roman or Saxon. She could find no argument against honor.

Marcus was what she had known, the world as it had been.

Wulfred and the world he had brought with him were what she knew now.

But what did she want to know?

The weight of her honor pressed against her, confusing her.

She knew Wulfred was relying on that honor and on the strength of her vow.

What was Marcus relying on?

Her love.

Melania turned away from the orchard, wishing she could turn as easily away from her thoughts. She had until the dawn to decide what she would do, which path she would walk and with whom. She would take that time, needing every moment of it.

She returned to the villa and went to her chamber. The day was mostly past, the roar from the triclinium had quieted; she wanted to be alone. She had much to consider.

Wulfred awaited her.

She did not want to see Wulfred. She was quite sure her feelings were visible on her face.

"Why are you here?"

He raised his eyebrows and grinned somewhat comically.

She did not smile in return; it was his smiles that confused her the most.

"Why aren't you with the others, in the triclinium?"

"Because I have a wife," he said, crossing his arms over his chest, dependably naked, and grinning at her. Or was it a leer?

Melania fidgeted nervously. That grin of his. . . . She had felt more comfortable with his open hatred than with . . . this.

"You're not afraid of a knife at your throat?"

"Am I not safe with you?" he countered.

"Am I not still Roman?" she practically hissed, reminding them both.

"You are my wife," he stated, typically unmoved by her anger.

"You married me to hurt me," she reminded.

"I have said so, and openly . . . however . . ." He paused and she felt her triumphant expression falter. "I also know that marriage is for life." He looked as awkwardly confused as she felt.

"Are you saying that there was some other reason for your manipulating me into a marriage ceremony? Something other than blind hatred?"

"Melania," he said softly, "women, Saxon wives, are honored. They are held in honor by their husbands and respected by the community. Saxon daughters are able to inherit. There is no divorce."

No divorce. In Rome divorce was rampant, and for almost any reason, or for no reason at all.

Of course, that was not true for Christians, but it disturbed her that the Saxons would have marriage practices closer to the Christian ideal than the Romans did. She was hardly eager to admit that to him; in fact, she silently cursed him for giving her yet another point of confusion.

"That's barbaric," she mumbled. "No divorce. Only a barbarian would conceive of such a thing. A marriage is a contract, and any contract can be broken. Many things could happen. . . ."

"Nothing will happen."

But things could. Jesus the Christ had even allowed divorce on the occasion of adultery. True, the world of Rome took a broader view of the issue, but even a follower of the Christ had a path of escape from marriage.

"What of adultery? Is there no divorce even for adultery?" she asked, somewhat panicked. How was she to get out of this barbarian marriage if there was no divorce?

"Nothing will happen," he repeated. He had not answered her question, she noticed.

"So says the barbarian," she said.

Wulfred smiled and walked toward her, backing her into a corner of the room. The light was just a golden memory now and the first few stars were out. She hadn't even eaten yet. Wulfred didn't look as if he cared.

Placing his hands on the wall and trapping her in the cage of his body, Wulfred grinned. It was definitely a leer.

"You can trust me to be a barbarian in certain ways, always."

"I don't need you to tell me that, Saxon oaf," she said. She had meant her words to be more tart, but the correct tone was difficult to achieve when he was brushing his lips against her throat.

"Probably not," he said against the soft skin of her neck, "but don't you want to know how and in what ways?"

"Absolutely not." Her denial had come out as a whisper and sounded almost seductive. Shameful.

"I will tell you anyway," he said as his lips moved to the curve of her breast. Even through the cloth she felt the burn. "Every night you will meet the barbarian. You will meet him on your back." Her stomach dropped to her knees and rolled helplessly. "He will be rapacious, demanding, insatiable, like all barbarians."

He kissed her nipple through the fabric, and the flame of his tongue lit her like an autumn fire. She threaded her hands into his hair and held him there, willing him to push aside the cloth, unwilling to degrade herself by asking that he do it.

"And when the barbarian comes through the door, what does a Saxon woman do?" she asked. She had to get his mouth off her. He couldn't win her desire this easily.

Wulfred lifted his head, his eyes blue and flaming, and kissed the tip of her nose. "She submits to him."

Melania pulled his head back by her grip on his hair and smiled triumphantly into his face. "And there is the difference between Saxons and Romans. A Saxon woman would submit. I will enjoy!" And she brought his mouth down to melt against hers.

She awoke before dawn and watched Wulfred in the weak light of morning. His body lay sprawled on the couch, his limbs long and straight and corded with muscle now relaxed in sleep. His head was thrown back, his long throat exposed, and one muscular arm supported his head as a pillow. He was naked and he was beautiful.

He was a great mystery to her.

He was gentle and he was a warrior. He could be funny when he was not being stern. He came from a barbaric society that had more finesse in its structure than she would ever have imagined. He had defended her against his own. He had married her and he believed it was for life.

But what did she believe?

She believed that she was very, very confused.

And Marcus waited.

There was no confusion in that; Marcus waited and she would go to him. He deserved at least that from her. He deserved so much more.

Melania left Wulfred sleeping in her chamber. The triclinium was quiet, except for the sound of sporadic snoring. She went to the stable and collected Optio, who, for the first time, gave her no trouble other than to spit on her palla. Optio she would give to Marcus. Marcus had need of a horse. No one saw her and no one followed her; she left freely and went straight to the apple orchard thinking not of the days of her father, but of today. Today the legions were gone. Today Saxons camped in her villa. Today she had left a Saxon warrior, a husband, asleep on her couch. And tomorrow?

The sun had risen above the horizon when she reached her destination. Marcus waited for her, tall and straight and proud. She knew, in that moment of first eye contact, that he would not beg for her to come, and her own sudden sense of relief shamed her.

Melania tied Optio to the worn fence of the orchard and retrieved the bag from between the two rocks. She carried it to Marcus as if in ritual, and it was a ritual of sorts. They both knew that.

"Will you come?" he asked quietly.

Claudia Dain

Her throat closed around sudden tears and she could only shake her head no.

"I knew." He smiled sadly. "It was in my heart that you would stay, though I cannot fathom it. Oh, Melania," he whispered, and took her in his arms. "How can I leave you? I don't care about the villa," he whispered fiercely, holding her tightly against him, "and I care more for you than for revenge. What holds you here?"

"It is not the villa that holds me, and it is not revenge," she answered, putting into words for Marcus what she had struggled to understand for herself. Saying it made it clear, and she gained strength with each word. "It is the Saxon. I . . . belong to him in a way I can't explain."

"I can explain it," he said roughly, without releasing her from his embrace.

"Oh, Marcus!" she flared, backing away from him so that she could stare into his eyes. "You understand nothing and condemn everything! How can you explain it when I cannot? Do you think I would ever have planned such a moment as this if I were given the authority to plot my own destiny?"

"Melania"—he smiled, pulling her back against him—"all fire and spark. Tell me, are you as fiery with your Saxon?"

"I am." There was defiant pride in her answer.

"Does he object?"

Now Melania smiled. "He hasn't yet."

"He must be an unusual man."

All she knew was that Wulfred accepted her, without censure or disappointment. What more was there? Had her father ever given her as much? She could not answer Marcus for her silent tears.

They rocked in gentle rhythm, arms around each other, in as much peace as there could be in such a moment of sorrow.

"His name?"

"Wulfred," she said.

"Wulfred," he repeated. "I will remember it."

"And what of you? What of the west? Will you go there?" She was desperate to keep some part of him in her present; he was going into a future she could not see and would not share.

"You have heard of Artorius, who is gathering men to fight. He is now in Segontium, where the Saxon threat is the least. Artos, as he is called, the bear cub, is forming a cohort of companions to fight against the barbari darkness."

"You will fight." She looked up at him, so dark and straight in the weak light.

"Fight the Saxons?" He smiled grimly. "Yes, I must. I will not stand idle while a civilization is eaten by wolves. It is my life I fight for, Melania." He looked down at her, his eyes gentle for a moment. "But I will not forget the name Wulfred. I will not seek to fight the man you love."

"I don't love him!" she protested, her color rising to match her outrage.

"You don't love him"—he nodded, smiling— "yet you stay with him, in his world, leaving your own. Of course, Melania."

"You don't understand," she mumbled, irritated and uncomfortable.

"Perhaps not," he said easily. "Lately there is little that I do understand."

"Nor I," she whispered, and buried her face against the fine wool of his tunic.

"What will you tell me of Hensa and what he plans?" he asked over the top of her dark head.

Melania stopped rocking within the circle of his arms.

"I know nothing of his plans." It was the truth, fortunately.

Marcus rubbed his hands up and down her back, soothing her, sedating her. "And his men? You must know their number since they abide with you. How great is his force?"

Melania stepped away from him, out of the warm safety of his arms, to stare him in the face. It was the largest step she had ever taken and she knew it. This was the point on which rested her honor. Surprising, but now that it had come, the moment was almost effortless, the way sharply clear.

"He leads Wulfred, Marcus."

"He leads many, all enemies of Rome."

How calmly they faced each other, how clearly they understood the meaning of this confrontation. A path that had been one, shared by them in love, was diverging.

"He is my husband."

"He is a Saxon."

Each sentence was a stone thrown at a love that was bruised with each toss, but they stood tall against the pain and the loss, their features calm and resolute. They were Roman, the two of them.

"He is my husband, Marcus," she repeated. "I will not betray him."

"He has betrayed you, Melania," he urged, his voice becoming urgent. "He has not protected the Romans from the Picts, as he swore to do."

Melania waited for the way to become cloudy and confused, but it did not. The path of honor was clear. She had learned much in her summer of the Saxons.

"He did not turn from his own honor, Marcus, which is what you are asking of me."

"How is this of honor? This is of love, our love, Melania."

It was true that the bond they shared was of love, a love so sure and strong that she did not doubt it, not even now. But she had a bond with Wulfred, too, and that bond had been forged daily on the anvil of honor with the hammer of truth. That bond had come to mean much to her somewhere during the passage of days spent in heated battle with him.

"What you ask of me," she whispered, gazing into his dark eyes, "he would not ask of me. Wulfred would not ask me to betray my own honor on any point."

Marcus opened his mouth to argue, and she knew what he would say. He would speak again of love, but she had the answer to that as well.

"Marcus"—she smiled tremulously—"he would not ask me to betray you."

It was the truth. He could read it in her eyes, and it put an end to their battle. They stood apart, in all ways separated, truly, for the first time. Only their love for each other remained, and it had been sorely bruised in this contest. But it was without condemnation that he looked at her, and she felt her eyes fill with tears at the loss she read on his face.

"You will be safe?" he asked, his voice hoarse with unshed tears.

She thought of Wulfred, his strength and defense of her against even his friends.

"I will be safe; give no thought to that. But you must travel west, as far west as there is to go. Go to a place where there are no Saxons. Go to a place of peace."

"I don't think there is any peace left on this earth, Melania. There is war everywhere."

"Not for you," she said with the force of prophecy. "You will find your place. And you will find peace. But it is not here."

"No," he murmured, kissing her forehead, "it is not here."

The dawn brightened into a misty morning. The birds were active and the ground moist; it was a good day for riding. And he had so very far to go.

"I will never forget you, Marcus," she cried softly. "I will love you always. Know that. Know that," she repeated desperately. She had so little to give him. "I love you," she whispered on a sob.

Marcus squeezed her once more and then picked up the bundle and walked away, leading Optio. Walked away from Melania. Walked away from the life he had known and the life he should have had, and walked toward the unknown and unfamiliar.

To Burn

Melania watched him until he was lost in the mist. He did not look back. She thought him wise not to do so. Turning, the mist cool against her wet cheeks, she looked up into the twisted branches of an old apple tree. It would produce no more. There was no more life in its branches; the energy had been leached out of it through season upon season. Feeling like an old woman, Melania walked with a heavy step back down to the villa.

Chapter Twenty-four

She didn't hurry. Each step carried them farther apart, and she found herself dreading each step. She would never see Marcus again; life was too uncertain and the distances too far in the hazardous world the Saxons had invented for them. She had just said good-bye to someone she had loved longer than memory, and she would never see him again.

Her heart struggled to beat.

Her eyes wept without permission.

Her mind told her with each breath that she had done the right thing. Made the right choice.

But her heart wept tears of blood, regardless.

As slowly as she moved, the villa appeared before her anyway. Home. She lived in a home full of strangers. Except for Wulfred; Wulfred she trusted in the way she trusted that a boat would float and that wood would burn.

He waited for her in the courtyard, looking somewhat grim. In fact, he wore much the same expression as when she had first seen him, peering down at her lying on the floor of the library, gasping for cool air. He could not be irritated because she had arisen and left their chamber before he did; he had done the same to her the day before. And she had not been pleased. Still, she had certainly not looked as solemn and forbidding as he did now.

"You return," he said, glaring down at her.

"Of course."

He nodded, taking her by the arm and leading her to the protection of the portico. It had begun to mist and the droplets hung heavily in the air before descending to quietly wet the ground.

"Did you doubt it?" she asked.

"Should I?" he said swiftly, leading her to the antechamber of the library.

The antechamber, where the Chi-Rho symbol of Christ had been painstakingly pieced into the tile floor in the time of her grandfather, was used as her place of worship. It was a closet in which to withdraw and seek the will of God. She prayed there daily, needing the solace of knowing that God was still at work in the world more with each day the Saxons stayed. What reason would Wulfred have to drag her there now? Did he want to pray with her? It seemed hardly likely.

Theras stood in the small room. Waiting? Dorcas

and Ceolmund were suddenly at her back. Melania turned to give Dorcas a searching glance, was met with an emotion-filled stare that she could not decipher, and turned again to Theras, her eyes full of questions.

"Shall we join in prayer together?" she said to no one and everyone. "I would enjoy the companionship, but didn't think you especially pious, Wulfred. Have you developed an interest in the one true God since residing among the civilized saved?"

Wulfred hardly spared her a glance, the oaf, but said to Theras, "Is anything else required?"

"Just her freely given vow before witnesses."

"Then all rests on you, Melania," Wulfred said, turning to give her his attention.

"I'm not surprised, but what, exactly, do you need from me?"

"Your vow," he said, his blue eyes piercing and strangely hot. "Your freely given pledge to be my wife."

She could only stare in shock. And horror.

"I have asked Theras," he continued, ignoring her insulting response, "about the marriage ritual for Romans. He told me that you are a follower of Jesus the Christ. I am prepared to partake of any ceremony that would please you."

How carefully he said the words. How carefully had he chosen them? He knew, he had to know, that a ceremony that invoked the presence and the power of the Christ would bind her to him securely. Of course he knew. He was no fool. His rituals might not bind her; hers would.

To Burn

Still, his motives could have been more generous than she'd suspected initially. He could just want her to have a ceremony that would have meaning for her, since he had all but tricked her into a Saxon marriage. Why prevaricate? He had most definitely tricked her into marriage. It was thoughtful of him to arrange for a marriage ceremony that would conform to her own beliefs.

Thoughtful? How stupidly sentimental she was becoming; he was plainly no fool. It would be best to look away from those unnatural and melting eyes while she thought this through.

If she spoke her vow, in Christus, then she would be bound by her own word to be a true wife to him.

He knew that.

Melania looked at Theras for some hint of his feelings on this turn of events. Theras's face was carefully blank. As it should be. This was her decision, and she would be the one who had to live with it.

Marcus would not share in this; he would be unaffected. She need not consider him. Even now he moved relentlessly west, away from her.

Marcus was gone. Permanently.

Had she not already decided where her future lay?

Melania looked again at Wulfred. He had said nothing to rush her or sway her. He had not attempted to bully her, though little good it would have done him. He understood that her answer would be her own and that she would hold to it. He understood much about her.

339

Claudia Dain

He understood much.

He accepted much.

She had told Marcus truly when she had said that Wulfred had never scolded her for her temper or her passion or her rages of feeling. It was the first time in her life any man had treated her so. Her father, for all that she loved him, had not been so tolerant of her volatility, and she had felt a buried sense of failure that she could not be more "Roman" in her deportment. She felt no such failure with Wulfred. In Wulfred's eyes, she could not possibly be more Roman than she was.

He stood formidable and silent and huge. He was a man who could force her to anything, or so he claimed, but he was not forcing her to do this. There was a freedom in her relationship with him that she had experienced with no one else, not even with Marcus.

Marcus had tried to bully her. Marcus, more often, had tried to gently manipulate her. Marcus had even lost his temper with her. Not so Wulfred. Wulfred, the savage barbarian, never lost control.

With him she could be exactly who she was. What greater freedom was there?

Facing him, the Chi-Rho beneath her feet, she took one large golden hand in hers.

"I will be bound to you as wife and I will serve you truly until my death. Or until I am cast off."

Wulfred did not smile; had he been so certain of her decision? *Oaf.* He took her hand in his, mimicking her, and said, "A Roman may abandon a wife when he tires of her, but a Saxon takes a wife for

340

life. I will not cast you off, Melania." The planes of his face were hard in the subtle light of the room but his eyes burned hot. She knew the look of him and was not afraid. "I will protect you from harm and provide for your needs."

He looked at Theras, silently asking if there was more to this ceremony of Christ.

Theras asked, "Will you, Melania, respect your husband?"

Melania looked up into Wulfred's hard warrior's face, her hand in his. He was an ox of a man: big and powerful and flatly magnificent. And, though she would lick fire before admitting it to him, he was wondrously handsome. She had never seen anyone like him in all her life; even the Saxons who now roamed her home could not challenge him. But she was not such a fool to bind herself to a face. No, against all she had ever been told, this Saxon had a mind. A keen and observant mind that was capable of intelligent deduction and cool reasoning. He also had remarkable control of his temper. He was not the unthinking brute she had believed him to be, though there was no reason to tell him of her change of attitude. He was arrogant enough already.

"I do respect him," she said, "and I will."

For once, she thought she saw surprise on his face, but he wiped it clean so soon that she was not certain.

"Will you, Wulfred," Theras continued, "love your wife?"

Wulfred looked down at Melania, studying her,

his face still while his eyes were full of turmoil. They had never spoken of love. It was hatred and a desire for revenge that they shared, not love. It had never been love. He was a man who spoke what was in his heart and was steadfast in his vows; if he loved her, he would have spoken of it. Now he was called to speak a vow of love to her, and she did not know what he would say. Her own heart trembled as she watched his eyes, afraid of what he would say. Afraid of what he could not, in honesty, say.

"Yes," he said, his voice a low rumble, "I will love her."

"Then you are one, in the eyes of the Christ and the Father and the Spirit," Theras pronounced solemnly. "May God bless you in your oneness."

Melania felt Wulfred's words roll through her as her mind tried to cling to his words. It was hopeless. She knew only stunned shock; her mind could not grasp the meaning behind his words. He had vowed to love her. Was it possible? Could all the turbulence and the anger they had shared have led them to love? She looked up at him, her eyes wide and measuring, trying to read him as she read the scrolls in her father's library. But he was not to be read. He was Saxon and illiterate; she could not read an empty page.

For the first time that day, Wulfred smiled fully, his teeth white and gleaming. She pushed away the hot brand his words had touched upon her heart and smiled at him in answer. Later she would ponder his vow of love.

"You should smile, Saxon," she said, letting her hand rest in his, "for you have joined your life to mine today."

"I joined my life to yours by Saxon ritual, little snake," he answered, his smile looking suddenly sharp. "I smile because, by your own will and by your own vow, you have joined your life to mine." He released her hand and gripped her hard by her shoulders, casting off his smile in the doing. "Now," he said. "Who had his arms around you in the orchard this dawn?"

Chapter Twenty-five

He could see the confusion in her eyes and gloated in it. So she believed in the mewlings of her little ceremony and believed that he wanted to please her. *Arrogant Roman*. He had tricked her for a second time into giving her vow. *Stupidly arrogant, ridiculously proud woman. Roman woman.* How could he have forgotten that she was Roman and therefore deceitful? Hensa was right: he had been a fool to bind himself by Saxon law to a Roman. She was the enemy, as she always had been.

"You use trickery and deceit, again, to win your way, Saxon," she blazed, her eyes points of fiery light. "Is this the way of honor?"

"This from the woman who stuck a finger down her throat to lose a meal and rob her body of strength?" he struck back, releasing her from his hold. If he touched her again, he would kill her for her deceit. And for the arms she had let embrace her. Roman arms. "Do not speak to me of deceit, Roman, unless you wish to instruct me."

Yes, she had deceived him. It galled him to admit it even to himself. She was soft and hot in his arms, and he had believed her passion to be for him alone; until he had seen her in the arms of a Roman warrior, for a man of such bearing could be nothing else. She had seduced him with her heat so that she could return to the arms of her Roman lover. And he had even begun to admire her, she with her rigid pride and unshakable honor. What honor in a woman who runs to a lover? What pride in selling her body to the enemy so that she could protect the cowardly Roman who hid behind her curves?

No pride and no honor. She was a Roman and she was . . . hideous. He looked down at her, ignoring the black fall of her hair and the vivid sparkle of her golden eyes and the delicate and proud line of her jaw. . . . Yes, he could ignore it all. But he had not been able to ignore her this morning. This morning he had felt her eyes scouring him even in his sleep and he had awakened with his manhood as hard as a fist. Thinking she went to empty her bladder, he had waited. When the wait grew tedious, he had become suspicious. With suspicion he had summoned Cuthred and Cenred and the three of them had tracked her.

Wulfred swallowed the bile that rose in his throat at thinking of how he had worried over her. He had thought her waylaid by Hensa's men. He had thought her defenseless and in need of a protector, and he had flayed himself with more vigor than any Roman had for leaving her alone and unprotected in a house full of Saxons seeking an enemy to best. And when his heart had begun to tear itself from his breast in anguish over her, he had seen her clutching the Roman to her bosom with all the fervor of a lover. Had seen her hold him to her in tearful parting. Had seen her give him Optio and watch with love-inspired tears as he walked away from her. Then he had known what it was she had done to him. All the love that was in her, she had given to the Roman warrior. Of course, she had deceived him; she was a Roman and they knew only the path to their own ends. But she had also tricked him into believing that there was something more than hatred between them—something of laughter and respect and trust.

Trust. With a Roman. He had been the worst sort of fool. He had been the imbecile she named him. But no longer.

"Then let us speak of pride, Saxon fool," she taunted.

"Let us," he countered. "What pride in sneaking off from a husband's bed—"

"It is my bed!"

"To meet another man! Is this the value you place on a vow? But I forget; you are Roman."

"You may have forgotten it, but I have not. I will not!"

"Certainly you will also not forget the man, the Roman, whom you held against you so passionately. And, speaking from experience, I am certain he will not have forgotten you. Cuthred and Cenred are pursuing him. When they bring him to me, you will have the privilege of watching him die. That is also something I pray to my gods you will not forget."

"You rant in your blundering Saxon way and I hear but one thing," she choked out, her rage a living heat. "You trusted me and found your trust betrayed. Why, Saxon?" she smiled with sharp cruelty. "I have never told you I feel anything for you other than blind hatred. Did you expect devotion? Loyalty?"

"Passion?" He smirked.

"Hatred is a passion. And I am very passionate where you are concerned."

How she turned everything, every moment between them, into a twisted distortion of what he had believed. She truly was a most adept deceiver.

"You have just sworn, by your own god, to respect me. Have you no passion for your faith?"

"I do," she said. "And I did not lie in my vow. I do respect you, for your strength and your leadership. My vows are genuine, unlike yours."

Never had he seen her so angry, and he had seen her angry often. He understood enough of her, or thought he had, to see that she used her anger as a shield. Anger was her response to fear, to danger, to sadness, to embarrassment . . . to love? No, she did not love. Not him. Did she fear? If she did, it was fear for her lover that had her blazing so hot and so high.

The small antechamber was now crowded with people, his people, and they crowded around his little Roman wife with glowing animosity. They but awaited his word to kill her. They would continue to wait. He would not kill her until he had the man she loved killed before her eyes. That man would die, because Wulfred would not share the smallest part of Melania with anyone; she was his. She had been his from the beginning.

Cuthred and Cenred elbowed their way into the room until they stood by his side. They were covered in sweat and bits of grass and broken leaves; they had chased their man far. Why did they come in alone?

"Wulfred"—Cenred breathed hard—"he escaped us. Your pardon."

"How is this possible?" Wulfred said furiously.

"He was horsed," Cuthred answered.

All eyes turned to Melania in blatant condemnation.

"It was *my* horse!" she shouted against their hate.

"Can you track him?" Wulfred said, ignoring his wife. At Cuthred's nod, Wulfred said, "Take what you need and go. Do not return without this man. Do not kill him. That is my pleasure."

"You take pleasure in killing a man who has left the spoils of battle to you? You would kill a man for leaving you to your victory and seeking a life for himself elsewhere?" she screamed, her hands curved like claws. Or fangs.

"I will kill him and take great pleasure in it for

lying with my wife. Unlike Romans, Saxons do not turn a blind eye to adultery," Wulfred said.

Melania pulled herself up to her full, petite height; such grandeur in one so small and delicate. She looked like a snake about to strike, and she all but spat her next words.

"I don't know what barbarities you practice in your Saxon hovels, but here, within the confines of Rome, a woman does not commit adultery with her brother!"

Chapter Twenty-six

He had not expected it, but the instant she said it, everything made sense. And while Melania could deceive, she had never lied outright. It would have made his life more pleasant if she did.

Looking at Theras, Wulfred asked, "Is this true?"

Theras nodded and said simply, "She has a brother."

"My word is not good enough for you, Saxon dog!" she screamed, the cords in her neck standing out in her rage. "You make me your wife, twice, and you take my word for nothing? A servant has more credibility than I? Listen carefully, Saxon pig, listen carefully so that you will hear every word, and I vow that every word is the truth." Pausing until the room grew still, she shouted, *"I hate you!"* Breathing deeply, she said more softly, "You swore to love me, and I knew it for a lie, but I thought that you trusted me. I have never done you an injury from the shadows, Saxon. I fought you openly. I did not promise to protect you while sharpening my knife. I did not vow to provide while planning your death." She paused, eyeing him coldly. It was the first cold rage he had seen in her, and it burned him more fiercely for the difference. Almost quietly, she said, "I have said that I respected you, but I see now your greatest strength is in deceit. You are without honor." There was a collective gasp from all lips, but not from his. He would take all she had to throw at him and not buckle beneath her wrath. She deserved to give vent to this rage. He deserved this abuse. "I do not respect you, Wulfred."

It was the first time she had said his name.

Silence, heavy and black, followed her indictment. None could argue against what she said; Wulfred had not trusted her when she had been worthy of his trust. She had spoken no lie.

But Wulfred knew that she had lied, though without realizing it. She said he did not love her. That was a lie. Now, when the breach between them was wider than it had ever been, he knew it for a lie.

Now, when he had broken whatever trust had been built between them, he knew it. Now, as she stood in stony and righteous distance, he saw what she had become to him. She was honor when honor was defeat and not praise. She was strength when strength was starved and bloody. She was truth when truth meant death. She was all he'd ever valued in life and she stood before him, as unbowed and proud as always, knowing no other way to be, scorning all other paths. Scorning him.

Why was it now that he knew he loved her?

There was the sound of angry voices and then a voice of command outside the antechamber. Bodies heaved as the newcomers pushed into the center of the tiny room, obliterating the Chi-Rho under their feet. Hensa appeared, dragging a man with him— a man with red hair and silver bracelets.

"Strange place for a meeting," Hensa remarked wryly. "My man, Sigred, had his interest stirred by the Roman woman—"

Wulfred pulled forth his knife and growled, preparing to leap upon his instant adversary.

"No"—Hensa held his arm—"not over a woman. Not over a Roman. He followed her and observed her having a covert conversation with a Roman warrior." Hensa eyed Melania with keen and malicious interest.

Wulfred looked down at Melania for just a moment as she stood in rigid fury to hide her fear. Whatever was charged against Melania, whatever was said, he knew where he would place his trust. He would not fail again.

"Sigred reports—"

"Cannot Sigred speak?" Wulfred interrupted.

Sigred smiled and said easily, "Of course, Wulfred. The Roman asked her about Hensa and about his plans for this rain-soaked land. He was one of Arthur's men and spoke of going west to join him in their battles against us. He would bring whatever information she gave him to Arthur and his cohort. Why would he ask her? Unless she is a spy."

Wulfred did not answer, but asked a question of his own. Like Sigred, his manner was easy—as easy as a swinging blade.

"And what was my wife's answer to these questions?"

Sigred shrugged. "I could not hear it."

Melania jerked forward in angry spasm, crying out, "Liar!" in hoarse Latin.

Wulfred pulled her back by the arm and held her firmly against his side. He would protect her even if she fought him every step, as was her way.

"You must be the only man alive"—he smiled, looking out across the men who had gathered for this sudden trial—"who cannot hear a response made by Melania."

He was rewarded by chuckles and outright guffaws from many of the men, certainly from his own. Hensa had not laughed. Nor had Sigred. It would be a pure pleasure to see to it that Sigred never laughed again.

"Who was the man?" Hensa asked, looking at both Melania and Wulfred. "Her . . . behavior with him was blatantly compromising, no matter what she did or did not say."

So. They would have Melania for any reason if treason could not be proved. Wulfred understood the game, praying to all his gods that Melania did not.

"He was . . . is her brother," he said calmly, projecting confidence with his very ease.

Hensa looked unmoved by that testimony. "Loyalty to her own blood would run strong, especially in a woman of such passion. And especially as she makes her hatred of Saxons no secret."

"You have said it," Wulfred said. "Nothing of this woman, my wife, is done in secret."

"Then her hatred is true," Hensa concluded.

Wulfred would continue no longer on this rabbit chase; Melania would not be condemned or saved because of her temperament.

"Is Melania being accused?" he asked outright.

It was that one question that gave Hensa pause. To make an accusation was a serious matter, never done lightly and never in haste. And Hensa was leader, an example; would his hate rule him, or would his head?

"If the man was her brother, the charge of adultery is invalid." Hensa paused, weighing the evidence. "But the charge of treason stands."

Wulfred did not hesitate. Melania was his. She had his trust and his love, though she did not know it.

"I stand as proof," he declared, his voice ringing against the walls of the tiled room. "Melania would not betray me, even to blood kin. This woman knows only the path of honor, no matter what trouble it brings her. If she betrayed me, her pride would demand that she proclaim it to my face. She has freely given her vow to be my wife, and Melania of the Romans would never betray her husband."

Wulfred looked out over them all, his eyes meeting without hesitation those of his brothers in arms. His hand was still upon her arm, his touch as solid as a tether and as gentle as goose down. He claimed her by his touch and by his word. "Her word is true. By her own vow she has taken a Saxon for a husband. Melania would not betray me. To anyone. I stand as proof to all that I have said."

Without pause his comitatus rose like a tide to cover rocks of destruction. Their voices rang out, as loudly as Wulfred's had done, proclaiming her innocence on the strength of their own honor. Melania would not stand alone against Hensa's condemnation.

"I stand as oath-helper," Cynric said firmly, standing to Wulfred's left. "What Wulfred says is true. She would not betray him."

"I stand as oath-helper," said Balduff. "Melania is true to her husband."

"I stand as oath-helper and declare that Melania is a loyal wife to her Saxon husband," declared Cenred.

"I stand as oath-helper," said Cuthred. "She would not fight against her husband from the darkness."

Ceolmund, who stood at Melania's back, shielding her from the hatred she could not see, said simply, "I stand as oath-helper. Wulfred knows the heart of his wife."

Melania felt the sting of hot tears behind her eyes. She would not let them fall and so disgrace herself or the husband who defended her so staunchly. His comitatus defended her; publicly and formally, they defended her. Why? When had this mob of hairy, naked men become her allies? Or were they more than allies? Friends? No, that could not be. Why had Wulfred defended her? Did he not hate and distrust her as she hated and distrusted him?

And she did hate him. She hated the man who stood so strong at her side, holding her hand protectively in his. She hated the man who had twice tricked her into marriage. She hated that he had distrusted her. She hated him so much that tears fled from behind her eyes, where they belonged, to flood her vision as she looked up at him. Impossible man to confuse everything this way. He had faced down his leader on her behalf. He had distanced himself from his people to stand in defense of her. *Oaf.* She would never forgive him for putting himself in such a precarious position. Could she ever forgive herself for being the cause?

"It is not your oath that must be given," Hensa said, clearly surprised by the support she had among his own. "It is Melania's, and she cannot be trusted because she is not one of us."

"She is my wife. I take responsibility for her actions."

"You knew she met with her Roman brother?" Hensa prodded, looking for a weakness and finding it.

"No," Wulfred answered truthfully, his expression almost pained.

What was coming? What was he protecting her from?

"Then . . ." Hensa drawled, clearly reaching some sort of conclusion.

"Then"—Wulfred took the initiative—"I propose an ordeal to settle the question."

The room almost flew away with the buzz of voices that his declaration inspired. Cynric clasped Wulfred on the shoulder, his own eyes filling with tears, and whispered warnings into his ear. Cuthred banged his seax against his shield and coughed roughly to hide his emotion. Balduff shook his head and looked down at his feet before looking up at her with an expression of melancholy. Ceolmund, behind her, laid a gentle hand on her shoulder in a comforting embrace. The tension was suffocating, yet she did not understand the cause.

Hensa eyed them both, his gaze long on Wulfred standing so protectively beside his wife. An ordeal . . . it was the way, yet he had not thought Wulfred so attached to his little Roman wife.

"An ordeal it shall be."

With that, the room dissolved of people. Melania and Wulfred were left alone in the antechamber, the Chi-Rho of the Christ appearing almost miraculously beneath their feet. The silence in that small room was frightening.

Wulfred still held her hand. She jerked it out of his grasp, angry because she wanted to throw herself into his arms and weep.

"What, under all of heaven, is an ordeal and why are you engaging in one? I know it must be some monstrous pagan ceremony designed to pacify your pathetic, pretend gods, but why is everyone so set on having one now? And what has this to do with the charge of treason against me?"

She was frightened; she could admit it, but she would not show it. Not now, not when it felt that the edge of the world was rushing toward her. She certainly would not show Wulfred her fear.

"There is nothing for you to fear," he began calmly.

"Oaf! Have I said that I am afraid? You will never hear such from me! I fear nothing you Saxons can devise, so just get on with your pathetic explanation of this barbaric Saxon ritual." His studied calm escalated her fear like wind fanning a fire.

"Your word, your honor, has been questioned. I will now prove you innocent of wrongdoing."

"Am I supposed to care that some filthy Saxons question my word? And do I need you to take care of me? I can well take care of myself, you insignificant barbari. . . ."

It would have been more convincing if she could have stopped those awful tears from falling.

"I took a vow"—he smiled gently, teasing her— "as you may remember?" He tugged the ends of her hair, urging her into the solace of his embrace. "It was to protect you. It is a vow I intend to keep."

"I remember," she grumbled, brushing her hands hard against her cheeks. "You don't need to prove anything to me."

"Don't I?" he all but whispered, then added

hoarsely, "Perhaps not, but I need to prove something to them."

The tension swirled all around them like the licking flames of a fire; she could feel it, and wondered that Wulfred could stand so quietly in the roar of such swirling heat. Something terrible was going to happen. This "ordeal" was some sort of horrible Saxon custom that would hurt Wulfred. She thought of his scars and shuddered. Wulfred must never be hurt again.

"Let me do it," she said, her voice rough with tears. "Let me do whatever it is."

"No, it is my place," he said, holding out his arms, inviting her to enter into that safe place near his heart.

She could not. She was too afraid. She had never known such soaring fear. And it was for Wulfred, not for herself.

"I think even your Christ would agree, Melania."

"Now you bring my own God against me?"

"I do what I can." He smiled softly, his blue eyes melting in their intensity. "You are less than cooperative, as I have said."

It was the truth; she had caused him little except trouble, as had been her purpose. Somehow, over the course of the summer, things had changed. Or maybe it was that she had changed. She no longer was as certain of the truth; the truths her father had taught her were insufficient to the times. The lessons she had learned, or, more accurately, the lessons she had been taught in childhood, were like smoke trails in the sky: thin, ragged, disintegrating.

Wulfred was solid, immovable, and she found reassurance in his unflagging strength. It no longer mattered that Wulfred was Saxon and she was Roman. Only Wulfred mattered.

Peace, Melanius.

"It has never seemed to stop you," she said with tearful wryness.

"Nothing stops me, Melania. Especially concerning you," he said softly.

Cynric came upon them then, his face as somber as Melania was sure hers was terrified. Never had she known such nameless panic; not even the attack of the Saxons had rendered her so enfeebled, because then she had known something of what was coming. Now all she knew was the roar of panic and the blinding blaze of imminent danger. And the danger was for Wulfred.

"All is ready, Wulfred," Cynric said. "They await."

They await.

Wulfred took one deep breath and then led them out of the antechamber, Melania's hand firmly in his. The Saxons, all of them, had formed two rows down the length of her courtyard. They stood with weapons out and shields up, and they stood staring at Wulfred. Releasing her hand, Wulfred walked to the end of the line, his spine stiff and his head high, looking each man in the eye, letting them measure his confidence in his wife and her honor.

Melania studied the scene, looking for the cause of her tumbling panic. She found it at the end of the row. There, resting quietly in a hot fire, was a length of iron, the end of which was beginning to glow red.

It was when Wulfred began to walk toward the glowing iron that she began to scream.

"No!" She ran forward and pulled him back, her arms wrapped around his waist. "Stupid, pagan barbari," she screamed, sobbing, "to do this! What does this self-mutilation prove? Except that you are a hopeless pagan and an imbecile . . ."

Wulfred turned within her arms and held her, his arms strong and sure while she jerked in her sobbing. He bent his head low—she could feel his breath on the top of her head—and she clung to him as he spoke.

"If you are innocent of wrongdoing, then I shall heal cleanly. Have no fear. Have no doubts," he whispered, kissing her brow. "As I have none."

"Why?" she cried, turning her face up to his, uncaring that the whole Saxon world watched them.

"Because I trust you, Melania," he said, kissing her softly on the lips. "Now give me your strength, not your fear-driven rage. This cannot be stopped. I would prove to them that you would never betray me. I would prove to you that I . . ."

He did not finish. He squeezed her gently and then turned again to face his ordeal, an ordeal she had precipitated. But she would not crumble under the weight of that guilt now. Now she would give him what he had asked of her. She would give him her strength and her courage and her faith that God would not allow this man to be harmed even in such a pagan ritual.

She watched him walk to the fire. She watched him with her spine stiff and her head up, as he had shown her how to do. She watched him pause as the iron spat heat up into the misty air and the flames engulfed the metal he must touch. She did not cry out; she would bite her tongue off first. She did not weep; her tears were blown dry by the heat of this ordeal. He would not see her weeping, he would not think that she in any way doubted him. She would give him her trust and her love.

Her love. She paused as the word took root, suddenly understanding that the seed had been cast long ago. Yes, he had her love. She would give him nothing less.

With his right hand, his sword hand, he grasped the glowing metal almost with eagerness. This he did for her. Melania's right hand clenched in futile imitation until she punctured her palm in shared sacrifice. The hiss and stench of burning flesh blew back to her almost immediately. She gagged down her sobs and faced him proudly. He turned in place and then, step by slow step, walked the length of that endless line of men. Walked back to her. With her love for him as her only prop, she watched him and waited for him, his every step echoing in her heart as the blood ran down her hand to the ground.

The Saxons banged weapons to shields, a sign of their approval. The pounding roar was nothing to her; she lived in a world of only Wulfred and he was walking toward her. She would be there for him. She would not fail. She knew the color had left her face, but she would stand as straight and tall as a lance for him. He would come to her, and when he did, the ordeal would end.

Four steps taken, five; he stumbled, but held firm. Six steps and then seven. His eyes were glazed and his skin covered in a sheen of sweat. On the eighth step he faltered and looked ready to drop to his knees.

Melania held out her arms to him, welcoming him, beckoning him. Wanting him beyond all the world, whether Roman or Saxon. Every dream she had ever had of her life lay in ashes at her feet; she took a step toward her husband and left the ashes of her dreams behind her, forgotten and unlamented. Everything she wanted in the world was walking toward her. Tears coursed down her cheeks, unheeded and unchecked; she could only hope that he could see what she felt for him in her eyes.

On the tenth and final step, he dropped the iron and fell into her embrace.

"I've got you now," she whispered against his skin, whispered the words she had longed to hear all her life. Words that a Saxon warrior had taught her as he held a frightened child. "I've got you."

Her words caressed him as she held him. She would not let him fall. She would never let him go.

"Never again will Rome cause you pain, Wulfred. This I vow," she stated over her tears as he closed his eyes against the pain blazing up his arm.

Chapter Twenty-seven

With the help of Cynric and Ceolmund, Wulfred had attained the chamber he shared with Melania. Melania had seen to it. She had also seen to it that Wulfred's hand was dressed properly and bound in clean wool. This first binding had to be well accomplished because it would be the only time the wound could be attended to; the purpose of the ordeal was for the wound to heal cleanly by God's design, not man's skillful intervention.

Monstrous, pagan ritual.

The only reason she would abide by their insane stipulations was because she knew that Wulfred would want it so. And she did not want him to think that she doubted the justice and honor of this Saxon system of determining guilt. But she did. It was barbaric. He was most likely crippled for life . . .

unless God truly did intervene. Miracles were not unknown, and if anyone deserved a miracle of healing, it was Wulfred.

Such an act of . . . love? Devotion? Such words tangled hopelessly in her mind when coupled with the thought of Wulfred, yet she did not know what else to make of his act of self-sacrifice. And all because he trusted her.

The tears rushed up and she let them fall. What good trying to stop them? They only came again. She had never cried so much in her entire life.

Perhaps she had not had cause.

Wulfred stirred in his sleep, and she brushed her hand over his hair. He had such trouble sleeping; the pain gnawed at him and would not let him rest. He had to rest. He had to aid the healing process. He had to defeat those bloodthirsty savages he called brothers.

Stupid tears . . . what good were they?

Of course, Wulfred, ever obstinate, did not see the need to remain cloistered and prone. He said the solitude added to the pain, that he wanted distraction. She'd laid her knife to his ear and promised him a quick one if he did not obey her in this. Laughing, he'd ceased complaining. For a time.

Not that they were truly alone. No, Hensa would hardly allow that for fear that she would tamper with the bandage, but she had won her way on a minor point by insisting that only Wulfred's men be allowed into his chamber. She saw no reason to have the enemy within while she fought for Wulfred's health.

If only she could persuade Wulfred to help her.

"Crying again?"

So he was awake.

"Is that your clumsy way of telling me that Saxon women don't cry? Because I can easily believe it. I have never seen an animal cry."

Wulfred smiled and carefully shifted his weight on the couch, keeping his bandage high and away from his body. She had wrapped the whole hand and now regretted it; she would have loved to know if his fingers were able to move, and to see their color. All was hidden beneath the bandage.

"I may be clumsy," he said, once settled, "but I don't cry myself sick."

"I am not sick and I am not crying."

It was true. The tears had stopped. She was too irritated to cry.

"Finally," he said, propping his head up with his good hand.

"You are a less than ideal patient," she said, straightening the sheet that covered his hips.

"You mean that I am less than cooperative? Good."

"I mean that if you don't rest, you won't . . ." She couldn't say it outright. She couldn't even speak about what would happen tomorrow. Tomorrow the wrapping would be removed. Tomorrow was the fifth day.

"Be able to rest some more?" He snorted, pushing himself into a sitting position. For all his care, she could read the pain that streaked across his face. "Come, Melania. I did not sleep so much even as a babe, and my back aches from lying here so long."

"I have never heard you complain about being in my bedchamber or on my couch," she said coolly.

Wulfred's blue eyes sparkled as he accepted her verbal challenge. "As I remember, and it has been long enough for my memory to be challenged, we did not spend much time on the couch."

"Your memory is challenged because of your own intellectual lack, not because of anything I have done."

"Exactly. You have done nothing that would mark my memory."

"You think to insult me? In front of witnesses?"

"Cuthred, turn your face to the wall," Wulfred instantly commanded, and Cuthred instantly obeyed. "Now"—he smiled, his eyes gleaming bright and hot—"do something that will mark my memory."

"A Saxon memory is a feeble thing, obviously," she said, looking askance at Cuthred.

"So obviously you must do something remarkable so that my weak Saxon mind will hold it. Can you do that, Roman?"

"I can beat you at any game, Saxon." She grinned, glad that he seemed distracted from his pain, willing to do anything to keep him smiling. "As you know."

"Prove it to me again. I have forgotten."

"Not surprising," she said, lifting the hem of her stola and placing one foot on the edge of the cot.

She lifted the hem slowly, his eyes a caress that

Claudia Dain

she could almost feel. Tilting her raised knee outward, she edged the length of fabric up over calf, over knee, over thigh . . . and was rewarded by the blue flame in Wulfred's eyes. He could see her, exposed to him, her black curls moist and twisted. Wulfred licked his lips and groaned, falling to his back. Melania would have grinned in victory, but she was having trouble breathing and her vision was becoming foggy. Wulfred ran his hand up her leg and she shivered. He did not stop. Did he consider himself the victor? He touched the throbbing between her legs and she swallowed her own groan, closing her eyes against the sensation. He pulled his hand away and his fingers were wet.

"See?" she whispered. "I still weep."

"These are the only tears I want from you," he whispered back, pulling her hem down reluctantly, glancing at Cuthred's back.

Melania sank onto her stool, her legs trembling. Wulfred licked his fingers and she gasped as if he'd stroked her.

"Cuthred," Wulfred said loudly, "bear witness that my wife has burned a memory into my poor brain that I will not forget."

Cuthred, turning back around, grunted in assent. He had little interest in conversation that did not directly relate to battle.

"I have won a small battle here today," Melania added, her breath easing into a normal pattern.

"No battle is small," Cuthred felt compelled to add.

"No," Wulfred smiled, "certainly not, though the adversary may be."

"I am not small," Melania said bristling. "I am of a perfect size by—"

"Yes," Wulfred interrupted, "by Roman standards. Did you ever think, little wife, that there are other standards of measure?"

"No," she said bluntly, "I never did. I have thought that I am certainly big enough for you."

While Wulfred coughed and choked on his spittle, Melania grinned pleasantly.

"I'll bring you wine, Wulfred," Cuthred offered as he quickly left the room.

"We're alone, for the moment," Wulfred said, his breath back.

"Is that significant?" she asked regally.

"I thought you might want to find out how big I can get." He leered.

"Certain parts of you are quite big enough already. Your head, for instance."

"Try another part," he suggested.

"I can't think of any. None has impressed itself on my Roman memory." She yawned.

Wulfred grabbed for her foot and jerked her off the stool where she had sat in superior complacency. She landed with a yelp just as Cuthred returned with the wine.

"Just in time, Cuthred," Wulfred said.

"For you," she muttered, rubbing her bottom. "Cuthred, make certain that Wulfred remains on that couch. Do not let him rise for any reason. Do you understand?"

"Retreating, Melania?" Wulfred grinned.

"No." She smiled sweetly. "Regrouping."

It was wonderfully satisfying to have both the last word and to leave him scowling.

The night of the fifth day eventually came. She didn't know if her stomach rolled with eagerness to have it all over or in dread that the bandage would be removed. She knew that Wulfred was only eager. But his hand pained him still and she did not think that boded well. Still, it could not be put off, and she would not have wished to prolong this agony of suspense.

Melania walked at Wulfred's side, Ceolmund and Cynric at their backs, when they entered the triclinium. She had made certain that Wulfred's hair was combed and his clothing immaculate, though he had hardly cared. Hensa, that imbecile, was sitting in the seat of honor. Fury rose in her, overwhelming her uneasiness, and she welcomed it. It was still her villa, after all; no matter that Saxon dogs had chosen to make it their summer residence. It pleased her to think of them as guests—rude, uninvited, unwelcome guests. Guests did not take the place belonging to the host. It was entirely possible that an ignorant savage would not know that. She would give Hensa the benefit of the doubt, for Wulfred's sake.

"Please," she said, "don't feel you must give Wulfred his seat. Be at ease at your host's table, as I am sure you have been since you descended upon us so unexpectedly. Tell me, when are you leaving?"

She could hardly have been more pleasant, all things considered.

Hensa gnawed on a joint of pork, the grease lubricating his cheeks, before deigning to answer.

"You must be very certain that the wound is healing cleanly to be so bold."

"I am certain of my own innocence, no one more sure," she answered.

"Except I," Wulfred added, placing his hand around her waist.

Even now, when she tussled with his war leader, he stood by her. Melania looked up at him, her eyes unknowingly blazing forth the contents of her heart for all to see. She would have been humiliated had she known.

Dorcas, seeing love shining forth so brilliantly from Melania's eyes, stumbled in surprise, spilling wine on Hensa. He drew back a casual and brutal hand to strike her for her clumsiness when Cenred spoke from his place behind Hensa.

"Please refrain from striking my intended wife." He had clasped Hensa's hand as he said it and now slowly released his hold, having made his point.

Dorcas, obviously stunned, ran from the room, tears warring with smiles on her face. Cenred grinned at her fleeing back, looked at Melania, and shrugged expressively, his grin comic and wry. Melania grinned back. At least one thing had gone right tonight.

One thing remained, and she could feel Wulfred's anxiety to have the bandage off and the matter settled.

"May I remove the wrapping?" she asked Hensa caustically. "Or would that be a breach of your heathen ethics regarding burn victims?"

Hensa did not bleed under her attack. She decided that he was grossly thick-skinned.

"Come, Wulfred," he commanded kindly. "Come into the room where all may see the decision of the gods. And the innocence or guilt of your wife."

Wulfred did not hesitate. She did. This talk of innocence and guilt was ludicrous; she knew she was innocent, but Wulfred's hand had blazed with pain from the first moment until this. Surely, if he had healed, the pain would have lessened?

"Bring a torch to us, Theras," she instructed, stalling for time. Was there nothing she could do? Her mind was a hideous blank. And the Saxons stood waiting.

"Here is the torch, Melania, and the oil," Theras said calmly, his eyes holding hers.

The oil. Oil. Good Roman olive oil, their last ampule. Theras continued to stare at her, holding the oil out to her as he held the torch. Oil . . . yes, oil! She knew what to do with the oil.

"I am a follower of the Christ who is named Jesus," she declared. "I ask that, without removing the bandage, I be permitted to pour oil over my husband's wounds and pray to my God for him."

"A strange practice," Hensa said, putting down his meat.

"I only follow the Christ's practice, for he was

known to anoint a sufferer with oil and heal him in this way. I only ask to follow the example of my God."

It had to work! Hensa had to allow it! Wulfred waited silently. She knew he was willing to allow her anything to ease her mind.

"I ask to practice nothing beyond my faith!" she urged.

"It is not our custom," Hensa said, stroking his throat thoughtfully.

"What of my customs?" she raged, stepping away from Wulfred, wanting both to protect him and to throttle Hensa.

"Let her," Cenred said. "The wrapping remains intact, which is our way. What can it matter?"

"It's not as if the oil will actually heal him," Bald-uff said.

Wulfred stepped to her side and pulled the end of her braid lightly. "It is Melania's guilt that is being judged. Let her own god judge her."

Hensa sat thinking, his inquisitive eyes never leaving Melania's face. She stood up to his scrutiny well, meeting him look for look.

"Agreed," he finally pronounced.

She wanted to cry with relief.

"Father," she began to pray, her voice soft and strong, "I follow you." She held the ampule to her bosom, embracing it, ignoring the men surrounding her to focus her heart, mind, soul, and strength on the one true God. "Take this oil and bless it. Use it to prove your power. Use it to show these people that you are the one God, the only God. And Jesus," she begged, "use it to heal my husband, as you have healed so many. Please, Father. Show yourself in this place."

The triclinium was silent, unnaturally silent. They watched as she uncapped the ampule. Watched as she poured the heavy oil over Wulfred's bandaged hand. Wulfred's eyes widened as the oil covered his hand; the pain that had smoldered there disappeared. Tingling and invigorating warmth bathed his hand and then vanished, leaving no sensation at all. No pain.

Nothing.

The pain he had understood; this . . .

He clawed at the wrapping, needing to see, dreading the worst. The dirty cloth fell to the floor and he stood staring mutely at his hand.

Impossible.

His head jerked up to look at Melania. She was staring at his hand and crying softly, her tears running into her open mouth, her hand clutching his shoulder.

Impossible.

"Show us," Hensa commanded, his voice revealing his grim expectation.

Wulfred looked at Hensa, at the men surrounding him, at his silently weeping wife . . . and held his hand aloft with a shout of pure animal joy.

It was a perfect hand.

It was a hand that had never touched fire.

It was a hand unburned.

The tumult that unblemished hand incited would have caused a lesser house to fall to its foundation.

"Is my wife innocent?" Wulfred shouted to them all, his voice a cry of victory.

Weapons pounded against shields as his answer. The roar of approval was thunderous, and he added his cry to theirs. Melania threw herself into his arms and he felt her tears on his chest. More tears. Would the woman never stop?

He knew a way.

"You are now one of us, Melania, accepted by all, proven by the god you serve."

"One of you?" She pulled back in his arms, the din of the clamoring men ringing against their ears. "One of you? I will never be one of the unwashed."

"Perhaps not," he conceded with a smile, "but you will live among them and speak their tongue and eat their food and raise the children of your womb in the Saxon way."

She pushed against his chest and freed herself from his embrace. She glared up at him, her anger lighting a welcome fire in her golden eyes. Her tears were gone.

"Because you say it? Because I have no choice and because you do not need my consent to force me to your will? Think again, Saxon! Think long and hard and perhaps you will recall that you have never yet achieved a victory over me!" Her hands were on her hips and she vibrated like a snake about to strike. "You have not broken my spirit, though I readily admit that I have been sorely pressed with this ever-growing throng of Saxons stinking up my home, but I am as strong today as on the day you crept in—no, stronger because of the indulgent care you have shown me. I did more work as a child of eight than I do here now by your command—"

"Then you admit that I am in command of this place and of you?"

"That is not what I meant—"

"How not, when you always speak exactly what is in your heart? It is one of your most engaging qualities." He grinned.

Melania lost some of her fire. "It is?"

"Yes," he said, running his hands down her arms to hold her by the hands. "Now admit it, Melania; you will stay by my side and be all that a man could hope for in a wife because you love me—"

"Just because I prayed for your hand—" she flared.

"As I love you."

The tumult of the triclinium had not quieted. They hardly noticed. It was a quiet moment for them, a moment when a new bond was being forged, a new contract. A new vow.

A new truth was born in that moment of time.

"You love me?" she asked, her voice small and sticking in her throat. She had never, ever, had anyone say those words to her.

"I love you," he repeated, his smile fading into solemnity.

She looked at the floor in happy disbelief, distantly noting that three more tiles had been worked loose. Her Roman villa was crumbling.

"And you love me," he said again. "You cannot

say the words in Latin, it seems. Shall I teach them to you in Saxon?"

"You are very arrogant," she mumbled.

"Perhaps, but also very sure."

"How can you be sure? I have not been sure, at least, not until recently," she stumbled.

"Melania"—Wulfred smiled, pulling her into his arms—"you blaze every thought from your eyes. I have seen your love when you stood with me in silent support against Hensa. I have felt your love because you yearn for my company as for no other. I have heard your love for me each time you name me 'oaf.' But it was when you, my little Roman snake, let your brother go, choosing instead to stay with me that I knew—I *knew*—that you loved me."

Melania wiped her eyes against Wulfred's bare chest, embarrassed beyond measure that he had reduced her to this. He was a very arrogant, very wise Saxon.

Melania looked up at her husband, glowing in his golden strength. He was a formidable man. It was one of his most engaging qualities.

"You will be wife to my heart and mother to my children, and you will never again know the slash of invader's steel. You are mine, Melania," he said softly.

She was his, hopelessly his.

"So be it," she vowed in answer, willingly losing herself in his eyes.

"These are words of love, Roman? I can see that I will need to teach you Saxon endearments; the Roman tongue does not have the words to tell the depth of your love for me, it seems," Wulfred grumbled with a half smile.

Balduff chose that moment to sweep her into a hug, spinning her around in his joy before releasing her to drink a long toast with Cenred.

"And you will not incite men's lust with your Roman wiles," Wulfred said, scowling after Balduff as he led her from the triclinium. "You will be a pure wife, with no hint of adultery."

The night air was wet and the sky thick with clouds; the moon hid behind a tattered edge that raced across the sky. It would rain again. Autumn had come.

"Why, Saxon? Because you pronounce that it will be so? When have I ever obeyed you?"

Wulfred swept her through the portico and out into the courtyard; he obviously had no desire to see the walls of his bedchamber anytime soon.

"You will in this."

He hurried her up the slope, ignoring the howl of a wolf as he made his way up to the rock that sliced the hillside. The clouds built and thickened as the wind abated. The rock was warm; the air was cool.

"Your punishments are nothing; they are rewards. Have I not been kept from all toil, given the best food and the best place at table? Have I not been made a wife instead of a slave? If these are Saxon deterrents, give me more."

Wulfred turned her face up to his with his thumbs, tracing the firm line of her jaw. The moon behind him lit the outline of his hair to white, etching lines of strength on the contours of his muscles. He emanated power in a world gone wild. He had given her love without qualification and without censure; never had she known such love. Never had she known such freedom. She would love Wulfred of the Saxons forever.

"There is no Roman divorce in the Saxon world," he warned softly, his lips brushing her temple before tracing a path to her ear. "The Saxon judgment against adultery is death, Melania."

Leaning into his caress, wrapping her hands in the golden length of his hair, Melania smiled wickedly.

"Yours? Or mine?"

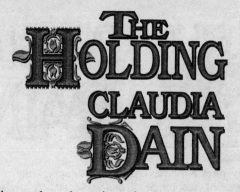

THE HOLDING
CLAUDIA DAIN

It is done. She is his wife. Wife of a knight so silent and
stealthy, they call him "The Fog." Everything Lady Cathryn
of Greneforde owns—castle, lands and people—is now safe in
his hands. But there is one barrier yet to be breached. . . .
There is a secret at Greneforde Castle, a secret embodied in
its seemingly obedient mistress and silent servants. Betrayal,
William fears, awaits him on his wedding night. But he has
vowed to take possession of the holding his king has granted
him. To do so he must know his wife completely, take her in
the most elemental and intimate holding of all.

___4858-2 $5.50 US/$6.50 CAN

They are pirates—lawless, merciless, hungry. Only one way offers hope of escaping death, and worse, at their hands. Their captain must claim her for his own, risk his command, his ship, his very life, to take her. And so she puts her soul into a seduction like no other—a virgin, playing the whore in a desperate bid for survival. As the blazing sun descends into the wide blue sea, she is alone, gazing into the eyes of the man who must lay his heart at her feet. . . .

Lair of the Wolf

Also includes the fourth installment of *Lair of the Wolf*, a serialized romance set in medieval Wales. Be sure to look for future chapters of this exciting story featured in Leisure books and written by the industry's top authors.

___4692-X $5.50 US/$6.50 CAN